*Happy reading
BJ Scott*

HIGHLAND HOMECOMING

B.J. SCOTT

SOUL MATE PUBLISHING
New York

HIGHLAND HOMECOMING

Copyright©2013

B.J. SCOTT

Cover Design by Rae Monet, Inc.

This book is a work of fiction. The names, characters, places, and incidents are the products of the author's imagination or are used fictitiously. Any resemblance to actual events, business establishments, locales, or persons, living or dead, is entirely coincidental.

All rights reserved. No part of this publication may be reproduced, stored in a retrieval system, or transmitted in any form or by any means (electronic, mechanical, photocopying, recording, or otherwise) without the priority written permission of both the copyright owner and the publisher. The only exception is brief quotations in printed reviews.

The scanning, uploading, and distribution of this book via the Internet or via any other means without the permission of the publisher is illegal and punishable by law. Please purchase only authorized electronic editions, and do not participate in or encourage electronic piracy of copyrighted materials.

Your support of the author's rights is appreciated.

Published in the United States of America by
Soul Mate Publishing
P.O. Box 24
Macedon, New York, 14502

ISBN-13: 978-1-61935-284-1

www.SoulMatePublishing.com

The publisher does not have any control over and does not assume any responsibility for author or third-party websites or their content.

I dedicate this book to my husband, Steve.

Without his continued encouragement and support,

I would never have realized my dream to become an author.

To my grandmothers, Barbara (Scott) Hopkins

and Gertrude (Scott) Parsons.

Born in a time when women struggled for recognition

and were still considered property under the law,

they were bright, intelligent, compassionate,

faced adversity with courage,

and were true heroines in the eyes of their families.

Both were a source of inspiration

I have carried with me throughout my life.

I someday hope to honor them by visiting

their birthplaces in Kirkintillock, Scotland

and St Helens, England.

Acknowledgements

There are always so many people to thank, so I will start with my critique partner, best-selling author Callie Hutton. Thank you for your friendship, keen eye, and constant encouragement, all of which kept me on track while this story was created. I would also like to thank Dorothy Wiley for her wonderful input and her part in making this book the best it can be.

I want to thank my husband, Steve, my mother, family, friends, and fellow authors for their continued support.

I want to thank Senior Editor, Deborah Gilbert, and the staff of Soul Mate Publishing for their faith in me as an author and their hard work and dedication to making my books shine.

To the readers who purchased my first two books, Highland Legacy and Highland Quest. It is because of you the third book in the series had to be written.

Chapter 1

Northern Coast of Scotland. Summer 1308.

Hooves pounded against rocks, surf, and sand as Alasdair Fraser pushed his mount beyond reasonable limits. Few things rivaled the thrill and exhilarating rush of mastering the powerful destrier between his thighs, controlling the magnificent beast with reins and will. The wind whipped through unbound hair and the tangy scent of the salty sea air filled Alasdair's nostrils.

He'd ridden hard all afternoon, hoping to reach the stronghold of his longtime friend, Jayden Sinclair. But the sun had slipped below the horizon, the twilight sky ablaze with orange, red, and purple hues. Darkness would soon be upon him and he'd be forced to make camp for the night. He licked his parched lips and his stomach rumbled. Many hours had passed since he'd last eaten, but a hot meal and a tankard of ale would have to wait. Water, oatcakes, and a bit of dried venison would suffice until he reached his destination.

He dug in his heels, and the steed surged forward. The more distance they covered before nightfall, the shorter the journey would be on the morrow. But as they rounded a bend in the shoreline, Odin faltered, reared up on his hind legs, then began to dance nervously from side-to-side. The battle-hardened warhorse didn't spook easily so Alasdair took heed of the animal's uneasiness.

With one hand resting on the hilt of his sword, the other fisting the reins, he carefully surveyed the immediate area. Nothing appeared out of the ordinary, yet the niggling of trepidation gnawing at his gut led him to believe there was something amiss. He nudged the horse's flank and the pair advanced with caution.

They'd only traveled a short distance up the beach when the sight of something a few yards ahead at the water's edge brought them to an abrupt halt. With his heart hammering in his chest, Alasdair cupped his hand over his brow and narrowed his eyes, trying to get a better look. The image came into focus and he could make out the unmistakable outline of a person sprawled out on the shore.

"What is it, Odin? Or, should I say, who is it?"

While this could be someone in need, it might also be a trap, an enemy or bandit lying in wait. Without hesitation, Alasdair slid from the saddle, pulled a claymore from the baldric slung on his back, and raced down the beach on foot. Stopping a few feet away, he sucked in a sharp breath.

"Mo chreach!"

He sheathed his weapon and took a step closer. A young woman, wearing nothing more than a thin nightrail, lay motionless in the sand, the waves of the incoming tide lapping at her bare feet.

"Mayhap a Selkie has washed up from the ocean's depths," he muttered and nudged her foot with the toe of his boot.

As a lad he'd heard many a tale of the legendary creatures, romantic tragedies about cunning seals that shed their skin then transformed into humans. They supposedly took the shape of beautiful women, waiting for unsuspecting suitors to whisk them away and marry them. Fishermen were rumored to go in search of these magical creatures and when they happened upon one, stole their pelt so they could not change back. They took the lass home to be wives and mothers, but if a selkie found their fur and returned to the sea, they left behind desolate, broken men.

Alasdair gave his head a rough shake. Only a fool believed in such fables and he was neither a religious or superstitious man. He made his own luck and governed his own fate. Whether he believed in myths mattered not.

As he moved closer, his pulse doubled and his groin stirred. A man would have to be blind to remain unaffected by the way the wet garment clung to her slender figure, narrow waist, and firm round buttocks. Waist-length, flaxen hair, the color of summer wheat, hung in a tangle of seaweed and sodden ringlets down the center of her back. With her head turned to the side, he noticed thick dark lashes resting on pale cheeks, and her lips held the blue-grey tint of death.

He squatted beside her. How did she come to be on the beach alone? Did someone attack her and, if so, was the scoundrel still lurking nearby?

Alasdair peered over his shoulder in all directions, but saw no one. Other than his own, no footprints marred the sand, leaving him to conclude that the waves had carried her to this spot.

Did she fall from a passing ship or lose her footing on a rocky crag and topple into the sea? A myriad of questions flooded his mind as he lifted her cold, limp wrist.

No pulse.

He pressed two fingertips to her throat. When he felt a faint heartbeat, he rocked back on his heels and blew out a sigh of relief.

Uncertain as to the extent of her injuries, he carefully rolled her to her back. He gazed down at her delicate features and breathtaking beauty.

Her drenched gown was almost transparent, leaving little to his imagination. Through the sheer fabric, perfectly sculpted breasts, tipped with pert, rosy buds summoned him for a taste. Long, shapely legs went on forever, and a nest of tawny curls guarded her most intimate place.

"Enough!" He gave his head another shake. She required assistance. He was not interested in getting involved with this woman, with any woman. Lifting a lass' skirt spelled nothing but trouble. Unlike his two younger brothers, he'd not be lured or swayed by a comely face and end up betrothed. He was a warrior dedicated to the Scottish cause and he had no use for a woman in his life.

He cursed beneath his breath. Why had the Almighty seen fit to bring him to this spot? Surely someone else was better suited to tend to her needs. Fate had indeed played a cruel trick and saddled him with an unwanted burden sure to complicate his life. But he could never walk away. No matter how unwelcome the task, he could not turn his back on someone in peril. Suffering from exposure to the elements, she needed his help, not lust-filled thoughts of a randy lad or the ranting of an insensitive oaf.

He brushed the sand from her face and scanned her body for visible signs of injury. While there didn't appear to be any broken limbs, he could not be certain unless he examined her more closely. But with the quickly rising tide and daylight fading, there was no time to tarry. Her shallow breathing, icy skin, and ashen complexion gave him cause for concern. In the past, he'd seen men topple from a horse or fall from atop a roof and appear unharmed, only to succumb to unseen injury a short time later. If this were the case, he feared there was nothing he could do but make her as comfortable as possible and wait for God to take her.

He swept a wisp of hair from her brow, revealing a dark, purple bruise above her left eye. When he called to her and gently tapped her cheek with the flat of his hand, she didn't respond.

By some divine miracle she hadn't drown. However, if he didn't get her off the beach and out of her wet clothes soon, she'd surely perish. He had no idea how long she'd been in the frigid water, but every minute wasted brought her closer to death.

Alasdair slid his arm beneath her slender shoulders and lifted her to a sitting position. The sudden movement caused her to cough and sputter. Seawater drained from the corner of her mouth and ran down her chin. He cradled her against his chest and wiped her lips with the hem of his tunic. "Easy, lass, I'll see you safe."

Finding somewhere warm was imperative and the Sinclair's castle was at least half a day's ride. Besides, in her weakened state, she might not survive the journey.

He glanced around the familiar surroundings, pondering his options when the hunting croft belonging to Jayden's father suddenly sprang to mind. He'd spent many days romping along this same stretch of shore with his friend while their fathers hunted and fished. But the trips ended when his da and older brother were killed in the massacre at Berwick on Tweed.

His throat tightened, a thick ball of emotion cutting off his ability to swallow. Despite the fact that nearly a dozen summers had passed since their deaths, thoughts of his parents and his two brothers, all slaughtered at the hands of the English, still swamped him with grief. Thank God Connor and Bryce had survived.

He shook the memories away and glanced down at the waif in his arms. She'd begun to shiver. Tenderness welled within him, as did the urgency to find her refuge.

The last time he'd been to Castle Sinclair was before the war desecrated his family, but if he recalled correctly, the hut was located only a few hundred yards up the beach. He hoped it still stood.

He scooped her up and moved across the sand with stealth. Odin followed, plodding along in his usual faithful manner. She continued to tremble and her teeth chattered, the pathetic sound increasing his pity for the lass, overriding his frustration with this unwanted burden. He had to move quickly.

Relieved to see the wattle and daub croft nestled amid a stand of oak, he shifted her flaccid form in his arms and quickened his pace. Within minutes they arrived at the small wooden porch. After taking the steps two at a time, Alasdair reached for the latch.

As he suspected, the hut was not locked. There was not much point. If someone wanted to get in, they merely had to pry open the shutters or break down the door.

The rusty hinges creaked as the oaken slab swung open. He ducked beneath the low-hung doorframe and entered. The one-roomed croft was shrouded in darkness, but as his eyes adjusted, he used the slivers of moonlight shining through the window to guide his way. Alasdair carefully moved toward a raised pallet on the opposite side of the room. He laid her upon it and covered her with a pelt he'd found at the foot of the straw-filled mattress.

Starting a fire was his first task. He rooted around on the floor in the corner, grappling in the shadows until he found the tinderbox filled with peat and several dry logs. After arranging the items in a pile on the hearth, he struck a flint he carried in his sporran against stone, creating a spark that set them ablaze. Candles were next. He lifted a thin piece of burning wood from the hearth and held it in the air like a torch. When he spied several tallow tapers hanging from the rafters, he snatched two, lit them, then placed one on a small table in the corner of the room. The other he'd planned to leave at her bedside.

A soft whimper caught his attention and he turned to see her thrashing about in a fit of delirium. Alasdair hurried to her side and set the candle on the table beside the pallet.

"Ut! Tapadh leat. Nay . . . chan eil mi," she muttered in Gaelic.

He leaned closer, but in her confusion he could only decipher a few of the words she spoke. Don't, she pleaded and then said she would not do it. Do what? He scratched his head. Obviously distraught, a distinct tremor of fear laced her words. But unless she woke up, he might never know what had happened to her.

She moaned and mumbled something he did not understand, but quieted when he ran his hand across her brow, as if finding some comfort in his touch. He stroked her cheek and she turned her head to the side. Her skin felt clammy beneath his fingertips and when she began to shiver again, one thing became very clear. He had to remove her wet clothes or his effort to warm her would all be for naught.

Alasdair stiffened his spine, threw back the covering, and sucked in a deep breath. He'd never undressed a lass without her consent. He'd bedded his share of women in the past, but they'd always been tavern wenches who'd had too much ale or women who were of questionable virtue and frequently lifted their skirt for coin. No respectable woman had ever taken a fancy to him, not the way they did his two younger brothers.

Connor and Bryce had been blessed with their mother's attractive features, sported finely honed, muscular bodies, and lush, dark locks. With his six-foot-six burly physique, what he considered to be average looks, and ruddy brown hair, Alasdair took after his father's side of the clan. He had not been graced with his brothers' good manners, ease in conversations, or quick wits. Especially Bryce, whose reputation for his ways with the ladies was known for miles. Rumor had it, fathers locked up their daughters when he rode into town, lest he steal their heart along with their innocence.

Alasdair heaved a deep sigh. When he was a lad, the other bairns called him a giant, an ogre, mocking him because of his height and large build. As a man he'd used his bulk to his advantage. No one dared stand in his way or challenged him. Not if he valued his life and limbs.

While a robust frame served him well on a battlefield or in an alehouse scuffle, women were frightened by his larger than average size and gruff demeanor. But mayhap that was for the best. He didn't want a woman in his life and preferred to keep them at arm's length. They could not reject him or pass judgment if he rejected them first. Besides, he'd never been comfortable around lassies and had no idea what to say when in their company. He usually uttered something foolish, offensive, or in many cases nothing at all.

She whimpered again, bringing his thoughts back to the task at hand. He reached for the laces on her nightrail, but hesitated as his hand brushed against the soft, pale skin of her throat.

Alasdair swallowed hard, steeling himself against the lustful thoughts swamping his mind, and quickly removed her sodden garment. Determined not to leave her exposed any longer than necessary, he dried her quickly, covered her nakedness with a layer of pelts and plaid, then tucked the coverings beneath her chin. Convinced he'd done all he could for the moment, he turned, then left the croft.

He came back a few minutes later with three large stones and buried the rocks amidst the hot embers in the hearth. Once heated, he'd position them beneath the bedding for added warmth.

Something hot to drink would help to bring her body temperature back to normal, but in her unconscious state, getting her to imbibe would prove difficult. Regardless, he emptied the water from his wineskin into a small iron pot and hung it over the fire to boil. When she woke up, he'd be ready.

He returned to the pallet, only to find her condition had worsened. Damp tendrils of hair draped the mattress. Her breathing was shallow, her lips and cheeks still devoid of color. He touched her hand, shocked that despite the heavy layer of covers her skin remained as cold as ice. He retrieved the heated stones and placed them under the pelt at the foot of the pallet, but it would take a while to get the desired effect.

There was only one way he could think of to warm her body quickly. He grabbed the hem of his tunic, yanked it over his head, and tossed it into the corner. His boots and trews followed. He drew back the layer of blankets and asked the Almighty to give him strength. This was not going to be easy.

By far the most beautiful woman he'd ever laid eyes upon, his heart raced at the sight of her lying before him. His body responded immediately, his rod hardening like a battering ram. He stifled the urge to moan aloud as he imagined her lithe limbs wrapped around his waist, the glorious rub of her thighs as he plunged in to the hilt. The mental picture of her writhing beneath him as he buried his aching shaft in her hot moist sheath made him dizzy with desire. But there was something more than lust coursing through his veins. A strange warmth in his belly, a flutter of anticipation in his chest, and a longing to hold her in his arms, to do everything in his power to keep her safe. Something he'd never felt before.

Under different circumstances, he wondered what it would be like to explore every inch of her goddess-like figure, to taste her luscious lips, to caress her silken skin, to make her his own.

For over two years, he'd fought shoulder-to-shoulder with Robert the Bruce and his fellow patriots. Helping to establish the king's claim to the throne and ridding his homeland of English invaders had become his primary focus. But keeping his unbridled need under control was going to be his greatest challenge. He might be a man of honor, but he was only human.

There must be some other way.

Alasdair scratched his head, desperately trying to come up with a viable option, but none came to mind. He'd run out of ideas and time. Left with no alternative, he slid in beside her, rolled to his side, and eased her back against his chest. Her body fit perfectly in the cradle of his thighs. Just as he somehow knew it would. He exhaled through clenched teeth. With her soft round bottom nestled against his groin, it was going to be a very long and painful night.

Chapter 2

Something soft tickled his nostrils, causing Alasdair to wake with a start. His first impulse was to leap from the bed, grab his weapon, and prepare to confront the enemy. He tossed his head back and groaned. He'd been a warrior too long. The only battle to be fought here was one with is own randy body.

He'd spent the night with the woman wrapped in his arms, his bulk warming her, his rock hard member pressed against the suppleness of her buttocks. It was a wonder he hadn't gone insane with need.

Her golden locks had dried into a sea of curls cascading across the mattress and draping his chest. He brushed the wisps of hair from beneath his nose, but not before he inhaled the scent of sea and heather. How could she be drenched like a wet hound when he found her on the beach, yet still smell so good? Alasdair's groin stirred and he chomped down on his lower lip to keep from moaning aloud.

He still could not believe he'd happened upon her. With a shoreline so vast, what were the odds he'd be in that exact spot when she needed his assistance? Was it divine intervention? He gave his head a shake. No God in his right mind would put a lass in his care.

Mayhap it was sorcery, a siren, or some other fae creature from the depth of the sea sent to tempt him, to capture his heart and bewitch his soul, then leave him broken and longing.

"Utter nonsense," Alasdair grunted. He'd set no store in fables when he was a lad and certainly did not believe in them now. Even if he was interested in settling down with a wife and family, which he wasn't, he'd never be fortunate enough to have a lass as breathtaking and desirable as this one. He shuddered to think of how she would react, the look of horror on her face were she to awakened now and find herself in the arms of a clumsy oaf.

Alasdair glanced down at the lass in his arms. Best he concern himself with tending her needs, then finding out who she was and where she belonged as quickly as possible. The sooner he rid himself of this unwanted charge, the better.

The fire in the hearth had burned down to a pile of glowing embers. While the room was still warm, adding more wood would be the first thing he'd do when he rose from the pallet. But instead of getting out of bed, he closed his eyes and inhaled another intoxicating whiff of her hair.

Just a few minutes more. What could it hurt?

Ribbons of sunlight filtered through the shutters, giving Alasdair a better idea of their surroundings. A heavy layer of soot covered the sparse, wooden furnishings and clouds of dust motes floated in the air. Shimmering cobwebs draped every rafter and judging by the musty smelling rushes on the dirt floor, no one had been to this place in a while.

He hadn't noticed the disheveled conditions of the croft when they arrived, but at the time, he could not afford to be choosy. Besides, a good cleaning would resolve the problem in a hurry. But then again, he had no intention of staying any longer than necessary, so it really didn't matter. He gazed at the woman's angelic face and his heart gave a tug. He cursed under his breath. The unwelcome reaction was the last thing he expected or wanted.

If his brothers heard how he'd spent the night, they'd refuse to believe it, and if they did, they'd never let him live it down. He could very well imagine the smug smirk on Connor's face, but Bryce would be rolling on the floor, consumed with laughter.

They'd quarreled often over the years, as most brothers do, but could always count on each other in times of adversity. Despite the frequent banter and bickering, they'd remained very close, especially after their parents and two brothers died at the hands of the English. While barely a man at sixteen summers, Alasdair, the oldest surviving son, vowed to watch out for his two remaining siblings, regardless if they liked it or not.

When Robert called for a break in the fighting, Alasdair had debated about going straight home to Fraser Castle. He knew his brothers and their families would be anxiously awaiting his return. Two summers had passed since the last time he'd seen Connor and Cailin. Their babe, Andrew, was only a few days old. According to missives he'd received from Connor, Cailin had graced him with another son this past spring.

Despite promises made to return before his niece was born, he'd missed the arrival of Bryce and Fallon's daughter, Elise. He still found it hard to believe his youngest brother, with his adventurous spirit and reputation for making ladies swoon, had settled down and married.

Guilt gnawed at his gut. Putting his own wants and needs before those of his brothers had never been an easy task, but he'd witnessed more than his share of death and destruction over the last few summers, so some time to relax and refresh before heading back into battle was exactly what he needed.

His brothers would not be pleased, but they'd get over their anger in time. Besides, he'd see them soon enough. When he had sent word home to inform them of his plans, he also reminded them of the Bruce's intent to confront the MacDougalls and MacCanns before summer's end. He was positive Connor and Bryce would both rally to the cause.

The lass shifted in his arms, her bottom pressing against his groin. Certain she would awaken any minute and determined not to extend the torture any longer, Alasdair slid from beneath the pelt. He didn't think she'd be impressed or pleased to find a naked man in her bed. Let alone one who was clearly in a bad way. He stared down at his engorged shaft and stifled a groan as he took a few painful steps. He was largely endowed and the sight his manhood in all its glory was apt to frighten her to death.

After grabbing a length of plaid and securing it around his waist, he moved with stealth to the hearth, stirred the hot coals, then tossed several logs on the fire. He hung the pot of water over the blaze to boil, then took a quick look over his shoulder in the direction of the pallet before exiting the croft.

Odin grazed on a small patch of grass at the edge of the forest. In his haste to get the lass inside, he'd neglected to remove the animal's saddle and bridle. But his well-trained mount didn't appear to mind. He approached the beast with his hand outstretched, then stroked the horse's silky black mane. "You're a good lad. When we reach Jayden's castle, I'll see you get a large helping of oats and a good rub before I set you out to pasture."

The horse whinnied, bobbed his head, and pawed at the ground as if he understood every word.

Alasdair glanced toward the sea. A refreshing dip was just what he needed. The sun hung just above the horizon, a bright orange ball of light reflecting off water. He paused to take in the surroundings he'd cherished as a lad, stretched, and inhaled deeply, allowing the tangy sea air to fill his lungs.

More than once, he'd thought about moving to northern Scotland when the war with England ended. While he loved the mountainous terrain and lush valleys around Beauly—a small town near Inverness and home to Clan Fraser—something in his gut told him this was where he belonged.

A sense of calm and contentment washed over him as he stared at the waves lapping the shore. Taking a swim in the cold surf would not only wash the dust, sweat, and grime from his body and hair, but would hopefully cool the fire in his loins. Without further thought, he sprinted across the sand, dropped the plaid at the water's edge, then dove into the icy waves.

When Alasdair finished his swim, he dried himself off with his makeshift garment, then wrapped the woolen fabric around his waist before jogging up the beach toward the croft. After retrieving a satchel of provisions tied to the back of his saddle, he prepared to go inside.

He lifted the latch and called out, "Dinna fear, lass, I mean you no harm." She would be frightened enough in the presence of a stranger and his unannounced entrance might add to her uneasiness.

But his words went unheard. To his surprise, she never stirred or opened her eyes. He raked his fingers through damp hair as he approached the pallet. Her breathing was slow and even. When he touched her arm, her flesh was warm. Why hadn't she awakened by now?

Alasdair sat hard on a wooden stool beside the pallet and studied her face. Was there something more to her injuries he could not see, something he'd missed?

Her lips were no longer blue, but her cheeks were still devoid of color. He wondered about the blow she'd taken to the head and gently brushed the hair from her brow so he could examine her injury closely. The dark discoloration above her left eye had spread a little during the night and a bump was still prevalent. Could this be the reason she failed to rouse? If so, how long would it be before she awakened? What if she never woke up? His mind races with possibilities, each one worse than the one before.

He rose and began to pace. Things were not going according to his plans. By now, they should be finishing up with a simple meal of oatcakes to break their fast and preparing to depart. The thought of leaving her here and continuing on to Sinclair castle alone briefly crossed his mind. Once there, he could arrange for someone to come back and fetch her. Mayhap Jayden could send a healer and a cart.

Alasdair cursed and slammed his balled fist against the doorframe. He could not leave her alone today, any more than he could walk away when he found her on the beach last night. Until she regained consciousness, he'd have no choice but remain here, tending to her needs.

If their stay was to be an extended one, Alasdair knew he would need more provisions. The food he carried in his pouch, a couple of stale oatcakes and a bit of dried venison, was hardly enough for one meal, let alone ample supplies for a day, mayhap longer. A search of the croft turned up several barrels containing flour, oats, turnips, and dried fish. A variety of herbs hung by the hearth and he'd found a crock of honey on a shelf by the door. While not fancy fare, it would suffice until he could go fishing or hunting for a hare or deer.

After wolfing down a modest meal of oatcakes and water, Alasdair settled on the stool beside the pallet. There was nothing more he could do but to wait.

She could not decide which was worse, the relentless pounding in her head, or the nausea twisting her belly. She struggled to open her eyes, but closed them again when her vision blurred and the room began to spin. Her mouth was as dry as wood, her throat parched. She'd give anything for a sip of water.

The lass raised a shaky hand to her forehead, wincing when she touched a painful bump above her eye. She didn't recall hitting her head on anything. In fact, she didn't remember anything at all. Worse, she had no idea who she was, where she was, or how she'd come to be on this pallet.

Her thoughts reeled. This was ridiculous. A person doesn't just forget their name and past. But that is exactly what had happened. She swallowed against the bile rising from her stomach. What was her name? The harder she tried to remember, the more her head ached. Lauren. For some reason this name came to mind.

Is that my name?

Shivering as if suddenly encased in ice, she tucked her arms beneath the layer of pelts. Shocked to find she was naked, her eyes flew open. Her gaze darted around the dimly lit croft, but she didn't recognize her surroundings or the man bending over the hearth—a huge man wearing trews and nothing more. Fear caused her gut to clench as she frantically searched for something, anything, to protect herself.

An eating-knife on a trencher beside the pallet caught her eye. While not a deadly weapon, it might give him pause for thought if he intended to ravage her. She reached for the small dagger, but in her haste knocked over a tankard, the tinware cup falling to the floor with a soft thud.

The man whipped around, and her breath caught as he stalked toward her. Her eyes widened and a chill skittered along her spine as he neared the pallet. Panic squeezed her chest, making it impossible to breathe.

"Tha e mor." The words about his large size slipped out before she could bring her hand up and cover her mouth. To say he was big didn't do him justice. He was a mountain of a man, broad in the chest and shoulders, with heavily muscled arms and thighs. A tangle of auburn hair hung loosely around his face and shoulders. While his blue eyes were quite expressive, the rest of his features were hidden by a dense, unkempt beard.

He stopped at the foot of the pallet and cocked his head to one side. "Och, you're awake. What's your name, lass?" he asked gruffly. When she didn't reply he repeated his questions again in Gaelic. "Dè an t-ainm a tha oirbh?"

She tugged the pelt under her chin and glared at him. "Chan eil fhios agam."

"You dinna know your name?" He moved closer.

"Nay." She held one hand in the air, while clutching the pelt at her throat with the other. "Stad! Ma'se ur toil e." She prayed her plea to stop and not come any closer would be enough to deter him. Given she had failed to retrieve the dagger—not that it would prove useful against a man of his size and bulk—she had nothing she could use to protect herself should he decide to harm her.

Alasdair halted and held out his hands with the palms facing skyward. "I mean you no harm. Dinna be afraid."

"Wh-what am I doing here and where are my clothes?" She failed to hide the tremor of fear in her voice.

"Dinna fash, lass. I found you on the beach and your clothes were drenched. There was no choice but tae remove them. Otherwise, you'd have caught your death of cold. I hung them by the fire tae dry." He pointed toward the hearth, then moved closer. "You're lucky I came along when I did. I—"

"You removed my clothes?" Her heart slammed against her ribs, his words cutting through her like a dagger. What else had this brute done to her while she was asleep?

"Aye, then I covered you with pelts and placed hot rocks at the foot of the pallet tae warm you. I dinna know how you came tae be on the shore or why, but when I first happened upon you, I thought you had drowned. When I realized you were still breathing, my only concern was tae get you somewhere warm and dry."

"How . . . how long have I been here?" Her teeth began to chatter and she tightened her hold on the pelt, now fisting it with both hands.

"Two days. You have a lump and a nasty bruise on your forehead. I suspected you struck your head on something, mayhap the reason why you dinna awaken for so long. Do you remember how you came tae be in the water?"

"Nay." She squeezed her eyes shut and brought her hand to the tender spot above her left eye. Her head was throbbing, her mind in a foggy haze. She had no idea what happened. When she opened her eyes, he was standing beside the pallet, only inches away.

"My name is Alasdair Fraser. We were on our way tae the keep of my friend, Jayden Sinclair, when Odin sensed there was something amiss."

"Odin?" He wasn't alone? She sucked in a gulp of air and anxiously scanned the room for another man, but saw no one.

"My horse." He picked up a tin cup from the floor. "Would you like something to drink? I can fetch you some water." Before she could answer, he ambled across the croft, took something from a pot hanging over the fire, then returned to her side.

She did not know this man, but she was so parched. She stared at the small tankard he held in his hand and dragged her tongue across her cracked lips. She shook her head. While she desperately wanted a drink, her instinct told her to refuse anything he offered. For all she knew, he might be trying to poison her or to addle her wits so she could not fight off an assault.

"I made an herbal brew tae warm you, but suit yourself. I dinna plan tae force it on you," he snapped and slammed the cup on the table, the precious liquid sloshing over the sides. When he turned to walk away, she grabbed the hem of his tunic.

"Wait. I am verra thirsty and would welcome your offer."

This time when he handed her the cup, she drank greedily, emptied the vessel to the last, then handed it back to him. "Tapadh leat."

"You're welcome. I'll get you some more. Do you want something tae eat or would you like tae rest a little more afore we leave?"

"I dinna know you and am not going anywhere with you."

"Well, I canna leave you tae fend for yourself. A lass alone wouldna last a day."

She stiffened her spine and glared at him. "I dinna need you tae take care of me. I can . . ." She stopped mid-sentence and squeezed her eyes shut, hopping to block out the banging in her skull and swallowed against the bile rising in her throat.

"Are you all right?"

Calloused fingers brushed her cheek, and she detected a hint of concern in his voice. "I'll be fine. But I dinna know where I live." She had no idea who she was or where she belonged. If he left without her, where would she go?

"You have nasty bump on your head. I'm sure the events of your life will all come back you in a short while. Have you at least remembered your name?"

"Nay, but for some reason the name Lauren comes to mind. I wish I knew for certain."

Alasdair tilted his head to one side and smiled. "A bonny name for a comely lass. Dinna fash over it right now. Mayhap Jayden or his father will be able to help. They are likely acquainted with all the neighboring clans and must know where you belong."

"And if they dinna recognize me?" She nibbled on her lower lip. She wasn't sure what to think. If they were friends, mayhap they could solve the mystery of her identity. However, if they turned out to be her enemy, it would be better if they did not know who or where she was.

"We'll deal with that if the need arises. For now, I will call you Lauren." He smiled.

Her heart jumped and she didn't fancy the lascivious way he was staring at her. As if he was remembering her without her kirtle. She lowered her gaze and twisted the plaid covers around her finger. "I dinna mean to be a bother. I'm sure you're right. Once my head has cleared, things will—" She closed her eyes again and swallowed against the sudden upheaval churning her belly. Her head pounded and the room began to swirl.

"Are you hungry?" Alasdair asked, apparently oblivious to the turn in her condition.

"Nay, but I . . . I fear I might be sick." She brought her hand to her mouth and inhaled deeply through her nose.

Alasdair's face paled and he sprinted for a wooden bucket beside the door, returning as she emptied her stomach.

Since she'd had nothing to eat and very little to drink in two days once the herbal brew was ejected, retching and dry heaves replaced the vomiting.

Alasdair handed her a damp rag to wipe her face. "Is there anything I can do to help?"

"Could I have some water, please?"

"Do you think it wise?"

"Aye. My mouth is so dry."

When Alasdair returned with the cup, she limited herself to a few small sips. "Thank you." She lay back on the mattress and dragged her hand over her eyes.

"The blow tae your head must have been worse than I thought. Mayhap we will have tae stay here a day or so, until you are well enough tae sit a horse."

She picked up a hint of disappointment in his voice, but she didn't have the strength to argue or answer. Her eyes closed and darkness engulfed her.

Chapter 3

She struggled to open heavy lidded eyes, but quickly raised her forearm to shade her vision from the rays of blinding sunlight streaming through the window.

"Where am I?"

The sounds of someone whistling outside the croft and the rhythmic crack of wood being chopped answered her question. Her stomach clenched and panic squeezed her chest. She was in the cottage of a stranger and he could return at any minute.

He'd introduced himself as Alasdair Fraser, but the name meant nothing to her. Then again, she didn't remember her own name. The last thing she recalled was leaning over a bucket, retching, certain her head was about to burst. As the events of her brief encounter with the man who'd claimed to find her on the beach slowly returned, a myriad of questions worried her mind. How long had she slept? Why had he brought her here, and what did he plan to do with her?

A dull ache resonated in her skull, but mercifully the nausea and dizziness she'd experienced earlier had eased, at least for now. She shifted her position, lifted the covers, and gasped. She was still naked.

She squeezed her eyes shut and heat rose in her cheeks. While he'd claimed the removal of her garments had been necessary to save her life, this man had seen her as only a husband should view a maiden on their wedding night. Was she a maiden? Or was she already married, mayhap even a mother?

She shoved those concerns to the back of her mind. There were more pressing issues to deal with now. She scanned her surroundings in search of her clothes and a modicum of relief washed over her when she spied a nightrail on a chair near the hearth. It wasn't much, but it was far better than no clothing at all. Once covered, she could search for her gown and slippers. Now all she had to do was retrieve the garment before he returned.

Without hesitation, she slid to the edge of the pallet and dropped her feet over the side, an impulsive act that caused the room to spin. She inhaled deeply, then let the air leave her lungs in a slow, controlled breath. She repeated the action and waited for her head to clear.

Determined to obtain her clothes, she pushed aside her fear, wrapped a plaid around herself, planted her hands on the mattress, and rose to a wobbly stance. But as she tried to take her first step, a sharp pain knifed through her right ankle, and she crumpled to the floor.

The door swung open, striking the wall with a loud thud. "What in the name of St. Stephen are you doing?" The man had to duck beneath the doorframe to keep from bumping his head. He lumbered into the croft, across the room, then stopped at the foot of the pallet.

"I want my clothes, sir." The words spilled out before she could curb her tongue. Her heart rose in her throat, uncertain how he would react to her boldness.

"My name is Alasdair and all you had tae do was ask. I'd have gotten them for you," he replied, then crossed his arms over his broad chest and peered at her through narrowed eyes.

She shuddered at the sight of him towering over her, but managed to keep her composure. "There was no need tae bother you. I am capable of fending for myself." She bit down hard on her lower lip, having again spoken her mind without thought for the consequences. He did not look impressed.

"If that's so, how did you end up on the floor?"

"I tried to walk, but my ankle gave way." Tears welled in her eyes, but she refused to cry. She'd not cower before this man or show any weakness, even though her heart was pounding so hard she was certain he could hear it.

He squatted beside her. "Let me see."

"I'll be fine." She tried to tuck her feet beneath the plaid, but he caught her lower leg with his large, calloused hand. With a surprising amount of gentleness, he brought the injured limb toward him. As he examined her ankle, she chewed the inside of her cheek to keep from shouting out, the pain greater than anything she'd ever experienced.

"I dinna think it is broken. The bones appear tae be in line, but there is some swelling and bruising." He shook his head and rocked back on his heels. "This will delay our journey even longer," he grumbled.

"No one asked you tae stay with me. Besides, I am not going anywhere with you."

"That remains to be seen, m'lady." Before she could protest, he slid one of his arms around her waist, the other beneath her knees, and lifted her as if she weighed no more than a feather.

She fisted her hands in the plaid to hold it in place and twisted in his arms. "I insist you set me down. You may take your leave any time you wish. There is no need for you tae wait for my ankle to heal."

"I'll decide what's best. Stop squirming," he growled.

"Then set me down and leave me be."

"I am putting you back where you belong." He placed her on the pallet, and covered her with the pelts. "I still dinna understand what possessed you tae get up without assistance in the first place? You have been abed for three days and have eaten naught since I found you. You're bound tae be weak. The next time you want something call for me and I'll fetch it." His voice held a tone of authority, his features stern.

"I want my clothes," she pressed. "Why am I still undressed?"

"I dinna think you would appreciate it if I took the liberty of putting on your nightrail while you slept. You made it clear you were not pleased that I removed it. Even though, it was soaking wet and a matter of your survival." Alasdair retrieved her garment and tossed it on the bed. "Put this on. I'll give you some privacy, but I dinna want you getting up again, not until you're stronger and your ankle has had time tae mend."

"I dinna take orders from you or any man. I—"

"You dinna have a choice, m'lady." He cut her off before she could finish, then moved toward the door. But as he grasped the latch, he glanced over his shoulder and softened his tone. "Remember what I said. Dinna get up. You must rest your ankle if we hope to leave any time soon."

She stared at the nightrail. "Where are the rest of my clothes?"

"There are no others." Alasdair pinched the bridge of his nose and shook his head. Frustration echoed in his voice.

"I was not wearing a gown or slippers?"

"Nay. I thought it strange, but the fact you were on the beach at all gave me more reason for concern than your attire or should I say lack thereof."

"I find that hard tae believe. I would never leave my chamber wearing only this." She tucked the plaid under her chin and held the nightrail in the air. At least she didn't think she would. "Tae go out in public in only a—"

"Are you calling me a liar?" Alasdair's face contorted with anger, his eyes darkened, and the bulging veins on his neck were visible as he took a menacing step forward.

She swallowed against the lump forming in her throat. "Since I dinna know you I have no idea what you would or wouldna do. In fact, I have no idea what happened while I was asleep." She fought to keep her voice from cracking as she spoke.

"Trust me, m'lady, when I say that nothing happened. If I wanted tae claim you, I'd have done so by now, and it is not something you'd forget," he snapped and took another step in her direction. "You may be a comely lass, but I am not so desperate for female companionship that I would ravage you or any lass while she was unable to participate of her own free will. Even though a good bedding might just curtail your feisty nature and incessant need tae question everything I say or do. Your accusations are not appreciated."

"I dinna accuse you of anything. But I have no idea what transpired. I woke up in a strange place, wearing no clothes, and with a man I'd never seen before giving me orders. Surely you understand how it must appear?"

"Mayhap you'd rather I'd left you on the beach tae die. Tae do so would have made my life a hell of a lot simpler, but I couldna turn my back on someone in need. However, I am starting tae rethink the wisdom of my decision. You can rest assured I have no desire tae complicate things any more than they are already." He completed his tirade, spun around, and stormed across the room. "The sooner I can get you tae Sinclair Castle and out of my hair, the better," he grumbled and slammed the door behind him.

Taken aback by his candor and abrupt departure, she stifled the urge to shout out a response. Obviously this man had a short temper, and it would be best to tread lightly until she was well enough to travel. She wasn't familiar with the Sinclair Clan of which he spoke. They might be friends and able to help, but she could not take a chance they were her enemy. As soon as she was able, she would do her best to escape.

She moved her legs and moaned, her ankle throbbing with the action. She cursed her luck, but then decided that her injury could be a blessing in disguise. As long as she was laid up, she could not sit a horse, buying herself some time to devise a plan. Alasdair might even tire of waiting and leave without her.

Until her strength returned, she could only hope he'd meant what he said. That he had no desire to bed her or to do her any harm. On that thought, she closed her eyes and prayed. "Please, Lord, grant me a boon and return my memory. I also ask that you keep this man true to his word. I believe there is some goodness in him, but if I am wrong, please protect me from harm."

While she found his brute size, unkempt appearance, and gruff demeanor intimidating, she sensed her disgruntled benefactor had a softer side he was trying very hard to conceal. Despite her lack of memory, there was something hauntingly familiar about those piercing blue eyes and his crooked smile. But she could not possibly know him, otherwise he'd have said so. Wouldn't he?

The alarm she'd experienced the first time she saw him had dissipated, but that didn't mean she was ready to totally let down her guard. Nor was she prepared to trust him. She dismissed the notion, slid the nightrail over her head, then buried herself beneath the warm layer of pelts and plaid. The fact she was wearing nothing else when he found her was still perplexing. She blew out a sigh. Until her memory returned, there was no point in speculating.

"Mo Chreach!" Alasdair cursed aloud as he stomped toward the woodpile and picked up an axe. "How dare she accuse me of lewd behavior? I should never have stopped tae help the ungrateful wench. If only it had been in me tae keep on riding." He raised the tool above his head and brought it down on a log with a mighty whack, splitting the thick piece of timber in half with a single blow. "Marbhphaisg ort! After all I've done tae help her." He cursed and hoisted the axe again. "Women are nothing but trouble and I am best tae stay clear." This time he hit the wood with such force it splintered into several jagged chunks.

Alasdair couldn't help but wish he'd gone home to Beauly rather than planning a visit to see Jayden. Instead of tending the unappreciative lass, he'd be sitting in the great hall of Fraser Castle with his feet propped up, a tankard of ale in one hand and a leg of mutton in the other. His only concern would be whether he should go for a ride or take a nap. He didn't have to answer to anyone about his motives, as to where he ventured or how long he stayed. He liked having the freedom to do as he pleased.

Despite being the oldest surviving son, he'd given up his birthright the day he declined the elders' request to assume his place as Laird of Clan Fraser. The daunting responsibility then fell on the next in line, Connor. While he was not trying to shirk his duty, and excelled on the battlefield, Alasdair believed there was a lot more than brawn to be a good leader. Qualities he lacked. With a level head on his shoulders, a knack for organization, intelligence, and ability to command respect everywhere he traveled, Connor was the sensible choice for Chief. Named tanist until Connor's son, Andrew, reached the appropriate age, their youngest brother, Bryce, would take over should anything befall him.

Alasdair quickly crossed himself. While he held no store that simple thoughts or words could govern a man's destiny, he preferred to err on the side of caution. In any case, the clan's fate rested in capable hands.

"Damnation." His thoughts returned to his current situation and the beguiling woman inside the croft. "The last thing I needed in my life is a woman." He cursed again and took a swing at another log. He'd done his best to maintain his distance over the years and had built a protective wall around his heart that was virtually impenetrable. Not that he didn't appreciate a comely face or enjoy a tumble beneath the plaid with a willing lass, but he had no desire for commitments or love.

Were he looking for a bride, which he was not, a woman like the lass in the cottage would be the perfect choice. No one could dispute her breathtaking beauty and sensual curves, a body that would drive a man wild with desire. But aside from a comely face and a means to sate his lustful needs, there was no mistaking her spirit and tenacity. Passion flashed in her eyes when she spoke, and the proud jut of her chin made him smile. Refreshingly different from the shy, subservient way most women acted in his presence, the lass wasn't afraid to speak her mind. Were she a man, and the battle one of wits and nerve, he imagined she would indeed be a most formidable opponent.

"God's teeth! What are you thinking, man?" Alasdair gave his head a sharp shake. Where on earth had these thoughts come from? She'd all but accused him of taking improper liberties, questioned his motives, and insulted his honor. It would serve her well if he did get on Odin and ride away, leaving her to fend for herself.

The less time he spent with this woman the better. Look what happened to his brothers when they got involved with lassies. He liked his sister-by-marriage, Cailin and Fallon, and his brothers appeared to be truly happy. He was glad they'd both found contentment in marriage, but while a wife and bairns might be fine for some men, it was not for him.

Besides, a lady as fine as his charge would have no use for the big, clumsy buffoon he believed himself to be. Despite her effort to put on a brave front, he'd seen the look of trepidation in her eyes when they first met. It was the same expression he'd seen many times when introduced to a woman; one that led him to believe she would rather be horsewhipped than spend a minute alone in his company. He'd felt her tremble and heard the sharp intake of breath when he lifted her from the floor, caught the nervous tremor in her voice when she spoke. She might not remember who she was or where she belonged, but he could tell after spending a very brief time with her, that she was a lady of breeding and status . . . the sort of woman who would never give him a second glance or thought.

Alasdair gathered the wood and carried it to the croft. There was an ample supply to keep the fire going for the time being and he'd cut more if the need arose. While he did not fancy the idea of another confrontation with the lass, there were things that needed to be taken care of. Until she was able to travel, he'd have to put aside his frustration and ire, make the most of a difficult situation.

Before he'd gone to chop wood the first time, he'd hung a pot of soup over the fire to simmer and had made some oatcakes. Mayhap the lass would be hungry. He'd allowed sufficient time for her to get dressed and hoped after a rest and something to eat, she might be ready to travel. If not, he prayed she'd at least be more amiable. Despite what she insinuated, his intentions and behavior had been strictly honorable and he was not in the mood for another battle of words. He shifted the load of logs in his arms, sucked in a fortifying breath, and nudged open the door to the croft open with the toe of his boot, just as he heard her scream.

Chapter 4

No one could have entered the croft without him noticing, so when he heard her cry out, Alasdair could not imagine she was in any physical danger. If the thrawn lass tried to get up again without his assistance and had fallen, he'd not be pleased. He'd never met a more stubborn female. He dropped the heavy load he carried and entered.

Alone in the croft, she sat on the pallet with a pelt clutched beneath her chin. Wide-eyed and visibly shaken, the lass appeared unharmed.

"Are you ailing, Lauren?" he asked. Rather than approach the pallet, he stood in the doorway, waiting for her to reply.

She shook her head, but didn't speak.

Since she was in bed where he'd told her to stay and there was no apparent cause for alarm, he picked up the wood, then strode with purpose toward to the hearth. When he dropped the logs again, they hit the floor with a loud thud.

After stirring the fire and adding more peat, his thoughts turned to their meal. He plucked a wooden ladle from a hook on the wall, then swirled it in the soup he'd left simmering. The pungent aroma of boiled onions and turnip wafting from the pot caused his stomach to growl and he could not resist the urge to sample his culinary creation. He blew on the contents of the ladle, then brought it to his lips. After all, he did not want to sicken the lass with his cooking.

She didn't utter a sound, but was watching his every move, of that he was certain. "Are you hungry?" he asked, but did not turn around. "I've made some soup and oatcakes." He grabbed one of the baked treats from a trencher, broke off a piece, and popped it into his mouth.

She didn't reply.

"Are you feeling up to having a wee bite?" he inquired over his shoulder. "It might be simple fare, but will fill your belly." He retrieved a wooden bowl from a shelf by the hearth and filled it with broth and vegetables. "Well, are you hungry or not?"

He whipped around and found her staring at him, the pelts still fisted tightly under her chin. "First I couldna get you tae stop talking and now you willna answer me. Is this how the next few days are going tae be?" He approached her, carrying the bowl in one hand and an oatcake in the other. "Either you want this or I'll eat it myself. I've never been one to let good food go tae waste."

"Judging by the size of you, I dinna suppose you have missed many meals," she blurted out, bringing him to an abrupt halt at the end of the pallet.

"What do you mean by that remark?" He'd been mocked his entire life because of his size. Why should she be any different from everyone else?

"I only meant that you are a very tall, brawny man." Her cheeks reddened to a dark crimson and she momentarily glanced away.

"Are you going tae eat or should I toss it back intae the pot?" he growled.

"Leave the food there and I will try tae eat a wee bit once it cools." She nodded toward the table.

"As you wish, m'lady." Alasdair bowed at the waist in a mock gesture of subservience, but did not hide the sarcasm in his tone. This woman had a way of stirring his blood in more ways than one. "Will there be anything else, Madame? Have you any further orders, or am I dismissed?"

"I-I mean . . . The soup will be fine. Please put it on the table," she stammered, clearly taken aback by his hostile reply. "I dinna mean tae be a bother or tae sound ungrateful. Thank you. I am in your debt." She lowered her gaze.

Was he finally making some headway with the lass? At least she was no longer giving him orders or questioning his motives. When she glanced up, and he gazed into huge hazel eyes, brimming with tears, remorse for his boorish behavior gnawed at his belly. Now, he really felt like an ogre. "I dinna mean to snap at you."

"I understand and dinna blame you. I have not been very gracious. But we got off tae a bad start and neither of us has been very cordial." She quickly added, "I dinna know you or who I am for that matter. I am thankful you found me and for your kindness."

"Dinna give it another thought. As I already told you, I mean you no harm and am as anxious as you are tae be away from here." He placed the food on the table and backed away. "You really should try tae eat something."

The smile that curled her lips as she lifted the bowl of soup caught him completely off guard, giving his heart an unexpected jolt. Never had he been affected by a woman to this extent, and he was not sure he liked this newfound emotional turmoil one bit.

She brought the bowl to her nose and inhaled deeply. "The soup does smell wonderful." Her stomach gurgled. "I guess I am hungrier than I thought." She lifted the wooden spoon to her lips, then blew on the content before tasting it.

"There wasna much tae choose from, but I did what I could with the supplies I found in the larder. Some vegetables, herbs, and a bit of dried venison. If we are holed up here longer than a day, I will have tae go hunting."

"This is very tasty." She downed another mouthful and smiled.

Breathtakingly beautiful, she lit up the room. If this was a great hall instead of a hunt camp, he could only imagine how heads would turn when she entered. This time when she smiled, it was like he'd been horse-kicked in the chest and had the wind knocked from his lungs.

"You dinna strike me as a man who would be able tae cook."

"Nay? And what sort of man did you take me for?" Alasdair scooped out a ration of soup for himself, then sat on a wooden stool beside the hearth, giving them both some space while he tried to get his own thoughts under control.

She almost choked at his question, and he fought the urge to jump up and pat her on the back. "When you are at war and spend as many days in camp as I have, you either learn tae cook or starve," he said, hoping to ease the tension.

"War?" She raised a brow. "Who may I ask are you at war with?"

He heard a nervous tremor in her voice again. If what she claimed was true and she had no memory past the day he'd found her, it stood to reason she would question him on a subject. "It is not me personally who is at war, but all of Scotland. For many years the English have tried tae impose their rule and deny us the right tae govern our own country. King Robert the Bruce, the rightful sovereign, is doing his best tae regain his throne and oust the English vermin from Scottish soil."

"And you follow this King Robert?" she asked, then sipped another spoonful of soup.

"Aye, my clan has long supported the Scottish crown. My father—" He paused and crossed himself. "Lord, rest his soul, fought for the cause and when he was killed in a massacre at Berwick on Tweed, along with my older brother, I vowed tae avenge their deaths as soon as I was old enough tae wield a sword. This war has taken too many good men and women. The time has come tae put a stop to it."

"I'm sorry you lost your da and brother. What of your mam? Did you have any other kin?"

"My mam was killed the summer afore my da died. The English attacked our village when the men were out hunting, took the crops and livestock, then burned our crofts. The women were repeatedly used for their pleasure then put tae sword when the blackguards had their fill." He ran a shaky hand across his brow.

Memories of the torture his mother was forced to endure caused his stomach to churn and his heart to clench. A knot quickly formed in his throat and he coughed to clear it. "They did the same tae the bairns and old ones, those too feeble or too young tae join the hunt. My brother had only seen six summers and was among the wee ones slaughtered." He placed his empty bowl on the floor and turned his head so she would not see the tears welling in his eyes.

He scrubbed his damp cheek with the back of his hand and gave his head a shake. He'd never spoken to a woman about his past. Hell, he'd barely said more than a few words to a woman at any given time. He had never been comfortable around them and usually ended up saying something foolish or offensive. How had the lass gotten him to open up the way she did? This was the same person he was ready to throttle not more than an hour ago for her obstinacy.

Lauren lowered her head. "I'm verra sorry for your loss. It must have been very difficult for you, being so young and all. I canna imagine."

Alasdair's stiffened his posture. "These events happened more than a dozen summers ago and I am no longer a lad. True, my two remaining brothers and I were forced tae grow into men in a hurry, but we were proud tae join the cause and to do our part to see justice served."

"Do they live nearby?"

"Who?" Alasdair rubbed his hand across his chin and at least a month's worth of beard and stubble.

"Your brothers."

"Nay, Connor and our youngest brother, Bryce, live in Beauly with their wives and bairns. It is a small town near Inverness and a few days hard ride. My brother, Connor, is laird of Clan Fraser."

"Is Connor your older brother then?"

"Nay, I am the eldest."

She cocked her head to one side and studied him for a moment before speaking. "If that is so, why are you not laird?"

"I'm not, and dinna wish to discuss my reasons. Why must women always meddle in things that are none of their affair?"

"And you are not married? Have you never thought about taking a wife and having bairns of your own?" she pressed.

Alasdair's mood soured. Uncomfortable where the conversation was headed, he rose from his stool. He'd already shared too much and was not about to discuss his shortcomings and inadequacy as a leader or a husband with this woman. Best the conversation end here and now.

"Women are trouble and I have no use for one in my life," he snapped. "Have you had enough to eat? Would you like something tae drink?" He quickly changed the subject.

"There is nothing more I need."

He approached the pallet. "If you dinna want anything else, mayhap you should rest."

She studied his stern features, furrowed brow, and noticed the catch in his voice when she asked about his brothers and why he'd never taken a bride. This was obviously a sensitive topic of discussion and mayhap one best avoided. For a brief time, Alasdair had almost been approachable, and she'd started to let down her guard. But his gruff demeanor had returned and she decided to trust this man might be a huge mistake.

She shifted beneath the covers and winced when a pain shot up her leg and her ankle began to throb.

"Are you certain naught is amiss?" he asked, his voice softening a little. "When I was outside chopping wood, I heard you call out and wondered why."

"I fell asleep and had a bad dream. I wasna aware that I shouted."

"Aye, you screeched like the devil himself was dancing on your heels. What was the dream about?"

A sudden chill ran down her spine. She clutched the pelt beneath her chin again, the question making her feel ill at ease. "I dinna remember. I just know it frightened me. When I awoke, my heart was pounding and I found it hard to catch my breath. Why do you ask?"

"I thought mayhap it would give us a clue as tae who you are and where you belong. You still do not remember how you came tae be on the beach or your name?"

She shook her head. "Nay, but I wish I did." She shifted her position beneath the covers again then covered her mouth to stifle a yawn. "I am suddenly feeling verra tired. Mayhap a rest would be helpful."

Alasdair gave a curt nod and after taking the empty bowl, returned to the hearth. "The more rest you get, the sooner we can leave. I will tend tae my horse and then see if I canna find a hare or grouse for the evening meal."

She didn't reply, but watched as he moved with surprising stealth for a man of his build. He cleaned the bowls, placed them back on the shelf, then went to the woodpile. His sun-bronzed skin glistened in the firelight and her stomach gave an odd twist, her heart a little flutter as she observed the bunch of the muscles across his broad back, when he lifted several heavy logs and tossed them into the hearth.

She found herself wondering what it would be like if they'd met under different circumstances. She'd gotten lost in his deep blue eyes more than once and imagined that if he combed his hair and shaved off his beard, Alasdair Fraser might be quite handsome, in a rugged sort of way. Judging by his tone when he spoke about his brothers and the loss of his parents, it was obvious he had a caring, sensitive side, despite the front he presented to the world.

Had she lost her senses along with her memory? She closed her eyes and shook her head, then brought the back of her hand to her forehead to check for fever. While she might not know her identity or remember anything about her past, common sense told her it was wise to be wary of strangers. He'd told her more than once he was anxious to leave and planned to take her to the castle of his friend. She had no intention of going anywhere with him. However, until she was stronger and her ankle had mended, she was stuck here. She balled her fist and pounded it in frustration against the mattress. She'd have to bide her time, but vowed she'd be more cautious when interacting with Alasdair and leave on her own as soon as she was able.

Chapter 5

The roar of waves pummeling the ship's wooden hull was deafening. Icy rain stung her cheeks and a fierce north wind whipped through her tangle of unbound hair. She fisted the rail with both hands and called on the last of her strength in an attempt to remain standing upright on the slick deck. She wasn't alone. There was someone standing a few feet away, but she couldn't make out his face, and he offered no assistance. When the vessel pitched to the left, she lost her grip and toppled over the rail.

The only thing between her and the ocean's depths was darkness. In that prelude to what she was certain would be her untimely death, she prayed the Almighty would be merciful and forgive her earthly sins.

Her breath caught as she hit the frigid water and sank like a stone. Her nightrail tangled around her legs, but she kicked with all her might. They say your life flashes before your eyes when you are about to die, but there was no time for that. She was not going to drown without a fight.

Salt water stung her eyes and nose. Her lungs burned and her head felt like it was about to burst from the pressure. Panic squeezed her heart as she pumped her arms and legs in a desperate attempt to reach the surface. She tilted her head back and kicked hard, thankful when her face popped above the waves.

Gasping, she sucked in a much needed gulp of air, and then another. She'd managed to swim to the top, but was by no means out of danger. The storm raged on and a dense layer of fog hung over the water, making it impossible for her to see or get her bearings. Her body trembled uncontrollably and her teeth chattered. If she did not get out of the water and fast, there was no hope of survival. Even though it was summer, the stretch of ocean separating the Orkney Islands from mainland Scotland never warmed much above freezing.

Treading for her life, she turned full circle, searching for the ship. Her arms and legs felt like iron weights, growing heavier by the minute. How long could she keep this up before the ocean claimed her?

A sliver of moonlight poked through the clouds and she narrowed her eyes. Something large loomed straight ahead, but when she reached out to touch it, the object was closer than she thought. A sharp pain lanced across her forehead when she struck her head, then everything went black.

She awakened with a start and brought her hand to her brow. Was it a nightmare or had the events in her dream really happened?

This would explain how she got the bump above her left eye and ended up alone on the beach. However, the events leading up to her fall from the ship remained a mystery, as did her identity. She had no idea how she wound up onboard or why, but could not shake the gut-twisting feeling that in addition to the storm, something or someone posed an even greater danger on that fateful night.

Why couldn't she remember?

She pounded her balled fist against the mattress. It had been almost a sennight since Alasdair found her on the beach and her memory had yet to return. It would not be long before he insisted they leave.

So far, Alasdair had posed her no threat, but she could not be certain about the Clan Sinclair. In her dream, she'd seen the silhouette of a stranger who meant to do her harm, but not his face. Until her memory returned, she remembered where she belonged, and knew who attacked her, there was no telling what danger she might be walking into if she accompanied Alasdair to the castle of his friend. She could not go with him.

True to his word, he'd done nothing to harm her and had made no improper advances. He also kept his distance. In fact, she seldom saw her benefactor. Conversations between them, while civil, were kept to a minimum. He spent very little time inside the croft, which should have made her happy, but she could not help wondering what this man was about. Despite his gruffness, he'd made an effort to dust and clean, prepared and served her meals, saw to her ankle, and tended the fire.

At night, he slept on a pelt in front of the hearth, but usually rose before dawn and was nowhere to be seen when she awakened. His evasive behavior, moodiness, and grumbling beneath his breath while he saw to her needs indicated he grew weary of waiting for her ankle to mend, but she was in no hurry to leave.

Things were taking longer than either of them had expected. The swelling had gone down in her ankle, thanks in part to the cold, wet rags Alasdair insisted on draping over her injury a couple of times a day. The angry purple discoloration had faded to a greenish yellow tint and the discomfort had lessened considerably. But when he asked how she fared, if she thought she could soon sit a horse, she lied, telling him she had not healed sufficiently to walk or ride.

She also refrained from telling him that over the last couple of days, when he'd left the croft for extended periods of time, she had managed to stand and had hobbled to the table and back several times. But that was a secret she meant to keep to herself.

Guilt tugged at her belly. She would surely burn in Hell for her deception, but she did not really know the man or the people he planned to visit. Despite his kindness, a tiny voice in the back of her mind warned her to be cautious. Other than their brief discussion about the war with England and his brothers, Alasdair had revealed very little about himself, except that he planned leave and take her with him as soon as she was able to make the journey.

Her ankle was healing, but she had not come up with a means to get away, and even if she had, was not strong enough to effect an escape. Until then, she would continue to pretend her injury was worse off than it actually was. Hopefully buying her some more time.

In the interim, she needed to practice walking and rebuild her strength. Now was the perfect time. Alasdair went hunting at dawn. Before he left, he told her he'd not return until mid-afternoon, so she did not expect him back for several hours.

She slid to the edge of the pallet and allowed her legs to dangle over the side. Her stomach growled. She'd eaten very little at the evening meal and it was well past the time she would normally break her fast. She nibbled on an oatcake and a bit of dried venison Alasdair had left at her bedside before he departed.

After finishing the modest meal, she planted her hands on the pallet for support, and rose. She inhaled deeply, took one wobbly step and then another. Before long, she'd managed to limp to the hearth—farther than she'd gone in the past. Thrilled by her accomplishment and ignoring the pain, she turned, and walked, albeit with difficulty, back to the pallet. Winded from the exertion, she sat on the edge of the mattress, taking some time to catch her breath.

Determined to repeat the trek, she pushed herself to a stance, then gingerly moved forward, her eyes focusing on a stool near the fire. There, she'd sit and warm herself before returning to bed. She ran her hand through her disheveled hair.

"What I wouldna give for a brush and a looking glass."

A noise from outside caught her attention. She grabbed the edge of the table for support and her heart began to race. Had Alasdair returned early? Could it be a wild animal or, worse, another stranger who happened along? Mayhap the man who tried to assault her had returned to finish the deed.

She released the breath she held when she recognized Alasdair's voice. He was talking to Odin, but they were right outside the door. Her pulse sped up a notch. He'd be here any minute. She needed to return to the pallet or he'd know she had been deceiving him.

"Please, Lord, let me make it afore he comes in. I promise tae see the error of my ways and make amends," she muttered aloud as she quickened her pace. She could do this . . . had to do this.

In her haste, she knocked over a stool in her path. While Alasdair was certain to notice the seat was not as he'd left it, there was no time to set it right. Relief washed over her as she reached her destination and slid beneath the pelts. She crossed herself, convinced if she kept asking the Almighty for favors, she'd be doing penance for the rest of her days.

The door opened and Alasdair entered, carrying two fat hares. "It dinna take me as long as I expected." He moved across the croft, placed the game on a table, then glanced in her direction. His eyes stalled on the toppled stool. "Are you well, lass?" he asked as he picked it up. His brow furrowed, but he didn't ask how it got upended.

The lump in her throat made it difficult to speak. "Aye. I'm fine." When she finally forced out the words, she heard the tremor in her voice.

He watched her for a moment before he spoke again. Did he know she was lying?

"Are you sure you're not ailing? Your face is flushed and you appear tae be out of breath," he finally said.

"I told you I'm fine. I was sleeping and woke when I heard you enter. It must have startled me." She twisted a corner of the pelt around her finger. "I can see your hunt was successful."

Alasdair gave a curt nod. "Game is abundant at this time of year. I hope you like rabbit stew."

"Aye." She kept her answer simple. The less said the better.

"Guid. You need tae eat if you want tae regain your strength. Mayhap you should try getting up and putting some weight on your ankle. The weather is bonny and thought you might be tired of looking at these four dreary walls. If you like, we could go outside for a spell. It wouldna hurt for you tae get some fresh air."

"A change of scenery would be lovely, but I'm feeling very weak and am not sure I am ready to stand. I—"

"All the more reason tae get you up and about. You've been abed long enough." Before she could protest, he threw back the pelts, wrapped a length of woolen plaid around her shoulders, then lifted her into his arms.

"What do you think you're doing? Put me down." She gasped and brought her hand up to cover her mouth, while holding the plaid securely in place with the other.

"I'm taking you outside so you can get some sun. Would you rather I let you walk?" He arched a brow and waited for her to reply.

She shook her head. "Nay. You know I canna walk." Alasdair was not about to give in to her wishes, of that she had no doubt. So she decided it was best she go along with his request for now and not give him any reason to be suspicious.

He carried her across the room and nudged the door open with his elbow. "If you tire, we can go back inside."

The abrupt transition from the darkly lit croft into bright sunlight caused her to squeeze her eyes shut. She tilted her head skyward, hoping to catch the warmth, while the combination of forest scents, tangy sea air, and spring flowers filled her lungs.

She glanced around at her surroundings, hoping that something might jog her memory, but nothing looked familiar.

He crossed a small clearing, then set her down on a fallen log. "Are you comfortable?"

She nodded.

He flashed a crooked grin, then adjusted the plaid around her shoulders. "If you get too tired or cold let me know. I dinna want tae do anything that will further delay our departure," he said, then moved to a spot a few feet away and stared off into the distance.

His concern was touching, even if he did have a reason to wish her a speedy recovery. While she knew very little about Alasdair, she found herself admiring his finely honed physique and chiseled features, what she could see of them beneath the dense overgrowth of facial hair.

"You are a man of verra few words," she said in an attempt tae break the uncomfortable silence.

"I dinna have much tae say. But my brothers would argue that fact. They are forever accusing me of talking more than I should."

"Do you miss your brothers?"

"Connor and Bryce have their wives and bairns tae keep them busy."

"That may be, but it doesna mean you canna miss your kin. This is the second time you've spoken about them and their bairns."

His expression hardened. "I learned at a young age not tae count on anyone but myself." He absently touched a strip of plaid he wore around his upper left arm.

"Why do you wear that? I have noticed you never take it off."

He coughed to clear his throat and lowered his eyes. "This piece of plaid was taken from my mother's skirt. The one she wore the day she died. I wear it in her memory and tae remind me of a pledge I made as a lad tae avenge her death."

She noticed the glint in his eyes and catch in his voice. The topic of his mother's demise obviously caused him great pain. "I am sure she would be proud of the man you have become and your tribute tae her."

"She was a verra special lady and I miss her verra much." He brought his beefy hand toward his eyes and scrubbed it across his cheek.

The sentiment with which he spoke of his mother touched her heart and she choked back tears. She wished she could remember her own family. Was she close to her mam and da? Did she have any brothers or sisters? "You must have loved her verra much."

"If not for her determination tae see me hail and hardy, I am not sure I'd be alive today." He exhaled sharply and raked his fingers through his hair. "When I was a wee laddie, I was quite sickly. I know it's hard tae believe if you look at the brute I am now," he quickly added and laughed.

He drew in a slow deep breath before he continued. "She never gave up on me and wouldna let me give up on myself."

"A mother's love can be a powerful thing. She was obviously right. You grew tae be a strong, healthy man."

"Aye, but it wasna always like that. I was born early and the midwife told my parents if I survived the night, I wouldna likely live beyond a summer. But Mam would hear none of it." He absently touched the plaid cloth around his arm.

"When I was a lad, I spent many days abed. By the time I was ten summers, I had seen my share of healers, sorcerers, herbal remedies, blood letting, and leaches." He closed his yes and shuddered.

"That must have been horrible." The thought of the age-old practices, remedies and the slimy, bloodsucking creatures used to release the poison from a body was enough to make a person's skin crawl with disgust. Odd she knew what he was talking about, but still remembered nothing about herself or her past. "Yet you wouldna know that you had a rough start by looking at you now. I have seen verra few men of your size and strength."

"I might be the tallest and strongest son now, but believe it or not when we were growing up, my brother, Connor, and my older brother, Blaine." He paused and crossed himself. "May the Almighty bless his soul. They stood up for me when other bairns called me names or tried tae do me harm."

"You look like you could have taken care of yourself."

"Mayhap now, but back then, I was a tall, lanky lad with flaming red hair and a strong wind could blow me over."

"A lot has changed. You are no longer of slight build and your hair and beard, while they both have streaks of red running through them, are fairly dark."

"I took after my da. He had plain features, red hair, and blue eyes. My brothers resemble our mother, with their raven locks, brown eyes, and guid looks. I was never as handsome and it wasna until I reached manhood that my hair began tae change color. Tae be honest, I never thought it would. Even though as a lad I prayed for it nightly. You know what they say about red hair."

"I'm afraid I dinna recall."

"Tae be born with hair of fire is a curse."

"Dinna tell me you believe in such nonsense. I wouldna have taken you for a superstitious man." She shook her head and clucked her tongue.

"I'm not. But when you are a bairn and people taunt and belittle you, claim you were born under an unlucky star, you find it hard tae discount. There were times when even my brothers teased me about my appearance because they knew it would get a rise out of me. Especially Bryce. He never missed a chance tae annoy me or tae point out the fact that I dinna have his winning way with the lassies."

"If you were tae shave, you would be quite pleasing tae look at. I think I would find you verra handsome."

Alasdair stiffened his spine and his brows knit together. "It matters not if you find me appealing or not," he snapped. "I think you have been up long our first time and I best take you back inside." He stomped toward her and bent to lift her. "I'll make some stew while you rest."

"I dinna mean tae upset you. But if you were tae—" Given the sudden scowl on his face, she decided, she'd said too much, again, and it was best not to continue.

Without saying another word, Alasdair strode toward the croft with her tucked securely in his arms. It broke her heart to learn he thought so little of himself and believed he did not deserve the same kind of love and happiness his brothers had found. No wonder he went out of his way to put on a harsh front.

Chapter 6

After placing her onto the pallet, Alasdair quickly backed away. "Get some rest. When you awaken, the stew will be ready. Mayhap you can try walking a wee bit after we eat. The sooner we get you on your feet, the sooner we can be away. My friend Jayden must be wondering what happened tae me by now."

He was babbling like an idiot and didn't wait for her to respond. For some unknown reason, Lauren had gotten him to open up and talk about his past, again. But what bothered him more was the way his senses, every fiber of his being, came alive in her presence.

His body ablaze with desire, Alasdair needed some space between them. He'd not be swayed by a comely face or her flattery. He spun on his heel and exited the croft.

He paused on the porch, his heart hammering against his ribs, his palms sweating, and his loins on fire. The lass had burrowed under his skin and he dinna like it one bit. No matter how hard he tried to keep his distance and stay his randy thoughts, his pulse raced whenever he looked into her beautiful hazel eyes. Her delicate, sweet scent drove him wild, and when he carried her in his arms, the rush of heat and carnal need was stronger than anything he'd ever felt before. It was as if she had been made for him.

The soft lilt of her voice haunted his dreams and thoughts of her occupied his waking hours. What's more, with her feisty spirit, she commanded his respect. He actually liked the lass and being in her company. Was he losing his mind?

"Mo chreach!" he cursed aloud and gave his head a quick shake. It wasn't like him to be so distracted by a woman's wiles. Not that many ladies had bothered showing him any interest. He wasn't the sort of man women fawned over. Actually, the lassies seldom acknowledged his existence. They were too busy trying to impress his handsome younger brothers.

He clenched his fists and his blood began to boil when he thought about the one and only time a lass had prompted him to let down his guard. "Mhic na galla!" he cursed again as he remembered the humiliation and anger he felt when he learned he'd been played for a fool. He could still hear the crofters snickering when he passed them on the street.

He had just seen his twenty-third summer when Lillian MacCloud, a fae creature with ebony tresses, bewitching features, sea-green eyes, and kisses as sweet as honey, had all but thrown herself at him. She was the kind of lass he had only fantasized about and never believed would pay him any mind. At first, he thought it a ruse, a cruel trick, but when she persisted in her flirtation, he believed she truly found him appealing.

He'd fallen hard and was prepared to put aside his pledge to the cause, his vows to avenge deaths of his family members, and ask for her hand. When Connor cautioned him to beware, told him she was a cunning shrew, and had tried to tempt him in the same way, rage consumed him. Alasdair drew his sword, ready to lop of his brother head for speaking ill of the woman he loved. Had Bryce not intervened and supported Connor's claim, he might have gone through with the deed.

Unwilling to believe his traitorous siblings spoke the truth and determined to prove them wrong, he went to her family's croft, to ask her to marry him. When he came upon Lillian with Gavin Maclean, wrapped in each other's arms, and rolling in the hay behind the barn, the bugger's hand beneath her skirt, Alasdair had been devastated. When he challenged MacLean to a battle of swords and informed Lillian of his intent to propose, she'd laughed in his face and called him a buffoon.

"Women are selfish, conniving, and are not tae be trusted. I've managed this long on my own and dinna need one in my life," he grumbled as he trotted down the stairs, then raced toward the shore. Another dip in the cold ocean surf would get his muddled mind and lust-ravaged body under control.

Unfortunately, his plan failed and he emerged from the frigid water even more frustrated and confused than before he took the plunge. He dried off using a length of plaid, tugged on his trews and boots, then trudged up the beach, stopping when he came across a huge boulder and plunked himself down.

Things had not gone as planned and he had to put Lauren out of his mind. Hell, she could be married for all he knew. If not, a lass that comely would surely be spoken for. Given his penchant for bad luck, she most likely had bairns, too.

But what if she wasna wed? He scrubbed his hand across his bearded chin. Was what she said true? Could she possibly find him good-looking if he were clean-shaven and brushed his hair?

Nay. He slammed his fist on the rock, the blow causing his knuckles to bleed. He was only setting himself up for a major disappointment by even thinking such a thing. If she claimed to have any feelings for him, they would only be out of gratitude for saving her life or because she felt sorry for him. He didn't want her pity. Once her ankle healed, she would be anxious to see the last of him. Besides, Robert the Bruce was counting on him to rejoin the cause at the end of the summer. He'd pledged his sword, and if need be his life, to his king, and had no time or desire to court a lass. Or so he tried to convince himself.

She dragged her hand across her eyes, then cupped her mouth and yawned. How long had she slept? She glanced around the dimly lit room. A half-spent candle and the soft glow of the fire burning in the hearth provided the only light.

The aroma of stew simmering over the fire filled the room. Her stomach growled. Alasdair promised it would be ready when she woke up, but he was nowhere around. He'd been cross and evasive when he'd brought her back to the croft. Talking about his mother and his past obviously made him uncomfortable. She'd meant no harm in asking.

The door swung opened and Alasdair entered. "I see you're awake. The sun has set and the hour grows late. You must be hungry."

She sat up and narrowed her eyes as he stepped from the shadows and into the firelight. Her heart skipped a beat when she caught a glimpse at his face. Shocked, she noticed his beard was gone. Freshly washed hair had been pulled back and bound with a length of leather. How this man could think he was unattractive or plain was beyond her comprehension.

Her breath caught as she took in his rugged features, a straight aquiline nose, high cheekbones, strong, square jaw, straight white teeth, and expressive blue eyes. She could hardly believe this was the same man who'd been tending her needs for a sennight.

"Is something amiss?" he asked with a grin that caused her pulse to race and her stomach to do a wee flip.

"N-nay," she forced out the words. "I was surprised tae . . . um." The heat of a blush rose in her face and she glanced away.

He moved to the pallet and touched her cheek. "Are you ill? Your face is flushed. I hope it doesna mean a fever is brewing. Mayhap I kept you outside too long this afternoon and you caught a chill."

"I'm fine." She pulled away. "You shaved off your beard. I hardly recognized you."

"I grew tired of it and decided it was time," he answered.

"What do you have there?" Trying not to stare, she pointed to a long, slender, carved piece of wood he was carrying.

"I made you a walking stick. I thought it might help you to get around until you've regained your strength and your ankle is fully healed." He laid it across her lap, then took a step back.

She ran her fingers over a row of thistles carved along the length of the shaft. Amidst the prickly wildflowers was a single rose. "I canna believe you did this for me. You are verra gifted. When did you find the time?"

He shrugged. "While you were asleep. Carving relaxes me and I have put dirk to wood since I was a lad. When you spend as many hours abed as I did, you need something tae keep you from going daft." He held out his hand. "Let me help you tae stand."

"I'm not sure I'm able," she lied. If he knew how many times she'd walked on her own and not told him, he'd be furious. This was not the right moment to reveal her secret.

"You can and will." He slid his thick arm under her legs, one around her waist, then slid her to the edge of the pallet. "Lean on me if you dinna feel steady or find it too painful. If you dinna get up soon, you willna be able tae leave."

Her heart sank. He was still talking about departing. She winced when he placed her feet on the floor.

"Are you all right, lass?"

She softened at the concern and tenderness in his voice. "Aye. I just need a minute." Guilt tugged at her gut and she nibbled on her bottom lip. Would he know she was lying, that her injury had healed more than she'd let on?

"Take as long as you need." He supported her weight and pulled her against his chest. "You've been abed for many days. We'll take it one step at a time."

He held her so close, it was hard to ignore the clean woodsy scent of musk and man. Her knees buckled and before she could speak, he lifted her into his arms, carried her toward the hearth, then sat her on a wooden stool.

"We'll eat first and then you can try tae walk back to the pallet.

He dipped the ladle into the pot and scooped out a generous portion of stew. "The fare is not fancy, but will stick tae your ribs." He placed the trencher on the table before her and handed her an eating knife.

She folded her hands, bowed her head, and whispered a prayer of thanks over the food. While she was not sure what possessed her to do so, it felt right.

Alasdair halted. With the knife halfway between the trencher and his mouth, he waited until she finished speaking. "Best you eat afore it grows cold."

She picked up the knife, brought the stew to her lips, and blew on it before popping it into her mouth. "Your cooking skills never cease tae surprise me. This is delicious."

"I made plenty if you want more." Alasdair, downed several mouthfuls, then leaned back in his seat. "What prompted you tae say the blessing? Have you remembered anything about your past?"

"Nay, I recall naught," she lied. Again. She'd had several vivid dreams about being on a ship and falling overboard, of being in danger, and a confrontation with a man whose face she could not see. Alasdair had given her no reason to fear him, but she was still uncertain who she could trust.

"I find that hard to fathom. You should have remembered something by now. Your name perhaps." He tilted his head to one side and waited for her reply.

"I don't know my name for certain, but as I mentioned before, the name Lauren is all that comes to mind."

"Lauren. The name suits you well." he said, then touched the back of her hand. "Since I couldna keep calling you lass, I will continue tae call you Lauren, until you tell me otherwise."

She nodded and lowered her eyes, trying to concentrate on the food—anything but him. Hearing the name roll off his tongue sent a warm tingling sensation to her belly, and beyond. She enjoyed his company when he wasn't grumbling about leaving. He tried so hard to hide beyond his gruff exterior, and she was finding it more difficult with each passing day to resist the growing attraction she felt. But with no memory of who she was or where she belonged, to even consider the idea of being anything more than friends with a man was wrong.

They ate the rest of the meal in silence. When finished, Alasdair cleared away the dishes and returned to her side. "Are you ready tae walk back tae the pallet?"

Her stomach fluttered and her heart skipped at the thought of him enveloping her in his arms again. But he did not give her time to respond. He took both her hands, helped her to stand, then slid his arm around her waist.

"When you're ready, Lauren, we'll try taking a wee step."

She did not want to prolong this any longer than necessary, so shuffled her right foot forward and then her left. He remained steadfast at her side, taking the bulk of her weight on his hip.

"Excellent. You will be walking on your own in no time at all."

He didn't rush, waiting for her to take the next step and then another. Her mind raced as they neared the pallet. Now that he had her up and walking, he'd expect her to be ready to leave in the next day or so. She'd do her best to stall, but for how long? She could not accompany him to Sinclair Castle. She did not know why, but something in her gut told her it was not a prudent thing to do.

While common sense told her it would be dangerous for a woman to travel alone, and as foolish as it might be, she could not help believing that going with Alasdair would put her in far worse peril. She'd wait until the time was right, when he was away from the croft, and leave before he returned.

They reached the pallet and he gave her waist a squeeze. "You did well. Rest now and we will try again in the morning." He held the pelts while she climbed beneath them. "Is there anything you need?"

"Nay. Just some rest." She rolled over and closed her eyes.

"Sleep well, Lauren."

She didn't answer.

Perched on a stool by the fire, he watched her sleep, wondering how he was going to ever let her go. She was by far the loveliest woman he had ever seen, and she did not seem to be put off by his size, awkwardness, or lack of manners. But duty dictated that they part ways.

After tossing a log on the fire, he spread a pelt on the floor in front of the hearth, then lowered himself to the ground. He pulled the tunic over his head and tossed it on the stool, then did the same with his trews and boots, before settling beneath a length of plaid.

The last thing he wanted to do was lie on the floor and go to sleep. If truth be known, he wanted to slip beneath the covers, take Lauren in his arms, and make her his own. But that would not be right or proper. They were not betrothed and despite what people might think of him, he was a man of honor.

The women he'd bedded in the past had all been of questionable repute and none had been untried maidens. If Lauren was not already married or spoken for, he held enough respect for her that he would wait until their wedding night. But then again, if she did not get her memory back, he might never know for certain.

He slammed his fist on the floor. What the hell was he thinking? He was never going to take a bride. Especially one with no past. He was a warrior. There was no future for them, something he best not forget. He tucked the plaid around his shoulders and dozed off.

An ear-piercing scream disturbed his slumber and Alasdair jolted up with a start. Wasting no time, he climbed to his feet and raced to the pallet.

She tossed in a fitful sleep. Sweat misted her furrowed brow, tears ran down her cheeks, and she mumbled something in Gaelic.

"Ut! Tapadh leat. Nay . . . chan eil mi."

These were the same words she was shouting in her delirium the first night he'd found her. She begged someone to stop and said she would not do it. Again he questioned. Do what?

She thrashed beneath the pelts, her breathing now coming in sharp pants. As he was about to wake her, she screamed again and shot up in bed. He reacted on impulse, took her in his arms, and hauled her against his chest.

"Shhh. You're safe, lass. You had a bad dream is all."

She clung to his arm, her nails digging into flesh. Her entire body trembled. "Please dinna let go," she sobbed.

He continued the embrace until she stopped shaking and her breathing slowed to a normal rhythm. "Are you all right? Do you want tae tell me about the dream?"

She hiccupped and sniffled. "It was a nightmare, not a dream. I was in my chamber, asleep, when I felt hands touching my shoulders and heard a man's raspy voice. He told me not tae call out, that he'd admired me from afar for many summer, and meant to make me his own." She clung to his arm even tighter.

"I told him nay, begged him tae stop, but he tried to slide his hand beneath my nightrail. He said if I dinna do as he ordered and allow him to bed me, he'd kill me. He held a dirk tae my throat and told me tae lay still."

Rage roiled in Alasdair's belly and every muscle in his body coiled with tension. The thought that a scoundrel would dare to enter her chamber and try to take her innocence infuriated him. He fought the urge to express his outrage. He didn't want to frighten her any further. "Did you recognize the man?"

"The room was dark and I dinna see his face, but his voice was familiar. I was not about tae let him have his way and we struggled. I grabbed the dagger and in my attempt to break free, I stabbed him. He fell to the floor and I got out of the room as fast as I could. The next thing I knew, I was on the deck of a ship. A storm was raging and I was certain a wave would sweep me over the side."

"Where was the blackguard who attacked you? Were there no others on board to offer their assistance?"

"Nay, the storm was fierce and anyone on deck was busy with the rigging or trying tae keep the ship from capsizing." She paused and took in a gulp of air. "Then I saw him. He was holding his side and cursing. When he came at me with the dirk in his hand, I panicked. I let go of the rail, prepared tae run, but the vessel pitched and I fell over the side."

He continued to hold her and gently stroked her hair. "You must have been terrified. It was a miracle you dinna drown."

"I was certain I would, but fought tae reach the surface. I remember the fog and searching for the ship. I was so cold, I couldna feel my legs and my arms grew so verra tired. There was a break in the clouds and the ship was upon me. I must have hit my head on the hull."

"Do you know why you were on the vessel or where you were going?" He eased back and gently lifted her chin.

"I dinna know how I came tae be onboard or why. Just that the man tried tae rape me. I wish I could remember." She began to tremble again.

"It dinna matter. You have enough tae deal with right now. Trying tae force your memory tae return willna help. It will all come back in time." He brought her onto his lap, cradled her in his arms, and rocked her back and forth.

"I'm not sure I want tae remember," she sobbed, then buried her face against his chest.

He'd forgotten he was naked. When he heard her call out, the only thing on his mind was getting to her side, and he had not paused to pull on his trews. His body responded to her soft round bottom resting on his thighs, so he eased her onto the mattress, and tried to stand up, but not before grabbing a plaid and wrapping it around his hips. "Mayhap you should try tae get some sleep. We can talk about this in the morning." He tried to ease her back against mattress, but she struggled to remain upright. "Lay down, Lauren. I will return to my spot before the hearth, but am close by if you need me."

She clung to his arm and peered up at him with hazel eyes that melted his heart. "Please. I dinna want tae be alone. I fear the nightmare will return. Stay with me. I beg of you."

He swallowed hard against the knot in his throat. She was so frightened, how could he deny her this request? He raised the pelt and lay down.

She immediately snuggled up beside him, her head on his chest, her hand resting over his heart. Could she feel the way it thundered against his ribs, like a monster clawing to get out?

She closed her eyes. Thick dark lashes rested on pale cheeks and her soft pink lips were drawn into a tight bow. Oh, how he wanted to kiss her. Just once and he'd be satisfied. Or would he? She stirred and when her thigh rubbed against his rigid manhood, he stifled the urge to groan aloud.

She opened her eyes and peered up at him. "Thank you for staying with me."

Alasdair couldn't speak. In the soft glow of the firelight she looked like an angel. He lowered his head and brushed her brow with his lips. When she tilted her head back, he captured her mouth in an all-encompassing kiss.

Chapter 7

An onslaught of desire threatened to override Alasdair's good sense. He fought the urge to plunder Lauren's sweet mouth with his tongue, to lift her nightrail, to make her his own.

He broke their kiss and raised his head, knowing if he didn't stop himself now, he might not be able to harness the unbridled passion heating his blood.

"Forgive me." He forced the words out on a strangled breath. He swept an errant wisp of hair from her brow and locked his gaze with the wide, hazel eyes of a woman obviously shocked by his impulsive actions.

He cupped her chin, stroked her cheek with the pad of his thumb, then brushed it across her lips. "I dinna mean tae make inappropriate advances or tae take liberties. I—"

She pressed two fingers to his mouth, silencing him. "You have no reason tae apologize. I appreciate you staying with me, Alasdair. After my nightmare, I canna bear tae sleep alone."

This was the first time she'd used his name, and it sounded as melodic as the Celtic lullabies his mother used to sing. At a loss for words, he stared back at her and smiled, but inside, his stomach churned in turmoil.

What to do?

He'd rather be drawn and quartered than remain on the pallet with her lush, shapely body pressed against his side, and not sate his carnal needs.

She'd begged him to stay, so why shouldn't he take her?

But she also trusted him enough to seek safety in his arms. He could not betray that trust.

In the past, paying women to warm his bed had served him well. There was never any worry about commitments or the fear of being turned away, but the acts lacked passion and were devoid of sentiment. Lauren was different from the tavern wenches he'd bedded. Not only was she stunning, she was intelligent, tenacious, and brave. All qualities he admired.

Bombarded with an array of emotions he'd never felt before, he wanted to bed her, to take his time and explore every curve of her figure, to memorize the delicate details of her beautiful face, and to bring her to the heights of ecstasy over and over. He wanted to pump into her with wild abandon until she shouted out his name in pleasure, and he joined her in release. Yet, if he gave into temptation, he knew he wouldn't be able to walk away.

While he might be war weary and longing for peace, he'd not forsake his duty. Nor would he let desire cloud his judgement.

He believed the Almighty had spared his life when he was a babe for a reason. He'd defied the odds of survival at birth, overcame illness as a bairn, and had grown to a strong, healthy man. His destiny was to fight for the Scottish cause. He'd seen his share of horror over the last few years, countless battles, destruction, and senseless loss of life. To hang up his sword and targe, to settle down in a croft by the sea, and become a fisherman was a tempting thought. But he'd sworn his fealty to the Scottish King and vowed to avenge the deaths of his kin.

The Almighty was testing his resolve, of that he was certain. Why else would the Lord place her in his care? He didn't trust women and had vowed never to marry. But he'd also never spent so many days and hours in such close proximity with a lass. He'd gone out of his way to avoid contact with women. Especially ones as beguiling as Lauren. That way, he could not be rejected or disappointed.

In a moment of weakness, he'd stolen a kiss, but vowed that was as far as he'd allow his desires to go. Frightened and vulnerable, she'd invited him to share her pallet. But she did so seeking comfort, not because she wanted him to bed her. He'd not take advantage of that fact.

For a sennight, he'd fought the undeniable and rapidly growing attraction to the feisty lass. Lauren was everything a man could want in a woman and more, but she was not for him and never would be. Besides, he didn't know anything about her past and his own future was questionable at best. Even if he learned for certain she was not already married and she'd have him, he'd not take her maidenhead if they were not wed.

While some men had no issue with ruining a lass in order to satisfy their own selfish pleasure, he had no intention of taking her innocence, or of fathering a bairn he'd not be there to raise. Once he'd seen her to Sinclair Castle, he'd leave her in Jayden's trustworthy hands, and rejoin Robert. There was still time before the Bruce planned to confront the MacDougalls and MacCanns, but to stay with Lauren so near, or worse, to see her husband come for her, would be a crushing blow he did not wish to endure.

She snuggled at his side and he watched her sleep. He'd never tire of looking at her beautiful face. She stirred and when her thigh rubbed against his rigid manhood, he stifled the urge to groan aloud and cursed beneath his breath. Being an honorable man was certainly not all it was said to be. Mayhap he was a fool after all.

Lauren brought her hand up and covered her mouth, stifling a yawn. She opened heavy-lidded eyes and glanced around the dimly lit croft.

Alasdair was no longer on the pallet beside her and he was not asleep on the pelt before the hearth. She sat up when she heard the unmistakable creak of the rusty hinges on the door. "Where are you going? The sun has yet tae rise."

"I've need of a swim and then I am going hunting for grouse. I'll return this afternoon. I left a tankard of water and some oatcakes on the table beside the bed."

Before she could respond, the door closed. Alasdair was gone. She lay back on the pallet and brought her fingers to her lips. If she closed her eyes, she could picture his face nearing hers, just before he captured her mouth.

His breath was sweet and tasted of fennel. Although he'd shaved, the rasp of fine stubble had grazed her chin. Her stomach gave a tug and her heart fluttered. She liked kissing him and the way it made her feel all warm and tingly inside.

The recurring dreams about the events on the ship got more vivid and frightening each time she had one. The last nightmare had terrified her so much, she'd asked Alasdair to share her bed, a foolish act that could have had serious repercussions. Given her request and her enthusiastic response to his kiss, he might have mistaken her need for solace as an invitation to bed her.

Would that have been so terrible?

She had grown fond of him these last few days and found him quite attractive, despite his low opinion of himself. He'd saved her life and cared for her injuries when he could have chosen to leave her to fend for herself. From what she knew of him, he came from a respectable clan and had proved himself an honorable man by showing her nothing but respect.

She slammed her balled fist on the pallet. She knew many things about Alasdair, but she had no memory of her own past, aside from being attacked on the ship. She was not in a position to offer herself freely to any man.

Lauren sighed, then slid to the edge of the pallet and sat up. She'd been abed long enough. She nibbled on a dry oatcake and washed it down with a few sips of water. While she appreciated Alasdair's culinary attempts, she'd grown tired of the same bland fare and no doubt he had as well.

She spotted the walking stick he'd carved for her beside the pallet and snatched it up. He'd been so kind, the least she could do while he was away today was to make some bannock and mayhap some sweet rolls as a way of saying thank you.

Using the carved shaft for support, she rose to a wobbly stance, then made her way to the hearth. She gathered the ingredients she needed from the larder and set them on the table before sitting down and getting to work.

While her injured ankle made it difficult to move around the croft with ease, she managed quite well with the walking stick. She was getting stronger everyday. Soon she'd be able to leave. The thought of never seeing Alasdair again caused her heart to clench. But she could not risk accompanying him to Sinclair Castle.

Alasdair might be angry when he discovered she'd left, but then again, he might be relieved. Aside from one brief, but passionate kiss, he had shown no interest in pursuing her on an intimate level. The fact that he'd not tried to take things any farther when the opportunity presented itself, along with constantly making it clear he wanted to leave as soon as she was able, proved he had no plans for a future that included her. Best she put aside any foolish notions about Alasdair Fraser, and concentrate on her plans to escape as soon as she was strong enough. That is, if she could figure out where to go.

After she finished baking, had dusted, and tidied the

room, she returned to the pallet for a nap. Weary from overtaxing herself, she slid beneath the covers and fell asleep.

"How dare you betray my father? He trusted you with my safety when he sent you tae bring me home. When I tell him you attacked me, he'll have you beheaded." She stood with her back against the wall and glared at the man as he stepped from the shadows and approached with a dirk in his hand.

He reeked of whisky and it was evident by the way he staggered and slurred his words, he was well in his cups. In the past, she'd caught him watching her, but never for a moment believed he'd had indecent thoughts, or would try to force himself upon her.

"You've had too much tae drink and are not thinking clearly. Once you are no longer intoxicated, you will see this is wrong. Go back tae your cabin and we willna speak of this again." She tried to reason with him, but could tell by the scowl on his face, he was not about to back down.

"I have served your father since before you were born and he views me as a friend and advisor. Who do you think he will believe? You or me? Especially if I deny your claim and tell him you are the one who entered my bedchamber." He threw back his head and laughed. "Do you think he'd send me tae fetch you home if he thought for a moment you'd be in any danger?"

"You canna think this deed will go unpunished."

"It doesna matter. Once I have had my fill, I can always toss you overboard and tell your father you drown. A shame about the storm. I dove in and tried tae save you, but, alas, I failed, nearly losing my own life in the attempt." He shrugged and laughed. "Let's stop playing games and get down tae satisfying my needs." He turned the dagger in his hand then grabbed the crotch of his trews.

"I dinna find you appealing in any way and you willna touch me." She fought to keep the tremor in her voice under control. She'd not show her fear. She spotted the sword hanging on the wall above the brassier. If only she could reach it. One thing her father had insisted upon was that she learn to defend herself. She excelled at many of the tasks usually associated with men, and could challenge any man with a blade when on equal ground.

"My father has promised me in marriage tae another. Do you think he'd allow you tae dishonor me and disgrace the clan?"

"Your father is a fool. And if you're dead, how will he know? Why he has offered your hand tae Laird Sutherland is beyond me. The man is a barbarian and I would have been a much better choice."

"You hold no title or land. While I dinna wish tae marry Laird Sutherland and mean tae take up this issue with my da when we arrive on the mainland, I certainly have no desire tae become your bride and willna willingly enter your bed."

He closed the gap between them. "You have always been a feisty lass, something I have thought a good lashing would cure." He lunged forward and she grabbed for the dirk, but he outweighed her by almost one hundred pounds, and she was no match for his strength. Despite the uneven odds, she continued to struggle. She'd not give in without a fight.

Using the bulk of his body, he trapped her against the wall, her hands at her side. When he licked her neck and cheek, revulsion skittered down her spine and she thought she might vomit.

She tried to break free, but he refused to budge. Certain she was about to lose the battle, she felt another dirk at his side and slid it from the sheath. Without hesitation, she plunged it into his side. He yelled out in pain, staggered backward, then dropped to his knees.

She chastised herself for not taking better aim. A little higher and she'd have struck his heart, but had to act when she could. While the blow was not enough to kill the blackguard, it did give her a chance to escape. Without looking back, she raced from her chamber, up the steep wooden staircase, and onto the rain-soaked deck.

Gasping for breath, Lauren shot up in bed. She'd been attacked by her father's advisor, a man she'd called uncle and trusted with her life. While she still could not remember her name, she did recall she was on her way to be married to the laird of another clan. More than likely to end a feud or to gain her father land and wealth.

Now, more than ever, she needed to get away. If Alasdair took her to Sinclair Castle and they recognized her, she'd be sent home to her father, and forced to marry a man she dinna love. What was worse, she'd have to face the man who'd tried to rape her and attempt to convince her father of his deception.

Both options were unappealing, and she refused to be put in that position. But what if Callum was right? When she told her father of the attack would he chose to believe his friend and call her a whore? She shuddered at the thought.

The door opened and Alasdair entered. He carried a pair of grouse in one hand and a bouquet of heather in the other.

"I see you had another good day of hunting," she said as he totted the game and flowers across the croft, then set them on the table. "Are those for me?" She smiled and slid to the edge of the pallet.

He held up a fistful of fragrant purple blossoms. "I thought they might help tae freshen the air and add a wee bit of color tae the room."

"They're lovely.

He glanced at the hearth and a broad grin crossed his face. "I see someone has been busy. You baked these?" He tore off a piece of bannock and popped it in his mouth. He lifted the lid on a pot simmering over the fire, dipped in a ladle, then tasted the contents. "This soup is verra good. Have you grown tired of my cooking already?"

"Nay, but I thought you might enjoy a wee bit of a change. And I wanted tae show my appreciation for the fine care you've given me." She grabbed her walking stick and struggled to stand.

He was at her side in an instant. "Let me help you. Judging by how clean everything is and this fine food, I have no doubt you've overtaxed yourself. You must be exhausted." He wrapped his arm around her waist and drew her against his side. "Can you walk, or would you like me tae carry you?"

His touch made her pulse speed up and her legs grew weak. Why did he affect her so? "I—I'm fine," she stammered, then stiffened in his arms.

"About last night," he blurted out. "I must ask your forgiveness."

"Forgiveness?"

"I am sorry for kissing you and assure you it willna happen again."

He said the words with such conviction, it served to further reinforce her belief that he had no interest in her on a personal level. Then why did her heart race and her breath catch ever time he got close?

"Dinna give it a second thought. A bheil an t-acras ort?"

He tossed his head back and laughed at her question. "According to my brothers, I am always hungry. Come, and we'll enjoy the meal you've prepared."

With him steadfast at her side, she hobbled to the stool beside the table and sat while he dished out the food, then placed it before her.

"I havena had bannock or sweet rolls in many months." Alasdair tore off another piece and offered it to Lauren.

He dug into his meal with gusto. The man obviously enjoyed his food. Yet, while he had a very large-boned build, he was extremely well muscled and carried no extra weight. Again, she found herself admiring his fine physique and the way the fire lit up his rugged, chiseled features. The more time they spent together, the fonder she became of her benefactor. She'd miss him when she left and wondered if they'd met under other circumstances, if they would have found love.

They enjoyed their meal and engaged in light conversation. Alasdair proved to be quite entertaining, once he allowed himself to relax. He told her tales of his brothers and their antics when they were younger. She found his sense of humor refreshing. Something she would never have expected when they first met.

Despite their pleasurable evening, she was plagued by thoughts of her recent dream. Efforts to remain focused on Alasdair and their discussion were fruitless. She had to discover the truth. If she returned to her own clan, she would soon be married, mayhap to a man she dinna know or love. Should she tell Alasdair she remembered more about the man on the ship, that while she was not married, she was spoken for? Or should she keep her secret and pray that if they had more time together, he might find her appealing and fight for her hand? She decided on the latter, but if he believed her on the mend and ready to travel, time was running out.

Lauren covered her mouth and yawned. "I am verra tired and think it might be wise tae return tae the pallet." She placed her hands on the table and rose.

"Your ankle appears tae be healing nicely. We should be able tae leave soon. Mayhap on the morrow." He handed her the walking stick. "But I dinna think it wise tae overdo. Mayhap I should carry you?"

"I can do this." She took a step, but her legs gave way and she collapsed to the floor.

Alasdair was at her side in seconds.

"I guess my ankle isna as strong as I'd thought."

He lifted her and carried her to the pallet. "You need tae rest. If you canna travel yet, another day willna make a difference."

Chapter 8

Guilt tugged at her belly. Alasdair had shown her nothing but kindness and she hated to deceive him. Withholding information about the vast improvements in her ankle and the events she'd remembered in her recent dream was wrong. But she was convinced telling him might hasten their departure, not postpone it.

Despite her efforts, she couldn't shake the feeling of dread that squeezed her chest each time he mentioned the name Sinclair. If anything, the trepidation she experienced grew stronger. Her only option was to make Alasdair believe she was not quite ready to travel and use any means in her power to do so. She crossed herself when he wasn't looking and vowed beneath her breath to make amends, somehow.

"I am sorry tae be such a bother."

"You've no need tae apologize, lass. I should have taken things a wee bit slower. Can I get you anything afore I say goodnight?"

Why did he have to be so gracious? Lying would be easier if he'd show his gruff, stubborn side again.

She shook her head. "I've everything I need and appreciate all you've done for me. Tapadh leat." She glanced away, unable to meet his eyes for fear she'd give herself away, or worse, surrender to temptation and ask him again to share her pallet.

The thought of another kiss caused her pulse to race and her cheeks to heat. But after the first one they'd shared, Alasdair had made no attempt to repeat the act. True, he'd cleaned up his appearance and freshened his breath with fennel. He had shared a little about his past and even brought her flowers, but he also vowed he would never make improper advances again. Her heart sank. Mayhap he didn't find her appealing and was more anxious to be rid of her than she'd thought.

"Sleep well, Lauren. Hopefully, you'll feel better on the morrow."

When Alasdair turned to leave, she touched him. "Please . . ."

"Is there something you need?" His brows knit together as he stared at her fingers resting on his forearm.

"Last night when you kissed me—"

"It was a mistake and I promised it wouldna happen again," he said, then withdrew his arm. "I thought we agreed tae put it behind us."

"If you dinna find me appealing, I understand." She lowered her gaze and nibbled on her lower lip to stop it from quivering.

"I've told you afore, you're a verra comely lass. Any man seeking a bride would be proud tae call you his own. But I'm a warrior. I have sworn my sword and my life tae the Scottish King and I mean tae honor that vow. I have no desire tae marry and willna ruin a lass tae merely sate my desires."

"You have never bedded a lass?" She found that hard to believe. Alasdair was a brawny, virile warrior. If she were to wager a guess, she'd assume he'd warmed many pallets.

"I've not bedded a maiden," Alasdair growled and began to pace beside the pallet. "Why must women persist in badgering a man until he is ready tae erupt with anger? They are never happy tae let things be."

"Mayhap I wouldna be questioning you if I understood

your lack of interest in women and why you mistrust them so." The words spilled out before she could stop them.

Alasdair halted abruptly, his posture rigid. "While my personal life is none of your concern, I dinna fancy lads, nor am I a damned eunuch if that is what you think. If you must know, I have bedded and satisfied many women in the past, but never one who is untried. I havena and willna take a lass' innocence unless I'm prepared to marry her, no matter how attractive I find her." He pressed two fingers to the bridge of his nose and shook his head. "I demand we end this discussion now."

"I dinna know if I am a maiden or not," she muttered.

"A verra guid reason for me tae leave your pallet afore anything transpired." He threw his hands in the air. "You dinna remember your past and might verra well have a husband and babes waiting tae welcome you home. Once I've seen you safely tae Sinclair Castle, I will rejoin the cause. Chances are we willna cross paths again."

He was right. She didn't recall her past. But if what she dreamed was true, she wasn't married. However, she was betrothed to a man she didn't know and had been attacked by a man her father trusted and called friend. Mayhap she'd been mistaken, and if she told Alasdair about her latest dream, he might reconsider. But the information could also give him more reason to hasten their departure. Besides, until her memory fully returned, she could not be certain if the events in her dream really happened.

"You are an honorable man. I'd like tae think I am not the sort of woman who offers my virtue freely."

His voice mellowed. "I am not a saint by any means. I am human and do have needs. Leaving your pallet last night was one of the hardest things I've ever done. But you asked me tae stay with you out of fear, not passion."

"True. But it doesna mean I would refuse tae consider your courtship were circumstances different."

Alasdair swallowed hard against the lump in his throat. Did he hear her correctly? Had she said she'd welcome his courtship? Nay, like all women, she was only saying the words she thought he wanted to hear. He'd been duped by a lass' wiles and taken for a fool in the past. He was not about to do it again. Women only flattered and flirted with men like him when it suited a purpose.

"You dinna know me well enough tae make such a statement, m'lady. My thoughts are not nearly as pure as my actions."

"I've gotten tae know you better than you think these last few days. I can tell by the way you speak and how tense you become when the topic of women is mentioned that someone has hurt you verra deeply. However, just as all dogs arena black, not all women are the same. Then again, I'm not looking for a man in my life either." She rolled over, snuggled beneath the pelts, and closed her eyes.

He blew out a heavy sigh. Finally, she was ready to settle for the night and they could finish this conversation. Had it continued much longer, he'd have tossed his morals aside and silence her by climbing under the pelts, kissing her senseless, and finding his release.

He trudged back to the hearth. After tossing several large logs on the fire, he plunked himself on a stool. He removed his boots and his clothes followed. He glanced from the pallet to the pelt on the floor and back. There was no question where he'd rather spend the night. But he was not about to let down his guard, to open his heart to her, only to have it ripped from his chest if her words proved to be lie or a husband came to claim her. Regardless of what she'd said, he get any randy thoughts of Lauren out of his head.

But that was easier said than done. He lay there, staring up at the rafters for what seemed like hours, his mind racing with possibilities, his aching shaft engorged and ready. The soft lilt of her laughter echoed in his mind and he could smell the fresh, sweet scent of her porcelain-like skin. He pictured her naked body, the sleek feminine figure he'd beheld the night he'd found her on the beach and removed her wet clothes. He groaned at the conjured image of her sensual curves, pert round breasts, and the way her perfectly sculpted bottom fit into his lap. His groin stirred to the point of pain.

He could relieve himself using a man's oldest means, but with his luck, she'd awaken and catch him in the lewd act. It would be so easy to slide in behind her, and, buried to the hilt, ease his discomfort, while bringing her to the height of pleasure.

Why me, Lord? What did I do to displease you?

Again he questioned the Almighty's wisdom and wondered why he'd seen fit to torture him so. For the first time, he understood the inner turmoil his brothers had experienced when they met Cailin and Fallon. He'd teased them both relentlessly, was certain they'd lost their good senses, and could not fathom why any man that was right in the head would chose to tie himself down to one lass, to any lass.

He had no intention of perusing Lauren or any woman, but his conviction to remain on his chosen path didn't stay the lust and desire coursing through his veins. Walking the fine line between duty and desire was not as easy as he'd believed. Neither was dropping his guard or letting go of the past. Self-doubt and the inability to trust had been his constant companions, the reasons for the skeptical way he'd lived his life for so long.

He bunched a length of plaid under his head, rolled to his side, and focused on the fire—anything to get his mind off Lauren.

When Lauren awakened at daybreak and glanced around the croft, she wasn't surprised that Alasdair had left. Given his terse reaction when she'd brought up their kiss, the way he dodged her questions, and a sinking feeling of dismay grinding in the pit of her stomach, she was certain today would be the day he insisted they depart for Sinclair Castle. Mayhap he was outside readying the horse.

Time had run out. She should have told him about her dream. But second-guessing her decision now would do no good. When he returned, she would explain all she had remembered and, hopefully, he would decide to help, and not forsake her.

When she stood, her ankle felt much stronger than it had yesterday. The notion of running briefly crossed her mind again, but she had no idea where she'd go.

The morning passed quickly and she'd spent most of the time in conflict, trying to decide how best to broach the subject. When she heard two voices outside the croft, her heart all but stopped. Alasdair had returned. She recognized the deep timber of his voice right away, but who was he talking to?

She crept to the door and opened it wide enough to see two men standing a few feet from the croft and to hear their conversation. Alasdair's size and stance was unmistakable, but she could not see the face of the man who accompanied him. However, the cadence of his voice was shockingly familiar. Did she know this man?

"I'm relieved tae see you hale and hardy, my friend. I was worried when you dinna show up a sennight ago, as planned. What possessed you tae stop here rather than finishing the journey tae the castle? Other than when a few of my clansmen stayed here during the fall hunt, no one has used this place for many years. I havena been here since we were lads," the stranger said, then threw his arms around Alasdair and hugged him. "I've missed coming here and you."

"I was on my way tae your castle when I came across a lass on the beach. She had fallen, hit her head, and was needed my assistance," Alasdair replied. "I dinna mean to cause you any concern, but I couldna leave her alone and there was no way tae send word of my delay."

"A lass, you say? Does she have a name?" He stepped around Alasdair and peered toward the croft. "Is she inside?"

Alasdair nodded and followed as the man stepped onto the porch. "She wasna able tae remember much after she bumped her head, but she thinks her name is Lauren. Might you know her?"

"The name isna familiar, but I dinna know every new member of the clan. With the English on the run and so many villages destroyed in their paths, people show up all the time looking for a place tae live. Mayhap seeing her will jog my memory." He threw back his head and laughed.

"What do you find so funny?" Alasdair asked.

"I canna picture you playing nurse tae anyone, let a lone a lass. Is she at least a comely wench?"

"She's bonny enough."

"Well that explains the delay." The man thumped Alasdair on the back. "You've been at war a long time, my friend." His grin broadened. "I can only imagine what it would be like spending most of your time in the company of men. Without bonny lassies to warm your bed, it must have been pretty lonely. I canna blame you for taking the time tae rut with a willing chit."

"Nothing happened between us," Alasdair replied

gruffly. "She hurt her ankle in the fall, as well as her head, and wasna able tae sit a horse. I cared for her needs and tended her injuries, that's all. She is on the mend and I was planning tae leave on the morrow."

"Dinna get your back up, man. I was not implying you did anything wrong. Mind you, I am not so sure I could have found the same kind of restraint."

"That's because you are a swine and have no manners." Alasdair returned the man's slap on the back with such force it nearly sent him toppling off the porch.

"I wouldna try that again," the man growled. "I could beat you in a wrestling match when you were a bairn and I still can." At least a head shorter then Alasdair, the man glared skyward, his fists balled at his side. "Even if you have grown to be the size of a giant."

"A lot has changed in twelve summers."

"I'll say. The last time I saw you, a strong wind could blow you over and your hair was as red as carrots."

"I dinna need you tae remind me. And tae set things straight, few men could best me in a wrestling match. You'd be a damned fool tae try." Alasdair planted his hand on the man's shoulder and urged him toward the door. "Mayhap I should go inside first and make sure the lass is decent."

"Or mayhap we can go inside and she willna be." The man laughed.

She'd heard that whimsical cackle before. But her heart rose in her throat when the stranger's features came into view. Her trembling hand came up to cover her mouth. "Jayden," she mumbled aloud. The reason the Sinclair name made her feel ill at ease was now very clear.

Panic squeezed her chest and she found it hard to draw a breath. She didn't want him to find her. Turning on her heel and moving as fast as her legs could go—given they suddenly felt like iron weights—she made her way to the back door of the croft, and exited, just as the front door opened.

Chapter 9

"Not so fast, Jayden. We'll not barge in on the lass without giving her a fair warning." Alasdair shoved his friend aside, opened the door a crack, and called out, "Lauren. I've returned from hunting and have brought someone with me. Are you ready for visitors?"

When she didn't respond he forced the door open all the way, ducked his head beneath the frame, and entered the croft.

"Well, where is she?" Jayden asked as he pushed past Alasdair and stopped in the middle of the room. He planted his hands on his hips and surveyed their surroundings. "I can tell someone has been living here, but see no signs of a lass. Are you sure you dinna fall off your own horse and bump your head? If not, mayhap you were dreaming or imagined her."

"She was asleep on that pallet when I left this morning." He pointed to the empty bed.

"The pelts are askew and it appears someone slept there, but for all I know, it could have been you alone." Jayden bit down on his lower lip, stifling a grin.

"The lass slept on the pallet and I stayed on the floor." Alasdair spun around and his mouth gaped open. The pelt was no longer before the hearth. It was folded neatly and on the shelf. He was starting to question his own sanity.

Other than the rushes he used to cover the ground, the area in front of the hearth was bare. The trenchers and tankards they'd used for the evening meal were cleaned and stacked on a shelf beside the pile of pelts and plaid. He scratched his head. "She must have tidied up, but I have no idea where she could be. Mayhap she stepped outside for a breath of fresh air."

Jayden slapped him on the back. "You said she had a bad ankle and couldna get around well enough tae ride. She canna have gone far. Unless—"

"She was here. I swear on St. Steven's grave, there was a lass on that pallet when I left a few hours ago," he snapped. He'd had enough of his friend's cynical remarks, and there was no mistaking the patronizing tone in Jayden's voice.

Jayden shrugged. "We saw no sign of her when we arrived, mayhap she went out back for some reason."

"I dinna know why she'd venture out, but you might be right." He moved with stealth to the back door of the croft and yanked it open. "Lauren! Where are you at, lass?" A mix of anger and worry churned in his belly. Where had she gone? Had she wandered off and gotten lost, or had someone abducted her?

"Lauren," he shouted, but silence greeted him.

"You're wasting your breath, Alasdair. Either she's gone or never existed in the first place. I, for one, am parched. Come inside and join me in a drink. If we wish tae reach Sinclair Castle afore nightfall, we canna tarry here too much longer."

Scowling, Alasdair faced his grinning friend. With his hands clenched, he took a step in Jayden's direction. "I'd get that smirk off your face if you value your life. Something is amiss. Otherwise, she'd be here. Mayhap someone found out she was here and absconded with her." He slammed his fist against the wall. "Mo crèche! I should never have left her alone." He stormed past Jayden, who was still standing in the doorway.

"Dinna blame yourself for something you couldna foresee." Jayden retrieved two tankards from the shelf, then uncapped the wineskin hanging at his side. "Calm down, man, and have a drink." He poured some whisky into each vessels, then handed one to Alasdair. "If she were here, and I'm not saying she was," he quickly added, "Mayhap she just decided it was time tae leave. You are out here in the middle of nowhere. There isna a croft or village for miles. The chance that someone came along is slim. I'm sure she just remembered where she belonged and figured her family would be worried. I doubt she's met with foul play."

"I came along so that destroys your theory." Alasdair downed the content of the tankard, then slammed it on the table, knocking over the cup of flowers in the process. He scooped up one of the delicate blossoms, brought it to his nose, then crushed it in his fist. "She was here and my gut tells me she is in danger."

Jayden filled the tankards again. "Have some more whisky, then I'll help you search the area around the croft if it will make you feel better."

"I've had enough of your palver," Alasdair snapped as he fastened a baldric on his back, then sheathed his sword. He tucked a dirk in his boot and one in the leather casing at his side. "You can stay here and get drunk if you want, but I'm going tae find Lauren."

Jayden finished his drink and followed Alasdair out the door. "I'm coming with you. I want tae meet this mystery woman you've conjured up."

A search of the area turned up nothing. There was no sign of Lauren, and since the ground around the croft was primarily rock and fine stone, there were no footprints or hoof marks to follow.

His voice hoarse from calling her name, Alasdair returned to the cottage a short time later, tossed his sword on the table, then sat hard on the wooden stool. He dropped his head into his hands and released a heavy sigh of frustration. Jayden might be right and the lass had remembered who she was and decided to go home. But she could have waited until he returned and told him she was leaving. He'd have seen her safely returned to her family and then gone on to Sinclair Castle. He never wanted to be saddled with her care in the first place, so should be glad to be rid of her. Yet he could not shake the feeling she was in some sort of trouble.

"We've covered the area around the croft and there is no sign of your lass. Best you forget about her and we prepare tae head home ourselves." Jayden pulled up a stool and sat on the opposite side of the table.

"I canna leave until I find her."

"I understand your concern, but she's nowhere tae be found. I'm not convinced she was here tae begin with, but I canna tarry here much longer. Either you come with me or I leave without you. The choice is yours. My da is expecting me back afore nightfall and I dinna want tae deal with his wrath if I'm late."

"How is your da? I was so caught up in my own problem that I dinna ask about your kin. I hope they are well."

Jayden lowered his head and crossed himself. "The war with England has taken its toll on our clan as it has many others in the Highlands. I lost my two older brothers at Falkirk and my younger brother fell at Stirling Bridge. He died a sennight later. He lost an arm in battle and never recovered from the poison that ravaged his body."

"I'm sorry. So you are the only surviving son?"

Jayden nodded and poured what was left of the whisky into their cups. "Aye. I am the last and will sit as laird when my da passes. Not something I ever expected being the third son, but life doesna always turn out as planned."

"What of your mam and sister? How do they fare?"

"They're gone as well. My da is convinced my mother perished of a broken heart. Losing three sons was too much for her tae bear. Mam became ill after Torun succumbed tae his wounds and passed a fortnight later."

"And your sister?"

Jayden lowered his head and his expression grew sullen. "Edina died recently as well."

"I'm sorry." Alasdair patted his friend on the shoulder. How did it happen?" The image of Jayden's younger sister came to mind. A homely lass with more freckles than he could count.

"It happened while she was on a journey home from the Orkneys. She went there to foster with my aunt and her husband after our mother's death. Da bid her return, tae marry Duncan Sutherland so he blames himself."

"She was a young bairn when we used to visit. But I do recall a scrawny lass with stringy, yellow hair, brown eyes that seemed too large for her face, and a toothless grin. She followed us everywhere we went and was quite a pest."

"That she was. But I'd do anything to have her back and relive those days." Jayden stared at the drink in his hand and swirled the whisky in his tankard, rather than imbibing.

Alasdair immediately regretted his comments about Edina and wished he could take back the words. He studied his friend's downtrodden expression. Jayden had lost many members of his family in a short period of time. He could understand his friend's grief, given he'd lost two brothers and both his parents, too. But he'd callously spoken ill of the dead. "Forgive me. I dinna mean what I said about your sister."

"You spoke the truth." Jayden smiled. "She was not a comely bairn and was always under foot. However, she grew tae be quite a beauty and my closest confidant. Edina could outride most men and her talent with a bow and blade were unheard of for a woman. I guess growing up with four unruly brothers spawned her competitive spirit."

"You must miss her verra much."

"Aye." Jayden took a sip of his drink. "She was verra fond of you as bairn. She oft told me she was going to marry you when she grew up. Mayhap you dinna know this, but our fathers discussed the possibility of seeing the two of you betrothed on more than one occasion."

Alasdair choked on his whisky, sputtered, and coughed to clear his throat. "I find that hard tae believe. I wasna a good-looking lad nor was I the eldest son."

Jayden shrugged. "I only know what my da told me. But we dinna have to worry about that now she is gone." He bowed his head and crossed himself. "May she rest in peace."

"I lost my older and youngest brothers, along with both my parents at the hands of the English swine so I understand your loss." Alasdair cupped Jayden's shoulder and gave it a squeeze.

"If you are oldest surviving son, why are you not laird of Clan Fraser? I heard your younger Brother Connor was chief."

"Aye, I believed Connor was better suited tae lead than I was at the time. The clan elders offered me the seat in my father's place, but in the end it was Connor who accepted the title."

"You're right. A lot has changed in twelve summers." Jayden raised his tankard in the air, then finished his drink. "This was not the happy reunion I had planned. Drink up and we can be on our way. I promise once we get tae Sinclair Castle there will be plenty of food and wine, enough tae take your mind off your mystery lass."

"You go on ahead. I'm going tae search the woods around the croft again and wait until morning, in case she comes back. If she doesna return, I'll join you on the morrow."

Jayden stood and stretched. "Suit yourself, but I think it a fool's errand." He extended his arm in Alasdair's direction. "Dinna wait too long. I'll have Cook prepare a feast for your arrival."

Alasdair rose and grasped his friend's forearm, giving it a hardy shake. "Be sure and have two places saved at the table. I plan tae have the lass with me."

Jayden shook his head and exited the croft, leaving Alasdair very much alone.

Alasdair took another sip of whisky, but he'd not sit idly by and wait for her to return. He retrieved his sword and prepared to resume the search. He'd scour every inch of the woods and area around the croft until he found her.

She crouched in the bushes at the edge of the woods. Her legs cramped and she shivered from sitting on the damp ground, but she had to remain hidden. Her heart hammered against her ribs and she'd suppressed the urge to sneeze more than once. But she had to remain perfectly still. She'd overheard Alasdair and Jayden talking, and if she could hold out until morning, Alasdair would give up the search and leave. She'd then have time to decide her next move. Returning to her clan was not what she intended to do. Her goal was to remain hidden until Alasdair left. If he found her, he'd expect an explanation for her actions. The fact that she'd withheld the truth about her identity and her injuries would come to light. Why had she kept her dreams a secret? She wished now she'd taken the risk and explained all she'd remembered. Now if he found out the truth, he would never trust her again.

Seeing Jayden had prompted an array of emotions she didn't want to deal with. They had always been close and she could share her innermost thoughts without fear of ridicule. She missed him very much while living with her aunt. The one good thing, mayhap the only good thing, about her return to the mainland was a reunion with her brother. But the fact that he'd sided with his father on the matter of her marriage to Duncan Sutherland, knowing full well she'd object, was a hard blow to handle.

She'd escaped the confines of the croft just in time to avoid discovery and she silently thanked the Almighty for boons rendered. If she managed to get away, she could restart her life. One in a priory was not entirely out of the question. At least if she took her vows, she'd not be forced to marry a man she dinna love. If she was found and returned to her clan, duty dictated she go along with her father's wishes. Out of respect for her sire, she had no intention of disgracing him or her people.

But they would have to find her first.

Her legs were asleep and she wanted to stretch them, but any movement of the bushes could give away her hiding place, so she had no choice but to persevere. Her stomach growled and her lips were parched, but those basic needs were also things she had to put out of her mind until Alasdair was gone and she could return to the croft.

"Lauren!" His deep voice echoed in the clearing and seemed to bounce off the cliffs. Her heart sank at the thought of him spending fruitless hours searching for her, but to no avail. The fact that he was worried about her safety was touching, but she could not give in to the temptation to ease his mind by letting him know she was safe.

She peered through the thick bracken, shocked to see his trew-clad legs only an arm's length from her hiding spot. Did he know she was here? She closed her eyes and offered up another silent prayer. When she opened them again and saw him trotting into the woods, she blew out a ragged breath.

He'd been too close for comfort and the slightest movement or noise would have alerted him to her presence. Why didn't he just give up and leave with Jayden?

Thorns pricked her skin and one of the bushes caused her eyes and nose to itch. She brought her hand up to stifle a sneeze, but she was not able to stop it.

Had he heard her? Her heart raced when he reappeared in the clearing beside the croft. Alasdair craned his neck, peering in all directions, then stalked toward her. She chomped down on her lower lip and waited with bated breath for him to pounce.

Chapter 10

Alasdair shoved his hand into the bracken, latched onto her shoulder, and tugged. She offered no resistance, and when she was free of the thicket, collapsed at his feet. "What are you doing in there? I've searched for hours and was certain you had met with foul play. I demand you explain."

She rose to a wobbly stance and brushed the leaves and dirt from her nightrail. "I'm a woman grown and I answer tae no man." She raised her gaze, her chin held high.

"When I returned from hunting and you were gone, I thought you'd been abducted or wandered off, mayhap had gotten lost or injured. What demon possessed you tae do such a foolhardy thing?" He crossed his arms over his chest and glared down at her. While he was relieved to find her unharmed, rage twisted his belly. She had been hiding only a few feet from the croft and had deliberately ignored him when he called out to her. Not to mention she'd had Jayden thinking he'd lost his mind.

True, she didn't belong to him and never would, but she was in his care, and until such a time that she wasn't, he felt responsible for her.

"You'd best have a good reason for your careless actions. What have you tae say for yourself?" he badgered.

She stiffened her spine and glared back at him. "I dinna have tae answer tae you, but if you insist, I needed a breath of air and decided tae take a wee walk."

"Fresh air? You left the safety of the croft for some damned air? You could have opened the window shutters."

"Last night, you appeared so intent on leaving. I thought it best I stretch my legs and see how my ankle fared. I—"

"Are you daft?" He threw his hands in the air. "Do you have any idea how dangerous it is for a lass tae be out on her own without an escort? You could have gotten lost in the woods, met with a wild animal, or worse, strangers meaning tae do you harm." The thought of these prospects made him shudder.

"I'm no fool, Alasdair Fraser, and you are making more of this than necessary. I needed some air and you were nowhere around. I had no idea how long you'd be gone this time or where. You never bother tae say."

"Och, you'll not be turning this around onto me, lass. When I leave the croft, I do so for a guid reason. I am hunting, fishing, or fetching wood for the fire." He felt the heat of anger rising in his face and the pressure building in the veins of his neck. He opened and closed balled fists, inhaled deeply, then silently summoned his last bit of restraint.

"When I leave, it is necessary, but I know you are in the croft and safe. Or so I thought until today." he said through clenched teeth.

"I had my reasons also. I've been cooped up with nothing but four walls to look at for over a sennight. If I dinna get out for a bit, I thought I might go mad."

Lauren wrung her hands and shifted her weight from one foot to the other. She was no longer making eye contact when she spoke. What was she hiding?

"You may feel your jaunts away from the croft are warranted, Alasdair, and I have no doubt they are for the most part, but you are oftentimes gone from before dawn until dusk. I have no idea when or if you will return." She tried to move around him, but he blocked her path with his bulk.

"I dinna wander far and kept the croft in sight at all times, so dinna know why all the fuss." She sidestepped him and began to limp back toward the croft.

He lunged forward, clasped her upper arm, and spun her around to face him. "You'll leave when I say, and not until. We are not finished with this discussion." He tightened the grip on her arm.

She released a soft whimper and squirmed in an attempt to free herself of his grasp. "Let go of me, you're hurting my arm."

He lightened his touch, but refused to release her. Not until she told him the truth. She was hiding something and he meant to find out what that was. "I dinna mean tae hurt you, but you willna be going anywhere until you explain yourself, Madame." He took hold of her other arm and yanked her against his chest. "If you dinna wander far, why did you not answer when I called for you? What's more, why were you cowering in yonder thicket like a frightened kirkmouse? It is clear you could hear me shouting out your name, yet you dinna reply. I find that curious."

She bit down on her lower lip, still averting her eyes. When she didn't answer his question, he softened his harsh tone of voice and asked again, "Tell me why you were hiding in the bushes, lass?"

"Why do you care what happens tae me? You have made it clear more than once that you are anxious tae leave, tae pawn me off on your friend and his clan so you can rejoin the cause. I'd think you'd be happy tae be rid of me."

"You're wrong." Unsure what had possessed him to put aside his ire, he dropped his head and in a fury took possession of her mouth with a ravenous kiss. Her plump lips parted, allowing him to taste her sweetness. She fisted her hands in his tunic and he wanted nothing more than to fall to his knees, taking her with him, and find his pleasure. He had no doubt she'd surrender.

But he came to his senses before he could take things any further. He broke the kiss, and held her at arm's length. He gave his head a sharp shake. "Forgive me. I promised that wouldna happen again. But it doesna change what took place today."

"But you did kiss me and it must not happen again," she blurted out when she managed to steady her rapid breath enough to speak. "I canna do this . . . we canna do this. Is it any wonder I felt the need to get away?"

She was talking in riddles, but had managed to catch herself up and he narrowed his brow. "So you admit you were planning tae run away?"

"I'll admit tae naught. I told you, I needed tae stretch my legs if you planned on leaving for Sinclair Castle. Why is that so hard tae understand?"

His head started to spin. He'd never met a woman who could talk in circles, twist his words, and distract him the way she could.

He released one of her arms, cupped her chin, then raised it until her eyes met with his. "My friend Jayden thought me daft when I told him about you and then you vanished."

His heart twisted when she clasped his hand and glared at him with narrowed eyes.

"What did you tell him? I must know."

He immediately picked up a tremor in her voice. Was she frightened of Jayden for some reason?

"I told him I found you on the beach a sennight ago and brought you here tae take care of your injuries."

"What else did you tell him?" she asked, then sucked in a short, sharp breath.

"I told him your name, but it meant nothing to him. I insist you tell me what is going on, Lauren. Why did Jayden's presence make you feel threatened? Was he the man who assaulted you on the ship? I demand to know."

She shook her head and said nothing.

"Tell me. Was he the man who attacked you?"

"Nay. Jayden is not the man who attacked me."

"It is obvious by your reaction that you know him. Tell me how."

"He is my brother." She broke free of his grasp, spun around and ran toward the croft.

He stood there momentarily, his mouth gaping open in disbelief as she sprinted off like there was nothing wrong with her ankle. Had she lied to him from the start about everything?

His heart thundered in his chest as he raced after her, reaching the back door as she slammed it shut in his face. He tried to open the latch, but she was holding on to it from the inside and it wouldn't budge. He pounded on the wooden plank with his fist. "Open the door Lauren. Or should I say Edina?"

"Please go away and leave me be, Alasdair."

Her voice shook and he was certain she was crying.

"Open up. Now. You canna hold on tae the latch for long. Let go and step away or I'll break the door down," he ordered.

When she didn't answer, he pressed down on the latch with all his force then shoved the door open. He stumbled forward when it gave way with ease and stormed inside.

She sat on a stool before the fire, her entire body trembling. He stared at her in disbelief. This striking woman could not possibly be Edina Sinclair. The same homely, freckle-faced lass he'd known as a bairn. If so, Jayden was right, she'd grown into a stunning beauty. No wonder he didn't recognize her. But that didn't matter. He would take her to her father and do his best to forget her.

She might have a good explanation for her actions, but he didn't want to hear it. She'd lied to him, deceived him for her own gain, and he'd been made a fool of by yet another woman. He'd not feel sorry for her and had every intention of taking her to Sinclair Castle immediately, even if they had to travel all night.

"Get up," he growled. When she didn't respond, he took her by the wrist and dragged her to her feet. He felt no remorse for his roughness, nor would he let her manipulate him again.

"Where are you taking me?" She tried to dig in her heels.

"Home tae your clan, where you belong. The sooner we leave, the better. I'll find you something tae wear and we'll be off."

"Alasdair, please I canna go home. Let me tell you why I—"

He held his hand in the air before she could finish. "I'll listen tae no more lies from you. I dinna know how you managed tae fake your head injury, but everything since the day I found you has been a deception. A jest at my expense. Hell, you dinna even tell me your real name."

"I wasna lying. I did hurt my ankle, and I dinna know my name."

"Then why did you tell me it was Lauren?" he snapped.

"I never did. When I woke up, I honestly dinna remember who I was or how I came to be on the beach. You asked, and Lauren was the only name that came tae mind, but I never said it was mine. I swear on all that is holy."

He spat on the floor. "You wouldna know the truth if it jumped up and bit you in the arse. I saw the way you ran back tae the croft. There was no sign of a limp, yet last night I had tae carry you tae the pallet because you couldna stand." He made no effort to hide his ire. "Do you take me for an idiot?

"I admit that my ankle is much better than it was." She dropped her chin and studied her feet. "Mayhap I should have told you sooner, but I was afraid tae say anything for fear you would insist on taking me tae Sinclair Castle."

"When did you remember your real name? How long have you been playing me for a fool?"

"I dinna recall my name until I saw my brother today." She placed her hand on his forearm. "Please, you must believe me."

"Why did you run rather than greet him? He told me your father was devastated when he thought you'd died. To know his daughter was alive would bring him great joy."

"His four sons were my father's whole life. I've done my best tae equal my brothers on horse, with a sword, bow, and when hunting. I can outride and outshoot all but Jayden. Yet my da has never shown any interest in me. Aside from what he stands tae gain from a well planned betrothal tae the laird of a neighboring clan."

"You are betrothed?" He slammed his fist on the table. "Is there no truth in anything you've told me?"

"My father has promised my hand in marriage tae the future laird of the Sutherland clan. He is hoping to forge an alliance, but I havena given my consent. I dinna wish tae marry Duncan Sutherland and hope my father will reconsider."

"He doesna need your consent and he'll not repudiate his decision if the union will benefit the clan. I know your father and he is not the type of man tae be easily swayed." He paused and studied her blanched face for a moment. "When did you remember you were betrothed, or have you known all along?" She'd been lying to him from the start so why should this be any different. He clenched his fists at his side, waiting for her reply.

She lowered her gaze and twisted her hands. "Yesterday. I had another dream while you were away and I—"

"So you saw fit tae hold back that information from me as well," he growled. "You really must think I'm a damned buffoon. I fell for your ruse of being injured and you almost had me believing you were sincere and honorable." He spun around and stomped toward the door, intent on putting some much-needed space between them.

"Where are you going?" she asked. "Will you not let me explain?"

"There is no point in discussing this any further. I canna believe a word you speak."

"Alasdair, please." She moved toward him.

He held up his hand to stay her advance. "I have nothing more tae say. You'll find a pair of trews and a tunic in a canvas sack by the hearth. I'd suggest you put them on, lest you wish tae be presented tae your da in your nightrail. I'm going tae ready Odin. Be prepared tae leave when I return." He yanked open the door and hurried out of the croft.

Chapter 11

Edina retrieved the canvas satchel from beside the hearth and opened it. Inside, she found clothes that were far too large for her petite frame and bound to hang on her like a grain sack. But Alasdair was right. She didn't want to travel on horseback wearing only a nightrail, nor was it how she wished to be presented to her father.

If only Alasdair could find it in his heart to forgive her deception, would reconsider his decision to turn her over to her family, and offer to help her with her plight.

After putting on the trews and rolling up the legs so they did not drag on the ground, she donned the tunic and turned up the sleeves. She glanced down at her appearance and shook her head—certain she looked like one of the homeless waifs she'd seen on the streets of Edinburgh the time she'd accompanied her mother to the home of her clan. Actually, it was the second time she had been there. She was born in Edinburgh on one such visit, the reason why her mother chose to name her Edina. In Gaelic, it meant of Edinburgh, and her mam told her that while she now resided in the Highlands, the name always reminded her of home.

She missed her mother very much, but her thoughts quickly returned to her current situation. Alasdair was furious, and she really did not blame him for feeling betrayed. But she was not a devious person by nature. She'd done what she had out of necessity and never intended to hurt him. She really did not remember her name or what happened on the ship when he found her. Somehow, she had to make him understand. But given his ire when he stormed out of the croft, this was not the right time. Suffice to say, the journey to Sinclair Castle promised to be a long and dismal ride.

"Are you dressed and ready tae leave?" Alasdair poked his head in the door and their eyes met.

"Aye, as ready as I will ever be. While I do appreciate the loan of your clothes, I am afraid they dinna fit verra well." She wrapped her arms around her waist to keep the trews from falling off her hips.

Alasdair stomped across the room, yanked the drawstring from his supply sack, and tossed it at her. "Use this tae cinch the trews and make haste. The hour grows late and I want tae be away while we still have some daylight."

Despite the strong temptation to speak her mind and comment on his rudeness, she bit her tongue, deciding it was better to remain silent than to risk riling him further. Edina tied the rope snuggly around her waist, then picked up the satchel and began filling it with dried venison, turnips, and the oatcakes.

"What are you doing?" Alasdair crossed his arms over his chest and glared at her through narrowed eyes.

"I thought we might have need of a few things tae nibble on along the way. Have you a wineskin I can fill with water?"

He patted the deerhide flagon that hung at his side. "I've already taken care of that and have another on my saddle. We have a hard ride ahead of us and if you're quite finished dallying, I'd like tae get started."

She stepped forward and placed her hand on his forearm. "I know you're upset with me Alasdair, but you must believe me when I say that I never meant tae do anything tae—"

"I told you I dinna want tae hear your excuses. They mean naught from someone who has proved herself tae be a liar."

She stood her ground. "You promised tae protect me, Alasdair, tae keep me safe. Yet you are willing tae toss me tae the wolves without giving it a second thought or allowing me the chance tae explain," she replied sharply.

"I hardly consider turning you over tae your kin as a betrayal. As for an explanation, I have heard enough of your lies."

"My father and brother care not about my happiness. They plan tae hand me over tae a man I dinna know or love with no more regard than they would a prize steer or mare at an auction. What else would you call it?"

"I call it following Highland tradition, the way it has been for centuries. Without these practices where would we be?"

"Tae hell with Highland tradition," she replied, showing no remorse for cursing. Something a lady of her standing would never do. "If only you would believe me when I tell you I was injured and dinna know my name. I never meant to deceive you, Alasdair."

"I thought you were different from other women I have known in the past, but I was wrong."

"I believed you were different as well. But it appears you live in the past like my father and are not the man I hoped you were."

"Think of me what you will, but you can rest assured, m'lady, I willna be fooled by you again." He lifted her hand from his arm, then moved away. "I'll be outside and suggest you dinna keep me waiting any longer."

There was no mistaking the disappointment and distain in his voice. Edina wished she had told him the truth when her memory first returned, but it was too late and there was no going back. "I come anon. I just want tae gather a few more things."

Alasdair planted his hands on his hips, watching in silence as she picked up some eating utensils, two trenchers, and two tankards, then placed them in the sack with the food. While he never uttered a word, the scowl on his face spoke volumes. Certain she had what they needed, Edina walked toward the door, but stopped to pick up a length of plaid from the foot of the pallet, then draped it around her shoulders. Evenings could be very chilly in northern Scotland, even in the summer.

Walking ever so gingerly, she followed Alasdair to where Odin stood, sharp stones and gravel digging into the soles of her bare feet as she crossed the clearing. Large hands encircled her waist and before she knew it, he had lifted her onto the saddle.

"I had no boots tae offer you and even if I did, they'd likely fall off. I'm afraid your feet will have tae remain bare. If you unroll the legs of the trews, they will at least be covered." He didn't wait for her permission and proceeded to tug down the fabric.

"Have you another horse?" She glanced around, in search of a second mount. He could not possibly mean for them to ride into her father's keep together, especially if he was concerned about appearances.

"Odin is strong enough tae carry us both. You weigh no more than a bairn."

"For us tae ride on the same animal isna proper. What will my father think?"

"You should have considered that when you hid from your brother," he snapped. "A lot has happened since I found you on the beach that most people wouldna deem proper. Had you made your presence known when Jayden was here, you could have ridden home in his company. So unless you wish tae walk all the way tae your father's castle, I'd suggest you not question how I mean tae get you there."

"How long afore we'll arrive?" she asked softly.

"Too long," he grumbled then climbed into the saddle behind her. "Get yourself seated properly and hold on because I dinna mean tae waste time."

Her body tensed and her breath hitched when she felt the intimate rub of his muscular thighs and the warmth of his rock hard chest pressed against her back. When he encased her with arms of iron and grabbed the reins, the scent of man and musk made her dizzy with desire. She tried to lean forward, to put a bit of space between them, but he yanked her back so her bottom rested against his groin.

"You'll tire too quickly if you sit forward like that. You have nothing tae fear, m'lady. My intentions are strictly honorable and your virtue will remain intact." He didn't bother to hide the sarcasm in his voice.

Given the way her body reacted to his nearness and the fact he was still very angry, relaxing was not an easy task. She wiggled her bottom, flexed her legs and arms, then fisted the horse's mane. "I'm ready."

"Finally," was all Alasdair said, then he dug both heels into Odin's flanks.

The steed lunged forward. Were it not for her skill as a competent horsewoman, she'd have been terrified by the speed at which the horse covered the rocky terrain. At this rate they'd arrive at their destination well before nightfall.

Her stomach sank at the thought of seeing her kin and having to explain what had happened. Four summers had passed since her mother died and her da sent her to foster with her aunt. She was not the same complacent lass she used to be, and she was certain she'd not be able to accept her father's demands without protest.

Her parent's marriage was far from ideal, yet somehow they'd managed to tolerate each other for more than twenty summers. They'd met at court, when her father came to pay his respects and taxes to the former Scottish king and her mother caught his eye. Her mam had no desire to leave her beloved Edinburgh, or to marry a Highlander, but once the king sanctioned the union, she had no choice.

The only daughter of a powerful laird, Edina always knew her fate would be similar to that of her mother—an arranged betrothal, possibly to a man she'd never even met—but secretly dreamed she'd someday marry a man she loved. She had no doubt that her da would be pleased to see her, as would Jayden. But there were still the matters of explaining why she'd spent the last sennight alone in Alasdair's company, her objection to marrying Duncan Sutherland, and, worst of all, facing her father's advisor and dearest friend, the man who had attacked her on the ship and, like everyone else, believed her dead. Mayhap it would have been better if she'd drowned.

If he continued to push Odin without taking a break, he'd run the poor beast into the ground, but every moment with Edina nestled in his lap was pure torture. The sooner they arrived at Sinclair Castle, the better. However, when froth began to form on the horse's chest and withers, Alasdair eased up on the reins and the faithful steed broke from a brisk trot to a walk.

"Are we stopping?" Edina asked hesitantly.

"Only long enough for Odin tae rest and have a drink. There are still several miles tae travel afore we reach your father's castle." He brought the animal to a halt in a small clearing, slid from the saddle, then reached up to assist her.

"I can do it myself." She lifted her chin, pushed his hands away, and climbed down unaided. "You dinna need to coddle me, Alasdair, I can ride as well as any man."

"So I've been told," Alasdair grunted. Under different circumstances, he might have found her temerity appealing. He studied the determination in her eyes, but despite her effort to put on a stoic front, she looked weary. After being abed for a sennight, she was bound to be exhausted. Were he not so furious with her, he might take things a bit easier. But

Edina had betrayed him, lied to him for her own gain, just like every other woman he'd ever known. He refused to take any pity on her, or to slow their journey on her behalf.

He grasped the wineskin from the back of the saddle, took a drink, then tossed it to her. "Have some water and best you tend tae your needs. I'm not sure when or if we will be stopping again."

She took a few sips from the flagon before handing it back to him. "Thank you. I will use yonder thicket if you dinna mind."

He gave a curt nod. "Do what you must and make haste. Daylight is waning and I want tae arrive at your father's keep afore dark. We have enough tae account for as it is and being forced tae make camp for the night would only make things worse. As it is, I'll be lucky if I'm not drawn and quartered for tainting your reputation."

"Naught happened between us and my da will understand. He must. Our fathers were friends and you are an honorable man."

"When a father has what he believes tae be a guid reason to question his daughter's virtue, the past and honor holds no credence. I suggest you do what you must while I water the horse." He dismissed her with a sweep of his arm.

After rolling up the legs of the trews so they didn't drag on the ground, Edina moved toward a clump of bushes at the edge of the clearing. He watched the gentle sway of her hips as she walked away and his groin stirred. "Mo crèche," he cursed. After all that had happened, she still had the ability to make his pulse race and his blood heat. The sooner they got to their destination the better.

He whistled for Odin and his obedient mount trotted over and nudged his arm. "I've sworn off women my entire life and for good reason, lad." He stroked the horse's forelock, then scratched the animal's ear. "Be glad you're a beast and dinna have tae trouble yourself about such things." He fisted the reins and led the horse to a nearby stream to drink.

Edina cleared her throat with a soft cough before speaking. "I'm finished and ready tae leave whenever you are."

Alasdair remained silent. He squatted beside the water and refilled the wineskin before answering. "The sack with the food is tied tae the back of Odin's saddle. I suppose there's time for you tae have a wee bite afore we go." He didn't turn around or look at her.

"I'm not hungry. Best we be on our way," she replied tersely.

"Suit yourself. Dinna say the offer wasna made." He stood and before she could respond, he lifted her into the saddle, and climbed up behind her.

They traveled the rest of the trip in silence. He slowed the pace a little, but the gesture was for Odin's sake and not for the lass. Or so he told himself. Regardless of what happened between them, he was and would remain a gentleman.

By the time they reached the castle of the Clan Sinclair the sun had set. Alasdair's stomach twisted. He dreaded facing Jayden and his father after making a fool of himself, prattling on about the lovely lass he'd found on the beach and had spent more than sennight taking care of.

Despite telling Jayden nothing had happened, his friend was convinced he'd bedded the lass. Her brother would surely want to see him flayed when he found out the woman he'd told him about was his sister. The laird would want retribution and he couldna really blame him if he believed the worst. Were he her father, he'd likely react in the same way. Edina was a comely lass, and most men would have taken advantage of their time alone together.

Resolved to face what fate had in store for him, Alasdair stiffened his spine and kicked Odin into a trot. Best he get this over with rather than speculate the outcome.

As they neared the drawbridge, two burly guards stepped into their path. "Halt and state your business," the first said, then widened his stance and drew his sword. The second held a claymore in one hand, and with the other, lifted a torch in the air.

Alasdair stopped the horse and dropped the reins. He held his hands out to the side, his palms skyward. "My name is Alasdair Fraser and I come in peace. I wish tae see Laird Sinclair and my friend Jayden. They are expecting me."

The second guard took a step forward and gasped when Edina peered around Alasdair's shoulder. "Saint's preserve us!" He crossed himself, then moved closer. "She's alive. How can this be? We were told she drowned."

"What are you babbling about, man?" the first guard growled and stepped into the light.

"The laird's daughter, she's alive. May the Almighty be praised." The second man crossed himself again.

"Hello, Thomas. You are looking well," Edina said, then smiled at the second guard. "As are you, Clive." She bobbed her head at the first man. "I'm pleased tae be home, but am verra weary. If you would be so kind as tae raise the gate and allow us tae enter, I'd be verra grateful."

Clive nodded. "Aye, right away, m'lady." He jabbed Thomas with his elbow. "You heard the mistress, stop staring like you've just seen a banshee, open the gate, then fetch the laird."

"Och, there is no need to bother my da at this moment, Thomas. Mayhap he has already retired. In the morning would be soon enough."

Alasdair could hear the tension in her voice. She obviously dreaded facing her family as much as he did.

"Your father is in the great hall having his evening meal. He will be most anxious to hear of your return," Thomas replied.

Chains rattled and iron groaned as the large metal blockage inched skyward.

"I'll fetch the laird and Lord Jayden." Clive handed Thomas the torch, ducked beneath the partly raised gate, and raced across the bailey.

"I'd hoped to approach your da on my own," Alasdair grumbled as he urged Odin forward. He swallowed hard and the knot in his stomach tightened. Something told him things could only go from bad to worse.

The bailey was all but empty when they arrived. Aside from a few villagers, most of the clan members were in their crofts or at the castle taking part in the evening meal. A young squire sprinted forward and bowed as Alasdair reined Odin in and slid from the saddle.

"I'd be pleased tae tend your mount, m'lord." The boy's eyes widened when he looked at Edina. "Once your wife has dismounted," he quickly added.

"We're not married," Alastair replied gruffly as he helped Edina down. "Take care of Odin. Give him some oats and a good rub down afore you put him out to pasture." He handed the lad a piece of silver and patted his head.

"Oh, thank you, m'lord!" the lad exclaimed. He clutched the coin in one hand and grabbed the reins with the other. "I'll see him well fed."

"He dinna recognize you," Alasdair commented as he watched the lad lead the horse away.

"He canna be more than eight or nine, and I've been gone the better part of four summers. Judging by his age, I would think him not much more than a babe when I left. I was not quite fifteen summers when I was sent tae foster with my aunt and I am no longer a bairn. There are many who willna know who I am."

"What goes on here?" a loud voice bellowed, causing them both to spin around.

At the top of the stone staircase stood a tall man with a brawny build. It had been a long time since Alasdair had seen Laird Sinclair, but other than his graying hair, the man had changed very little over the years. Jayden flanked him, his face contorted with a scowl.

"Speak up, Fraser. Tell me how it is you arrive in the company of my daughter. A lass we believed lost at sea."

Jayden stepped forward and crossed his arms over his chest. "Best you explain yourself, Alasdair, afore I cut out your heart and feed it tae the dogs."

Chapter 12

"What have you tae say for yourself, man?" Jayden cast a lethal glare at Alasdair and fingered the hilt of his sword. "Explain tae me why you lied. You told me you dinna know the lass you claimed to find on the beach."

"I spoke the truth. When I came upon her, she was unconscious. I dinna have any idea who she was or how long she'd been there. At first I thought her dead, but when I realized she was still breathing, my only concern was tae get her out of the frigid water and tae find somewhere warm and dry, so I could tend her injuries. Who she was mattered naught."

Jayden's posture stiffened and he took a menacing step forward. "She wasna unconscious for a whole sennight. When she awakened, you should have come for me, or brought her home? Mayhap, you were more interested in sating your needs."

The words of his childhood companion cut through him like a blade. "What are you suggesting?" Alastair clenched his teeth, fighting hard not to lose his temper. Jayden and his father were understandably shocked to learn that Edina was alive, but he never dreamed his friends would question his honor.

"I asked her name, but she couldna remember. Nor did she recall how she came tae be on the beach. She took a nasty bump tae the head, so I figured her memory would return in time."

"You spent a sennight alone together and you told me you had no intent on marrying the lass you found. She's my sister. Damnation, man! Did you think you could defile her then cast her aside and no one would be the wiser?"

Momentarily at a loss for words, Alasdair raked his fingers through his hair. Given the circumstances, and if he were Jayden, he'd likely think the worst as well. But he'd not acted on his desires and refused to stand there and be accused of deeds he did not commit.

"Many summers have passed since I saw her last, and even you must admit her appearance has changed immensely. Edina is no longer a bairn of seven summers. She's a woman grown and looks nothing like she did when we were lads." Alasdair scrubbed his hand across his beard-stubbled chin. "Had I known her identity, I would have brought her home immediately."

"Instead, you took her tae my father's hunt camp, had your way with her, and damned the consequences?" Jayden growled. "For that, you will pay." He took another step in Alasdair's direction with his blade raised.

"Jayden, please, naught happened between us. If anyone offered tae speak up on Alasdair's behalf, I thought you would. He is your friend, as well as your guest. You canna possibly think he would do anything tae disgrace me or the clan." Edina stepped between the two men, glared at her brother, then focused on her father. "Da, things are not as they appear."

"Hold your wheest, daughter, and mind your place! I will speak tae you on this matter later. Right now, I want to hear what happened in the croft," her father growled and drew his own sword. "Only a coward hides behind a lassie's skirts."

Alasdair held his hand in the air. "Hush, lass, listen to your father, and mind your tongue. I dinna need anyone tae speak on my behalf. If your da and brother wish tae accuse me of something, let them speak their mind. I have naught to hide."

"Do you think me a damned fool?" her father bellowed. "You appeared at my keep, with my daughter in tow. She is barefooted and wearing men's clothing. According to what you told my son, the lass you found has been with you more than a sennight, yet she was nowhere tae be seen when he discovered you were staying at the hunting croft. If she had done naught to disgrace herself and dinna remember who she was, there was no need for her to hide from her brother."

"Father, you're mistaken. I swear it on my mother's grave, things are not what you think," she cut in. "Alasdair is the son of one of your dearest friends. He—"

"Silence! I've had enough of your insolence," Laird Sinclair shouted. "Andrew Fraser's character is not in question. He was an honorable man and a brave patriot. However, that doesna mean the son follows in his father's path. I've a mind tae flog the truth out of him, then see him drawn and quartered for his actions." Laird Sinclair's face reddened and contorted with anger as he searched the bailey. "Helen." He summoned a young woman standing a few feet away.

"Aye, m'lord." The lass scurried over and bobbed a curtsy.

"Take Edina tae her chamber. See she bathes, dons some proper clothing, then lock her door. I will speak with her when I am finished dealing with this swine." He pointed his finger at Alasdair.

"Come, m'lady. I would be happy tae assist you," Helen said.

"Nay! I'll not go anywhere until my father listens tae reason. There is something verra important that I must say."

"You will go tae your chamber. Your presence here and constant nattering only reinforces what I already believe tae be true," her father growled.

She raced to Alasdair's side and placed her hand on his

forearm. "I'm sorry this has happened, but you must speak up in your own defense and make him understand."

"I order you tae obey me this minute, Edina. Go with Helen tae your chamber and wait for me there," Laird Sinclair insisted.

"But, Father, I need tae—"

"You need tae heed what I say. I summoned you home tae marry the soon-tae-be laird of the Sutherland Clan, not for a dalliance with the first scoundrel you came across. You have disgraced me and the clan with your actions." Her father gestured with a sweep of his hand toward the castle. "Do as you are told and leave me tae settle this unsavory matter. I'll not hear another word from you."

"You arena helping me, lass. Do as your da asks," Alasdair whispered as he lifted her hand and placed it in Helen's.

"Please, m'lady, leave this for the men tae handle. I will pour you a hot bath. Once you've changed intae your own clothing and have had a wee bite tae eat, you'll feel much better."

"Why won't anyone listen tae me?" Edina protested.

"You'll have your chance tae speak with da when he is finished here. Go with Helen. You have caused enough of a palver for one day." Jayden clasped her by the wrist and dragged her towards the keep. "Alasdair is right. You are not helping, only making him look guilty of the charges."

Alasdair battled the urge to intervene as Edina was led away. He did not approve of the callous way her brother and father treated her upon her return, and under normal circumstances would not stand by and allow her to be forcefully taken against her will. But with armed guards surrounding him, and her irate sire to deal with, he was in no position to stop them.

After Edina and Helen entered the keep and slammed the door behind them, Jayden turned to face Alasdair. "Does what we shared as lads mean naught? I canna believe you would betray me in this manner," he spat. "I've heard tales of your younger brother, Bryce, and his way with the women, but thought you were different."

"My brother's reputation, while grossly exaggerated, is not up for discussion," Alasdair responded sharply. "I will say this only once. I dinna treat your sister with the utmost respect. At no time did anything of an improper, intimate nature happen between us. If she was a maiden when I found her, she remains so. I willna be accused of something I dinna do. Fate brought me tae her on the beach, I tended her injuries, and no more."

"Are you saying you dinna find Edina appealing or worthy of your attention? Are you questioning her virtue?" Jayden asked, anger resonating in his voice.

"You are twisting my words. There is no denying that your sister is a comely lass. Tae say I wasna tempted by her beauty would be a lie. But aside from women who lift their skirts for coin, I dinna bed a lass unless I am prepared tae make her my bride. Since I never intend tae marry, I wouldna dishonor Edina or any maiden in this way. I take great offense that you would think so little of me."

"I've heard quite enough from you, Fraser!" Laird Sinclair moved forward. "Either you confess the truth or spend the night in the pit while I decide your punishment."

"I have already told you what happened. If you see fit tae reprimand an innocent man, so be it. But I will not grovel at your feet or beg mercy for acts I dinna do." Alasdair crossed his arms over his chest and waited for the chief of the Sinclair clan to respond.

"Take him tae the pit!" Laird Sinclair ordered. "Put him in irons and post a guard. After I have spoken with my daughter, I will decide what is to become of him. Mayhap after spending the night with the rats, he will rethink his lies."

Alasdair offered no resistance when two guards grabbed his arms. "That willna be necessary," he stated calmly while pulling free of their grasp. "I will come with you. Lead the way."

He accompanied the guards across the bailey to an opening in the ground surrounded by a pile of stones. One of the men lit a torch and guided Alasdair down a steep, narrow tunnel. The other followed behind.

"This place isna fit for man nor beast. But it will serve the likes of you," the first guard said as they entered a narrow underground cavern.

"Chain him up and let us take our leave. The rancid smell is making my stomach turn." The second guard gagged and covered his mouth with his hand.

"Aye. I agree," the first guard replied. He led Alasdair to the back of the pit, fastened iron bands around his wrists, then rattled the chains attached to the mud wall. "That should hold you until Laird Sinclair decides what tae do with you. I'd be praying for a fast decision and a quick end if I were you."

During his years as a warrior, Alasdair had found himself in many undesirable situations. He'd suffered hardship, inclement weather, starvation, illness, and had even seen several pits in his day, but he had never been the one imprisoned. The dojon at Fraser castle was a palace compared to this dark, dingy cesspit.

The air was heavy and he tried to suck in a deep breath, but the disgusting stench of damp earth, decaying rushes, and human excrement caused his stomach to revolt. He choked down the bile as he watched the guards make a hasty retreat down the tunnel and the light fade to nil. The squeal of rats and a tug on his boot, reminded him he was not alone.

This was not how he had envisioned spending the night, and suddenly imagined what it would be like to be buried alive.

He shook his head, unable to fathom how he ended up in this predicament. He'd been on his way to visit friends and a much-needed rest from war. He happened upon the lass and couldn't in good conscience leave her to die on the beach, so offered his assistance. He'd tended her injuries, denied the strong attraction and desire to bed her on more than one occasion, and returned her to her family as soon as he realized her identity. Yet here he sat, awaiting his fate and sharing his last hours on this earth with what could be disease-ridden vermin.

He yanked on the chains, but they were firmly secured to the wall. Unable to see his surrounding and somewhat grateful for small mercies, he sank to the ground and tucked his knees up close to his chest. This was going to be a long night, one during which he did not plan to sleep.

His mind wandered to the castle, to Edina, and his heart sank. While he was still furious with the lass for deceiving him, and would not ask for her hand, he'd become quite fond of her and admittedly a bit possessive. He wondered how her father would deal with her, and if he would believe her story. She'd already suffered enough humiliation and he hoped her da would listen. Somehow, he doubted that. To make matters worse, she was to marry a man she didn't even know. If he would still have her.

A brief bout of pity gave way to a surge of anger. "She lied tae me and will get what she deserves. Edina is just like the other women I've met in my life. I swear if I can find a way out of this mess, I will leave, and forget about her," he vowed aloud. He could not allow himself to fall prey to her beauty and whiles again. It was because of her deception he was imprisoned in the first place. He cursed and dropped his head, resting it on his knees.

Who was he trying to fool? While there was no hope of a future with the beguiling lass, getting her out of his mind was not going to be an easy task. Figuring out a way to avoid execution even harder.

Chapter 13

A click of the lock caused Edina to spin around. Her heart pounded in anticipation. Had her father finally come to speak with her and give her a chance to explain?

The door swung opened and Helen entered the chamber carrying a wooden tray laden with an assortment of vegetables, a wedge of cheese, a pot of honey, a loaf of bannock, and a tankard of mead. "You arrived after the evening meal, but Cook put together a few things tae tide you over until morning. The drink will warm you and help you sleep," she said cheerfully.

"I'm not hungry and I dinna wish tae sleep." Edina paced the room. "Why has my father not come tae see me? Have you any word of Alasdair?"

Helen shook her head. "I know naught what keeps your da and havena heard anything about Lord Fraser, m'lady."

"I canna believe my father treated Alasdair so disgracefully and gave you orders to lock me in my chamber."

"I'm truly sorry the laird dinna herald your return in a more joyous manner. I am sure he will come anon, realize he has made a mistake, and have a change of heart." Helen placed the tray on a table in the corner the chamber, then faced Edina. "I've missed you verra much and am pleased tae have you home. Even if it is only until you are wed."

"I dinna wish to marry. Especially a man I have never met. I would rather take the vows and spend my life in prayer. I will tell my father so when he comes to see me. If he ever arrives." Edina blew out a heavy sigh, then sat hard on a stool by the hearth.

"I'm told the young Laird Sutherland is a guid man and according tae some, quite handsome. His father is one of the most powerful chiefs in all the Highlands and his son will soon take his place." Helen arranged some food on a trencher, then faced Edina. "In the least, he is not as auld as most of the suitors who have asked for your hand."

"I dinna understand why Duncan Sutherland asked for my hand. He has never laid eyes on me."

"You are considered quite a prize, m'lady. News of your beauty has spread across the Highlands and an alliance with your father is coveted by many of the local lairds. There have been many offers."

"If Duncan Sutherland is as handsome as you claim and his father so powerful, why is he not already married?" Edina asked.

Helen shrugged. "Rumor has it that he was betrothed tae his cousin, a lass from the Clan Mackenzie. But that ended when his father took ill and announced his son would take his place as head of the clan. The old laird met with your da and offered him an alliance, cattle, and a chest of gold if he consented tae the union. Once a betrothal was agreed upon, your da sent a missive tae King Robert. Since he is trying tae unite the clans, the Bruce sanctioned the nuptials."

"I've always known that my fate would be dictated by my status as the laird's only daughter. Just as I know being bartered for with less regard than livestock is common, but hoped I would be spared the anguish." Edina dropped her head into her hands.

"I wish there was something I could do tae help," Helen said as she placed her hand on Edina's shoulder.

"Mayhap there is." Edina raised her head and clasped the maid's hand. "We have been friends since we were bairns. I begged my da tae let you accompany me tae the Orkneys, but he refused. If you could leave the door unlocked, mayhap I could depart afore my father arrives."

"Och, nay, m'lady. Please dinna ask me tae defy the laird. William, son of the village cobbler, and I were handfasted last fall. He has already spoken tae my father and had planed tae ask your da for permission to marry me this verra night. I canna risk your father's wrath." Helen lowered her head and glanced away. "We are verra much in love and hope tae be wed on the summer solstice."

Edina rose and tugged Helen into a tight embrace. "Dinna give my request another thought. I willna ask you tae do anything that might jeopardize your wedding plans. But if you could find out what has become of Alasdair, I would be truly grateful. I am about tae go out of my mind with worry."

"Are you in love with Lord Fraser?" Helen asked bluntly.

Edina's spine stiffened and she took a step back. "Nay. Why would you ask such a thing?"

"I dinna mean tae speak out of turn, but your face does light up when you say his name and he is dashing in a rugged sort of way. You did spend a sennight together and I only thought—"

"You thought the accusations my father made were true," Edina snapped. "I told my da that naught happened between Alasdair and me, and spoke the truth."

"I meant no disrespect and would never question your word, m'lady. Please forgive me." Helen dropped to her knees and bowed her head.

"Alasdair saved my life and cared for me when I was ill. I am indebted tae him for his kindness and if he is wrongfully punished because of me, I couldna live with myself. I only wish tae know he is well and unharmed."

"Best you be thinking about your betrothed and not another man," a deep voice bellowed from the doorway.

Laird Sinclair strode across the room and paused a few feet from where Edina stood. "Well? Are you ready to tell me what happened while you were in Fraser's company?"

"Where is he?" Edina squared her shoulders and raised her chin. "I demand you tell me at once." The words left her lips before she could stop them.

Her father's brow creased and his face twisted in anger. "You demand? I am your father and your laird, best you remember your place. Is this obstinacy the reward I get for sending you tae foster with your aunt?"

"You expect a reward for sending me away when I needed my family the most?" Edina replied curtly. "I was still a bairn, had just lost three of my older brothers in the war with England, and my mam died a few weeks later. You and Jayden were all I had left." Tears streamed down her cheeks, but she held her head high.

"I suffered the same losses," he replied coldly. "You were a lass of fourteen summers and I did what I thought was in your best interest. I would have sent you tae a priory had I known you'd be ruined by your mother's sister."

"I was fifteen. My aunt is a kind and loving woman. She saw in me strengths and abilities you are too blind tae see. It isna too late tae send me tae a priory. I would rather take the vows than be sold in marriage tae a man I dinna love."

Laird Sinclair spat on the floor. "Love? There is no need for useless emotions in a marriage. Your mother and I were not in love and we managed tae have four fine sons."

"And a daughter," she muttered under her breath before speaking up. "My mother ... may the Almighty rest her soul." She paused and said a brief prayer. "Was a fine lady, in good standing when she met you. Aye, she did her duty, married you without love, tolerated your touch, and bore your sons, but she was never content. A happy woman doesna die of a broken heart."

Laird Sinclair slammed his balled fist on a nearby table. "Enough! You will not speak tae me with such disrespect. I am your sire and you will honor me as such. You know naught about our union. It was arranged tae benefit the clan, and your mother never complained about her lot in life."

"She was a saint and wouldna find fault in anything or anyone. But that doesna mean she was happy. I am not my mother and dinna wish tae marry Laird Sutherland."

"You will do as you're told. Duncan was on his way tae fetch you when word came that you'd been lost at sea. I—"

"So he believes I am dead. Then I dinna see a problem," Edina cut in.

"This union has been sanctioned by the king and will benefit the clan immensely. I sent a missive as soon as you arrived, informed Duncan that you are alive, asking him tae honor our agreement and come for you as soon as possible."

"I canna believe you did that without at least telling me first. Why—"

"So I see the rumors are true." A man sauntered across the chamber and stood at her father's side.

She sucked in a gulp of air and steeled herself against the fear and loathing bubbling up from the pit of her stomach. "Callum," she said on a strangled breath.

Before her stood her father's advisor and dearest friend, the man he'd entrusted with her safety and charged with bringing her home to be wed. The same man who stole into her chamber and tried to rape her.

"Is it true Alasdair Fraser found her on the beach and they consorted in sin for over a sennight?" Callum blurted out. "I am shocked and appalled by the news. I trust you will see them both punished accordingly."

"I was equally shocked," Laird Sinclair growled. "Both deny the tryst, but I dinna believe them. Laird Sutherland will be here soon and I dinna know how tae tell him she has been ruined. I wouldna blame him if he doesna wish tae marry a wanton woman."

"I am not ruined. I told you naught happened between Alasdair and me."

"There are ways tae tell. Shall I summon your physician, m'lord, or call for the village midwife? Either can determine if her maidenhead remains intact," Callum said with an evil grin.

"Helen, fetch my physician." Laird Sinclair dismissed her with a sweep of his hand.

"Right away, m'lord." The lass bobbed a quick curtsy and hurried from the room, but not before offering Edina a sympathetic glance.

"I willna be subjected to this humiliation," Edina protested. "My word should be enough."

"I see that in addition to picking up the morals of a stray cat, the lass has developed a viperous tongue. Something a good lashing would quickly resolve," Callum said smugly. "If she were my daughter, I wouldna tolerate her insolence."

"I can imagine you'd do many unspeakable things were you my father. Thank the Almighty you are not." Edina raised her chin in challenge. She'd not back down from this blackguard. She had to tell her father what happened on the ship, but feared he'd not believe her. The conversation she'd had with Callum on the night he attacked her, along with his threats to ruin her reputation if she crossed him, flooded her mind, but she refused to back down.

"You'll not speak tae Callum in that manner. Mayhap he was right about the need for a firmer hand," her father interjected.

"It doesna surprise me that she took up with Fraser. If I dinna know better, I'd say the whole thing was arranged. He will rue the day he got trapped in her web. A night in the pit afore he hangs will give him time tae think about his actions." His sinister smirk broadened. "He has her tae thank for his demise."

"The pit! Father you canna be serious. How could you put Alasdair in such a horrible place? He saved my life and despite what you think, he is a decent, innocent man."

"He should have thought of the consequences afore he stole your virtue," Callum remarked snidely.

"If anyone is tae be punished, it should be you," Edina reiterated sharply.

Callum's eyes narrowed and his expression darkened. "I have no idea what you are talking about."

She swallowed hard and summoned her courage. If what Callum predicted was true, her father would side with his friend, but Alasdair's life depended on her proving that his trusted advisor was the liar and a scoundrel.

"Well?" Her father crossed his arms over his chest and glared at her. "Dinna draw this out. What have you tae say?"

"The night I fell overboard, Callum entered my cabin after I'd retired and took intimate liberties. He tried tae bed me against my will." She finally forced out the words.

"Is this true?" Her father spun around to face his friend.

"She lies! Will you take her word above that of your advisor and longtime friend? She is trying tae divert the attention and guilt from Fraser by telling a grave falsehood."

"I'm not making this up, Father. He came intae my chamber. He was well in his cups at the time and told me he'd admired me for some time and wanted to bed me. He called you a fool for promising me tae Laird Sutherland and threatened tae kill me if I told anyone what he'd done."

Callum began to pace. He threw his hands in the air and approached her father. "I have no idea why she has concocted this story, but may she be damned in Hell for her lies."

"We struggled and I cut him with his dirk. I tried tae get away but he chased me ontae the deck and he—"

"You canna believe I would do such a thing," Callum protested. "Mayhap she was dreaming and imagined the entire thing. That would explain how she ended up on deck rather than in her cabin where she belonged."

"Let her finish." Laird Sinclair raised his hand in the air, silencing his friend.

"I wasna dreaming. Callum tried tae rape me and when I resisted, he threatened to cut my throat. I managed to get away and ran to the deck. There was a storm and then when he came at me again, I lost my footing and fell overboard."

"Did anyone witness this?" Her father dragged his hand across his bearded chin.

"She has no witnesses because it dinna happen. I have served you faithfully for many summers. Both as your confidant and your friend. I admit that I saw her on the deck, but swear I never laid a hand on her. When I went to tell her it wasna safe tae be out in the storm she acted like I was the devil himself. She started shouting, told me if I came any closer, she would jump intae the water and her death would be on my head. The ship pitched and when she fell over the rail, I dove in and tried to save her." Callum glared at Edina as he spoke.

"That isna how it happened. If what I say is a lie, he willna mind removing his tunic. He will have a gash on his left side, just below his ribs."

"I have naught to prove and willna do it," Callum replied.

"Why was I not told about your confrontation aboard ship when you returned. You told me Edina fell overboard in the storm and you tried to rescue her, but you never mentioned her strange behavior."

"I-I dinna think it important. She was dead and you were so distraught. I dinna see any point in adding to your anguish," Callum stammered.

"Take off your tunic," Laird Sinclair ordered.

"But m'lord, I—" Callum protested.

"Remove it now!"

Callum grumbled a curse, grasped the hem of his shirt, and tugged it over his head.

Laird Sinclair's mouth dropped open and his eyes widened at the site of recent wound on Callum's left side. He summoned the guard standing by the door. "Arrest him."

"I can explain. This isna what it appears," Callum pleaded as the guard grabbed his arm. "I cut myself on the rail when I tried to save her. You must listen to me."

Laird Sinclair shook his head. "You've said quite enough. Take him to the pit."

"I canna believe you would take the word of a whore above mine. She is a wicked temptress. If truth be told, she came to my cabin and offered to lay with me, not the other way around," Callum shouted when the guard grabbed his arm. He broke free and stumbled toward his friend. "Is this how you repay me for my service?"

"Is this how you prove your loyalty and maintain my trust?" Laird Sinclair replied. "I canna stand the sight of you. Take him away."

"You'll see. She is evil." Callum continued to call out as the guard dragged him down the hall.

"I am so glad you listened tae the truth, father. Will you now release Alasdair?"

"This doesna change anything in regard to the charges against Fraser. Callum may have attacked you and will be punished, however, the fact remains, you spent the last sennight in the company of a man who wasna your husband."

"You summoned me, m'lord?" The door opened and the clan physician entered. Helen followed.

"Aye. It appears my wayward daughter has seen fit tae offer her innocence tae a man who is not her husband. She denies the act and claims she is still a maiden." Laird Sinclair took Edina's wrist and ushered her toward the physician. "I want you to examine her and settle this once and for all. A man's life depends on the outcome."

"Father, please dinna do this. I swear on my mother's grave. I speak the truth." Edina choked back a sob.

"If you have naught tae hide, then you have no reason tae object," her father growled.

Edina drew in a slow deep breath to steady her nerves and faced the physician. If allowing this man to examine her would prove her innocence and save Alasdair, so be it. "Verra well. If this it the only way I can prove what I say is true, I will do as you request. I have naught tae hid." She followed the physician as he moved toward her pallet.

"Lay down and raise your skirt," the man ordered then turned to face her father. "Would you like tae be present while I do this, m'lord?"

"That willna be necessary." Laird Sinclair strode toward the door. "Neither will the examination."

"M'lord?" the physician asked.

"I have changed my mind. Your services will not be needed." Laird Sinclair summoned the guard standing in the hallway with a wave of his arm. "Go to the pit and bring Alasdair Fraser tae my chamber. I am ready tae pass judgment." After issuing the orders, he stormed down the hall.

Chapter 14

"Get up. Laird Sinclair wishes tae see you," the shadowy figure towering over Alasdair growled, then kicked his boot.

Alasdair raised his head and narrowed his eyes in an attempt to focus in the dim light of the man's torch. "Why does he wish tae see me at this hour? I expected tae have until morning afore he stretched my neck."

"I am only following orders. He summoned me and told me tae bring you tae his chamber right away. Best you not keep him waiting."

Alasdair unfurled his legs and slowly rose to his feet. He groaned and stretched, the cold and dampness from the ground having stiffened his joints. "Lead the way. I'd just as soon get this over with quickly. I dinna fancy spending my last night on earth curled up on the ground in this dark, dank hole, with rats for company."

The man grunted. "If I were you, I'd be happy for any time I had left." He spun around and headed down the twisting tunnel.

Alasdair followed a few steps behind, but paused to draw in a deep breath as they emerged from the pit and into the crisp night air. He glanced skyward, wondering for a moment if mayhap his parents and brothers were watching over him, if they were awaiting his arrival in Heaven.

Without saying a word, the guard led him across the bailey, into the castle, up a steep staircase, then down a long hallway, halting when they came to a large oak door at the end of the corridor.

"Wait here. I will make the laird aware of your presence." The guard knocked on the door then entered, leaving Alasdair alone in the hallway.

Alasdair's gut knotted with uncertainty. Prepared for the worst, he could only surmise that his fate had been decided. The question was when would he be executed and how. He could try to escape, but was certain the castle guards would be upon him before he reached the curtain wall, if he even made it out of the keep.

The guard returned a few minutes later and pointed toward the door. "Laird Sinclair will see you," he announced then trotted down the hall.

Puzzled by the man's hasty departure and at being left unguarded, Alasdair sucked in another fortifying breath, and entered the chamber. "You wanted tae see me, Laird Sinclair?" he asked, then waited for a reply.

Sinclair's head jerked around. "Aye. Please come in, lad," he said and waved him in with a sweep of his arm.

More confused than ever by the laird's change in demeanor and jovial tone of voice, Alasdair stepped forward, then halted just inside the room.

"It appears I've made a grave mistake and I wish tae apologize for the way you've been misjudged." Laird Sinclair moved in Alasdair's direction with his hand outstretched.

Alasdair crossed his arms over his chest and widened his stance. Uncertain he wanted to hear the laird's apology after the way his honor had been questioned or the shameful way Edina had been treated, he said nothing.

"Och, I dinna blame you for being angry." Laird Sinclair lowered his head and gave it a shake. "I know you were treated poorly upon your arrival and some serious accusations were made. I was wrong. If only you could find it in you tae forgive this old man's mistakes."

"What made you change your mind?"

"After speaking with my daughter, I realized you were both telling the truth." Laird Sutherland raked his fingers through his hair and shifted his weight from one foot to the other.

"And what brought you tae that conclusion? You were so convinced she had brazenly surrendered her innocence and that I had eagerly taken advantage of her."

"Err . . . um . . ." Sinclair mumbled and dragged a shaky hand across his bearded chin. "It appears Edina was attacked on the ship as she claimed and fell overboard trying to fend off the culprit. By the mercy of the Almighty she dinna drown and was washed ashore, where you found her and tended tae her needs. For that I am eternally grateful."

"Did she say who it was who accosted her?" Alasdair asked. He fisted his hands at his side. "Tell me his name. I will find the swine and see him flayed."

"That willna be necessary. The man has already been arrested and awaits his punishment."

"Tell me his name."

My advisor, Callum, the man I charged with Edina's safety, is the blackguard responsible."

Anger twisted Alasdair's gut. It was bad enough she'd been attacked, but the thought of someone Edina knew and trusted committing the heinous offence infuriated him. Would that he had a few minutes alone with the man. He'd never harm another lass as long as he lived. Which, if Alasdair his way, would only be only enough time for him to draw his sword and run the bugger through.

"The man just came forth and confessed? I find that hard tae believe given the consequences," Alasdair replied.

"Nay. He tried to plant more seeds of doubt by insisting that Edina was a wanton woman. He claimed she entered his cabin, offered him her virtue, then became enraged when he declined. He also did his best to convince me that you violated her, and suggested she be examined by my physician."

"You believed Callum's word held more credence than that of your own daughter and would have allowed her tae suffer the humiliation?" Alasdair did not bother to hide the shock or disgust in his voice. "What kind of father would do such a thing?"

"One who believed his bairn was dead and was not thinking clearly when she returned after spending a sennight alone in a man's company. A man who wasna her husband."

"Most men would be thrilled tae learn their bairn was alive. Yet you chose tae think the worst, despite what we told you. You treated her like a whore, and me, like a rapacious fiend whose only thought was sating my carnal needs." He was not about to make this easy on the laird. While he could understand how it must have looked, there was no excuse for the way Edina had been unfairly accused by her own kin.

Then again, how was his own reaction when he discovered Edina's true identity or the assumptions he'd made any different from those of her father and brother? He, too, had condemned her without giving her a chance to explain, and assumed like all the other women he'd trusted, she had deliberately gone out of her way to deceive him for her own gain. Mayhap, he'd been wrong as well.

"I was elated tae see Edina, but furious tae learn she had been alive all this time and living in sin. Or so I thought. Put yourself in my position and tell me you wouldna think the same things," Laird Sinclair responded with his hands outstretched at his sides, the palms facing skyward in question. "My daughter is a comely lass and you are a braw, virile warrior."

"That doesna mean anything happened between us. You could have taken my word, rather than making accusations without first hearing what I had tae say." Edina entered the chamber with her brother in tow. "There is more than one Sinclair who owes Alasdair an apology." She placed her hand on Jayden's shoulder and shoved him forward.

Alasdair coughed to clear his throat. His chest tightened and his palms began to sweat the minute Edina entered the room. He longed to hold her, to sweep her up into his arms and apologize for being a fool, for doubting her. But with her father and brother present, he was forced to stifle the urge.

"Edina is right. I am as guilty of jumping tae conclusions as my da. I should have known better than to question your honor, and am verra sorry." Jayden lowered his eyes and shuffled his feet.

"While I dinna approve of the way Edina was mistreated and never wish tae see the inside of your pit again, it appears you both realize you were in error." After a moment's pause, Alasdair held his arm out to Jayden. "If I had a sister and found myself in a similar situation, I might have reacted in the same way."

Jayden grasped Alasdair's wrist and hauled him into a tight embrace. "Thank you, my friend. I willna doubt your word again."

"And your sister's word?" Alasdair asked.

"I have already apologized tae Edina, but willna discount what she has tae say either." Jayden took a step back. "You have always been like a brother tae me, Alasdair, I should never have doubted you."

Alasdair turned to face Laird Sinclair and bowed. "I accept your apology, m'lord."

"An act of contrition isna enough tae make adequate amends. Accompany Jayden tae the stable and take your pick of any mount and saddle. I will also see you are compensated with silver and other treasures as well. I—"

Alasdair raised his hand. "That willna be necessary. I have a trustworthy mount and dinna want your money. Only your promise that you willna doubt your daughter in the future."

Jayden jabbed Alasdair in the ribs. "Are you right in the

head, man? Take what he offered. Getting my da tae part with his coin or his livestock doesna happen often." He tossed back his head and laughed.

"The gesture is a generous one indeed, but I consider his renewed faith in me and Edina as payment enough. What do you plan tae do with the man who attacked her?" Alasdair asked.

Laird Sinclair blew out a heavy sigh. "Sending Callum to fetch Edina home proved tae be a grievous mistake. He has been my advisor for many years. I also trusted him and never dreamed he would behave in such a dishonorable way."

"He will be punished accordingly," Jayden interjected. "Right now, he has taken your place in the pit and is awaiting my father's decree. If I have my way, he will be gelded, then drawn and quartered. Even that is too good for the blackguard."

"I have yet tae decide his fate, but mark my words, he will never hurt Edina again," Laird Sinclair said with conviction.

"I'd like tae speak with Edina privately if you will grant us some time alone." Alasdair glanced at the lass. "We have a few things tae discuss."

Laird Sinclair gave a curt nod and moved toward the door. "Come, Jayden, we will give them some time tae speak. But keep in mind she is betrothed and I am expecting her future husband tae arrive at any time," he commented over his shoulder.

Laird Sinclair's words hit him like a blow to the gut. While he was in no position to ask for Edina's hand, the idea of her in another man's arms caused his blood to boil.

"Father, after all that has happened, I canna believe you still expect me tae marry Duncan Sutherland."

"I've given my word. The wedding will take place," her father replied and left the chamber.

"Jayden, you must try tae reason with him, make him change his mind. Please. I dinna wish tae be married tae a man I dinna know or love."

Jayden shrugged. "He sent word of your return the minute he found out you were still alive. You know once Da makes a decision on something, he doesna change it. Best you resolve yourself tae the union," he concluded then left the chamber.

Visibly upset about her upcoming nuptials, Edina threw her hands in the air, then fisted them at her sides. Her brow furrowed and she released a heavy sigh as her brother strolled down the hallway. "I must find a way to convince my da to break the pact he has made with Duncan's father. I dinna wish tae marry and my brother doesna appear to be of any assistance."

"Your father gave his word, and a man's word is his bond," Alasdair replied. "This alliance will help tae unite the Highland clans."

"I'm not a piece of property to be bartered for. My mother married my father for all the wrong reasons and I willna follow in her path."

"You dinna have a choice, Edina. As the laird's daughter, it is your duty to marry as he sees fit. This has been the way of it for many centuries, and old traditions are not about tae change any time soon."

"You could speak up on my behalf," she blurted out, her face flushing red. "Please. Will you talk tae my da?"

"I have no influence on your father's choice of a suitor. He has selected the man he thinks best meets the needs of the clan." Alasdair wished there was something he could do to help, but even if he was prepared to admit he'd developed feelings for the lass, he held no title and had nothing to offer.

There was a time when he would have been considered a strong contender for her hand, but he gave up that chance when he declined his birthright and his brother was appointed as laird of Clan Fraser in his stead.

"My wishes mean naught tae anyone and I would rather go tae a priory than marry without love." She sank onto a chair beside the hearth and buried her face in her hands.

Alasdair studied her downtrodden expression before he spoke. Something her father had told him weighed heavy on his mind. "I canna believe you were willing tae suffer the humiliation of an examination by the clan physician tae prove my innocence."

"Again, I had no choice. If my father demanded it be done, I was helpless tae object," she replied, her eyes trailing the floor.

"According tae what your da said, you gave your consent and were prepared tae go through with it willingly. That was until he decided tae believe your word. Why would you do such a thing?"

"I decided it best tae endure the embarrassment tae clear my name and yours. I couldna bear the thought of you being hanged for a deed you dinna commit. Not that it matters."

"It does matter, Edina." Alasdair stepped forward and lifted her chin. "No one has ever been willing tae make such a sacrifice on my behalf."

His heart twisted when she gazed at him with tear-filled eyes. "Then do something tae stop the wedding. You could ask for my hand. Unless, you dinna find me appealing."

Alasdair grasped her hands, helped her to her feet, and tugged her against his chest. "You are the most beautiful woman I have ever laid eyes upon. If I were in a position tae marry, I could think of no other I would rather spend the rest of my life with."

Before she could respond, he lowered his head and captured her lips.

Chapter 15

Edina clung to Alasdair's tunic and her lips parted, welcoming his kiss with equal enthusiasm. She tasted even sweeter than he remembered, and his groin stirred, the tantalizing scent of heather and lavender making his head spin. He wanted her more than his next breath, and damned the consequences.

A voice inside his head told him this was wrong. He had no intention of taking a bride and had no right to lead Edina on. He battled the desire and lust coursing though his veins, but she affected him in ways no woman had ever done before.

Heaven help him.

He fisted one hand in her silky, flaxen tresses, holding her head in place, while he slid his other palm along her spine, coming to rest on her bottom. They fit together so perfectly, he'd swear she'd been tailored for him and him alone. Could she feel his heart pounding against his ribs like a beast trying to break free?

He cursed beneath his breath and broke the kiss as reality, not to mention, his senses, slowly returned. She was betrothed to another man and would never belong to him. He held her at arm's length. "Forgive me, Edina. It appears I again find myself guilty of taking liberties I have no right tae take. Were your father tae return and catch us together in an embrace, everything we have done tae clear our names would be for naught."

Despite his effort to put some distance between them, Edina refused to let go of his shirt. "You are obviously attracted tae me, Alasdair. Why else would you kiss me with such passion? I must confess, I find you quite pleasing, and have since I was a wee lass. But I was not sure you felt the same way about me. I was after all quite a homely bairn." Her bottom lip quivered as she lowered her gaze, but her grip on his garment held firm.

For a moment Alasdair saw before him a spindly, seven-year-old, freckle-faced lass, with stringy blond hair, huge hazel eyes, and a toothless grin. He gave his head a sharp shake and the image of a beautiful, beguiling woman returned.

"Neither of us was what one would call comely, especially me. You are breathtaking now, Edina."

"As are you, m'lord." She stroked his beard-stubbled cheek. "I always found you appealing. Even when you called me a pest." She raised her chin and smiled.

His heart twisted and his stomach clenched. Turning his back on Edina and leaving Sinclair Castle was not going to be easy. "I was a tall, lanky, lad, naught but skin and bones. I find it hard tae believe any lass would find me attractive."

She placed two fingers against his lips. "You're wrong. I found you quite handsome and even . . ." Her voice trailed off as she lowered her head.

"Even what?" Alasdair lifted her chin.

Tears welled in her eyes but she managed to hold them at bay. "I hoped that some day we might marry. I know it tae be a foolish notion, given I wasna a bonny lass and you were the son of one of the most powerful lairds in all the Highlands. Jayden teased me relentlessly about my crush. But I once overheard our fathers talking about the possibility of our union and it gave me hope."

"I wasna aware of such a pact. Not until Jayden mentioned it. Our fathers were friends, but as the second son, I was tanist tae my older brother. Had he not died along with our father at Berwick on Tweed, he would now sit as laird of Clan Fraser. Mayhap he would have been your husband."

Edina crossed herself. "Forgive me for saying this, but your brother is dead and you are now the eldest son. I am sure if you asked my da, he would give consent."

Alasdair backed away and shook his head. "Nay. I might be the eldest son, but my brother, Connor, is laird of Clan Fraser. I have no wealth, land, or title, so our joining would serve no purpose. Not like a marriage between you and Duncan Sutherland." He stared into eyes filled with anticipation, and wished he could tell her what she wanted to hear. But there was no future for them. Every moment he remained in her presence made it more difficult for him to leave.

He squared his shoulders and held her at arm's length. "Your hand has been promised to Sutherland and you must honor your father's wishes. I have no desire tae marry and will be leaving tae rejoin the cause verra soon. That is where my destiny lies," he concluded with conviction and in hopes of putting an end to his attraction to the lass and she to him.

"It doesna have tae be that way. I would gladly run away with you if you were tae ask. I would make you a good wife, I promise. In time you might even come tae love me. Please give it some thought."

If only she knew his true feelings.

He heard the desperation in her voice, but had to remain strong. "My mind is set, Edina, and your father wouldna stand for your defiance. He'd hunt us both down and see me hanged. There is nothing I can do tae change what is about tae take place. Jayden is right, best you accept your fate and prepare for Duncan's arrival." He spun around and strode out of the chamber.

Dashing Edina's dreams and leaving her standing there was difficult. But there was no choice and a clean break was for the best. Or so he tried to convince himself as he raced down the stairs and into the great hall, searching for a tankard of ale, mayhap many, given the way he was feeling. Helpless and defeated were two emotions he was not accustomed to and he did not like either in the least.

"Did you settle things with my sister?" Jayden asked as he joined Alasdair in the great hall and motioned for him to sit at the table. He opened the clay jug he carried and poured the content into two tankards.

"What have you there?" Alasdair reached for the pewter cup.

"Uisge beatha, the water of life and the finest whisky in all of Scotland. You look like you could use some."

Alasdair snatched a tankard and downed the content in one gulp. He wiped his mouth with the back of his hand, then held the vessel out in Jayden's direction. "More."

After obliging his friend's request, Jayden sat back in his chair, and sipped on his own drink. "Your mood is foul. The conversation you had with Edina must not have gone well."

"It went fine." Alasdair emptied his tankard for the second time and held it out to Jayden again. "Things are as they should be and I dinna want tae talk about it anymore."

Jayden poured another drink for each of them. "At this rate I will have tae carry you tae your chamber." He laughed.

Alasdair narrowed his eyes and glared at his friend. "I willna need you tae carry me anywhere," he growled. "If you dinna wish tae share, I can find my spirits elsewhere."

"Nay. That willna be necessary." Jayden raised his hands in a gesture of compliance. "Have all you want." He pushed the jug across the table toward Alasdair, then rocked back in his chair. "You're a grown man and know your limits. If you wish tae drink yourself senseless, I willna stand in your way." He hesitated a minute before asking. "Were we wrong tae believe there was nothing between you and Edina?"

Alasdair slammed the tankard on the table, sprang to his feet, then planted both hands on the slab of oak and stared at Jayden. "I thought we were through with that discussion and had put it behind us?" he said through clenched teeth. "If you wish to end this matter once and for all, I will meet you outside in the lists." He fingered the hilt of his sword.

Jayden placed his hand on Alasdair's forearm. "Calm yourself, man. I am not saying you did anything tae defile my sister. But that doesna mean you dinna have feelings for her. Even if you willna admit tae them. I've seen the way you look at her. If you wish tae speak about it, I will keep your secret."

"I have naught to discuss or tae hide. Edina is a beguiling lass, but she is betrothed to Sutherland and that isna about tae change. I have no plans to wed and intend tae rejoin Robert the Bruce in his quest tae rid Scotland of the English."

"If you can wait tae leave until after the wedding, I will join you. I'm sure Robert will welcome another sword."

Alasdair shifted in his chair. It was hard enough to imagine Edina in the arms of another man, but to attend the ceremony and hold his tongue was another story. "I canna make any promises." He sat hard on the chair and picked up his tankard.

Edina paced her chamber like a cornered animal. She didn't realize how much she cared for Alasdair until he'd stormed out of the room and possibly out of her life forever. Had she fallen in love with him?

While her heart fluttered every time he came near, the cadence of his deep voice made her swoon, and his touch excited her, she had tried to rationalize her response to him as being normal. He had saved her life and cared for her when she was injured. What she felt was gratitude. Wasn't it?

She couldn't believe she'd asked him to marry her. He must have thought her daft or at the least, a desperate fool.

"What am I tae do?" Edina muttered aloud.

"I beg your pardon, m'lady?"

Edina whipped around. "Helen. I dinna hear you knock."

"I did, but you dinna reply so I assumed you dinna hear me."

"What is it you want?" Edina asked, her mind still preoccupied with thoughts of Alasdair.

"The hour is late and your father sent me tae help you get ready for bed. You've had a verra busy day and you must be exhausted." Helen crossed the chamber and took a nightrail from a hook on the wall. "Would you like me tae brush your lovely hair?"

"Nay," Edina snapped, her response more abrupt than she intended. "I'm not tired and dinna need help getting ready for bed."

Helen lowered her eyes. "I dinna mean to intrude."

Remorse tugged at Edina's belly. She had taken out her frustration with Alasdair and her upcoming wedding on her lady's maid. The only person she could truly call a friend. Mayhap, the only person she could confide in and trust. "Forgive me, Helen. I dinna mean tae be rude or harsh with you. I have a lot on my mind, but had no right tae speak tae you the way I did."

Helen bobbed a curtsy. "Och, you have naught tae apologize for. You have been through quite an ordeal and I hold no ill will against you."

"Thank you." Edina released a deep sigh and sat on the end of her bed. "I value your friendship and dinna mean tae be difficult. I would appreciate your help."

Helen handed the nightrail to Edina. I've missed you verra much. It saddens me tae think you will only be home for a brief time. Your father said he expects your betrothed to arrive on the morrow and plans tae see you married as soon as possible."

"I need no reminders." Edina lowered her head, cradling it in her hands. "I must find a way tae get my da tae change his mind. I dinna wish tae marry Duncan."

"I understand, and wouldna like tae be forced tae marry a man I dinna know or love. I am so fortunate. William and I have been betrothed since we were bairns. I love him with all my heart and could not bear tae marry another. He told me he feels the same way about me."

"You are very lucky. I wish I had a choice," Edina said, then smiled as an idea popped into her mind. "Did you not say Duncan Sutherland was once betrothed tae his cousin, a lass from the Clan Mackenzie?"

"Aye. He was tae marry her this summer, but those plans changed when his father made a pact with your da." Helen shook her head. "The young laird must have been heartbroken when he learned of the arrangements."

"It appears neither of us will be entering into this marriage of our own accord." She paused and pressed her finger to the side of her nose. "Mayhap if the lass were here, Duncan may find the courage tae challenge his father's decision."

"What are you suggesting, m'lady?"

"I must find someone I can trust tae ride tae the Clan Mackenzie's stronghold and convince the lass tae come afore the wedding takes place. Surely if Duncan loves her, he will fight for her hand and free me of my burden."

"It might work, but is there time?" Helen asked. "I could ask William tae go."

"Do you think he'd be willing tae help me?"

"If I ask him tae do it, I'm sure he will. He has a difficult time refusing me." A blush rose in Helen's cheeks. "If you wish, I can go and ask him now. The sooner he leaves the better."

A knock on the door caused them both to turn. Jayden strolled into the chamber. "I thought you'd want tae know. A messenger arrived a few minutes ago from the Sutherland Clan. Duncan is expected tae arrive on the morrow."

Edina's heart sank. Time was running out. She turned to face Helen. "Could you see tae that matter we were discussing?"

Helen nodded. "Aye. I will take care of it right away." She turned and scurried down the hall.

"Please make haste," she called after the maid.

"Are you all right?" Jayden slid his hand over Edina's shoulder. "You were verra upset with me earlier, and I canna say that I blame you."

"I'll be fine," Edina replied softly.

"I wish there was something I could do tae get Da tae reconsider, but he is certain this marriage will benefit the clan and has given his word."

Edina moved to a small casement window and peered into the bailey. "I believe the Almighty has a plan for me and He will decide my fate," she replied.

"Please say yes, William," she muttered under her breath as she watched Helen race across the bailey toward the cobbler's wattle and daub hut.

Chapter 16

A rap on the door awakened Edina from a fitful sleep. Was it morning already? She felt as though her head had just touched the pillow. She opened heavy-lidded eyes and glanced around the room. Rays of sunlight slipped through the cracks around the shutters, heralding a new day. The dreaded day she'd meet her betrothed and her life would be changed forever.

It wasn't too late to run. If she slipped out while many of the clan still slept and the men who were up and about were busy training in the lists, she could be miles away before anyone knew she was missing.

But where would she go? Alasdair was right. Her father would find her and bring her back to marry Duncan. Known for her temerity, she was not one to give up easily, but honestly saw no options but to comply with her father's demands.

Another knock, a little louder than the first, caught her attention. "Who is it?"

"Helen. I've come tae help you dress. May I enter your chamber?"

Edina sat up and stretched. "Aye, come in."

The door swung open with a loud creak when the maid entered. She carried a basin of water across the room, placed it on a small table by the window, then opened the shutters, and peered into the bailey. "It is going tae be a bonny day. I thought you might like tae freshen up afore you join your father in the great hall tae break your fast."

"I dinna wish tae get up. Ever." Edina flopped back on the mattress and covered her eyes with her forearm. "I am not ready for this day tae start. There is naught to look forward to, only heartache."

Thoughts of Alasdair flooded her mind, the taste of his kisses, the possibility of a brighter future . . . had he felt the same way about her as she did him. But he'd made it clear he had no intent of complicating his life with a wife and bairns. He planned to rejoin the Bruce and she'd never see him again.

"You're wrong, m'lady. Everyday we live is a blessing. The Almighty doesna give us more tae bear than we can handle." Helen smiled and moved toward the bed.

"If only that were true." Edina bowed her head and wrung her hands. "I have to face Callum today and I canna stand the sight of him. But I must be present when my father passes judgment and determines his fate. While the blackguard deserves tae be punished, it willna be an easy task for Da tae determine his fate. They have been friends for many years and he was verra disappointed tae learn he had been betrayed by Callum."

Edina stood and joined Helen by the window. "Once that unsavory chore is done, I will spend the rest of my day waiting on tender hooks for Duncan tae arrive. Mayhap he will be delayed, or not come at all. One can only hope."

Helen's expression sobered. "You dinna hear? I was certain someone would have told you."

"Told me what?" Edina asked. "I havena spoken tae anyone since Jayden left my chamber late last night." Helen definitely had piqued her curiosity.

"Callum is dead, m'lady," the maid blurted out.

"Dead? Are you certain, Helen?" Edina could not believe her ears.

"Aye. Apparently, he pretended he was ill, and attacked

his guard when the sentry went to check on him. Laid the poor man's head open with a wooden stool, he did, then made his escape."

"If he got away, how do you know he's dead?" Edina's heart began to race. She remembered the look of pure evil on Callum's face when she told her father what had happened on the ship. His threats to get even if she betrayed him were foremost in her mind. Would he make good on those threats?

"Several of your da's men gave chase. They followed him ontae the cliffs and in his haste, Callum lost his footing and plunged to his death." Helen crossed herself and muttered a prayer.

"Did anyone see the body?" Edina needed to be certain.

"Nay. It was verra dark, but the men tracking him said there was no way he could have survived such a fall. They will search for him today, but fear his remains have been washed out tae sea. In my opinion it was a fitting end after what he tried tae do tae you."

Relief washed over Edina and she released the breath she'd been holding. "That may be, but it is a horrible way tae die."

"And you think death by hanging is what he would have preferred?" Helen asked.

"What Callum did tae me and the duplicity is inexcusable, but I dinna believe my father would have sentenced him tae hang. He more than likely would have banished him, the humiliation and alienation from the clan being a fate worse than death."

"It matters not. The scoundrel is dead, and I say good riddance." Helen retrieved a kirtle, gown, and slippers from a shelf by the door. "Once you've washed up, you'd best be getting dressed. Your da and brother are waiting for you. And I am sure lord Alasdair will be there as well." A grin tugged at her lips.

"I care not where Alasdair Fraser is or what he is doing." Edina lied. "He can take up residence with the devil for all I care."

Helen's eyes widened. "Och, you shouldna say such things. I dinna mean tae upset you. I thought—"

"Well you thought wrong. What Alasdair does from here on is none of my concern." She tugged the kirtle over her head and the gown followed.

"Forgive me. I suppose if you are getting married, thinking about another man wouldna be prudent." Helen lowered her gaze and began to wring her hands.

Again remorse for overreacting and taking her frustration out on Helen seized Edina's gut. "You have naught tae be sorry for, but beating this dead horse willna help. My only hope is that Duncan doesna want this union any more than I do, or that William can convince Duncan's cousin tae come afore the wedding."

"He left as soon as I bid him go. I hope he makes it in time," Helen replied then crossed herself again. "The Almighty willing he will be successful in his quest."

"I hope you're right, Helen. I hope you're right.

"Did you spend the entire night here?"

Alasdair struggled to open eyes that felt like anvils. He groaned aloud. "Leave me be, Jayden. Where I slept matters naught." Why had his friend disturbed him? It had taken him all night to finally fall asleep.

"I dinna care where you slept, but it is time tae break our fast and you are sprawled out in my father's chair. I expect him tae arrive any minute." Jayden picked up an empty jug from the floor and place it on the trestle table beside another. "It appears you dinna spend the night entirely alone. You finished off one flagon of whisky, and nearly emptied another. I would imagine you must feel like you've been dragged behind a herd of wild horses." He laughed.

Alasdair found no humor in his friend's comments and wished he would lower his voice. Better yet, he wished Jayden would leave. "I can hold my spirits and feel fine," he lied. In truth, his stomach roiled, his head was about to burst, and his mouth tasted like he'd been chewing on dry wood.

"Well if you ask me, you look a might green about the gills. My father will be here soon and Edina will be joining us. What will she think if she sees you are well in your cups at this hour of the day?"

Alasdair belched and spat on the floor. If possible, his mood soured even more than it was already. "No one asked you. I dinna care what she thinks. Once Duncan Sutherland arrives she will be busy planning her wedding."

"Say what you want, but I know differently. You're smitten with my sister, so there is no point denying it."

"I'm not smitten with anyone. Besides, she is spoken for and her marriage to Sutherland will benefit both your clans," Alasdair snapped. Were his true feelings for Edina that obvious?

"You look at her like a lovesick hound whenever she is around. I know she is promised tae Duncan, but if you wish tae offer for her hand, I can speak to Da on your behalf."

"You're wrong and know naught what you're saying," Alasdair replied curtly. "If you are truly my friend, you'll drop the subject and mind your own affairs. Better yet, do your best tae convince Edina I am not the man for her and her marriage tae Duncan is a wise choice." He almost choked on the bitter words.

Jayden slid his arms under Alasdair's shoulders and hoisted him to his feet. "I'll help you to your chamber so you can get some sleep. You may feel differently once you've rested and your mind has cleared."

"I can rest from now until the day I die, but I willna change my mind. Women arena worth the trouble and your sister is no exception," Alasdair growled. "Now if you will point me in the direction of my chamber, I will leave afore she arrives." He reached for the near-empty jug, brought it to his lips, then cursed when Jayden snatched if from his hand.

"You'll not be needing any more whisky. Come, I will show you tae your bed." He clutched Alasdair's arm in an attempt to lead the away, but he jerked free.

"I can walk on my own and dinna need a nursemaid." Alasdair drew in a ragged breath, reclaimed the jug from Jayden's hand, and took a wobbly step, followed by another. He staggered into the hall, but as fate would have it, Edina approached from the direction he was headed.

He cursed beneath his breath. There was no way he could avoid a conversation with the lass. He squared his shoulders, raked a shaky hand through his hair, and put on a false smile as Edina and her maid drew nearer. "Good day, ladies." Alasdair bowed, then stumbled, finding it hard to stand steady. "You look tae be in good health, Edina. I trust you slept well." The words were slurred and even he could hear the hint of sarcasm in his tone.

"You're drunk and smell like you slept in a vat of whisky." Edina crinkled her nose, waved her hand in front of her face, and took a step back.

"Aye, but not drunk enough." Alasdair brought the jug to his lips and took another swig. He swiped the back of his hand across his lips, then belched loudly. "Now if you lovely lassies will excuse me, my friend and I are going to my chamber." He patted the jug, then took another sip.

"If you ask me, you've had quite enough," Edina replied tersely.

The disapproval on her face spoke volumes, but Alasdair was beyond caring what she thought. Mayhap she would see him for who he truly was and be glad she was betrothed to

Sutherland. "I dinna ask your opinion and dinna care what you think," he replied, then muttered a ribald curse in a barely audible voice.

Edina's eyes widened when Alasdair pushed past them. "How rude. Best you go and sleep it off," she said as he staggered down the hall and out of sight.

"Oh my, he is quite unmannerly," Helen remarked. "I can see why you wish tae distance yourself from the brute."

"He has obviously imbibed too much of my father's whisky. I have no doubt it was supplied by my brother." Edina's brow creased. When she met up with Jayden, she would tell him what she thought. "He is usually not so discourteous. He should—" How could she be defending Alasdair? She gave her head a shake. He cared not what happened to her and she needed to rid her mind of the man and concentrate on how she was going to convince Duncan this marriage was a mistake.

"Good morning, daughter." Laird Sinclair strutted down the hall toward them. "Did you sleep well?"

Edina jumped, startled by her father's presence. Had he witnessed the exchange between her and Alasdair? "I'm doing as well as can be expected given my life is about tae end." She lowered her gaze and stepped aside so Laird Sinclair could pass.

"You are exaggerating, my dear. Marriage to Duncan Sutherland is the beginning of a new life and a union that will greatly benefit the clan. You should be proud and pleased he agreed tae be your husband."

"I am not pleased and I dinna want tae wed Duncan or any man who is not of my choosing. I wish there was something I could do or say tae get you tae change your mind." Edina brought her hands together as if in prayer and waited, hoping her father might show some indication he would reconsider.

"You have known since you were a wee bairn the day would come when a husband would be chosen for you. Now be a good lass and join me in the great hall. I asked Cook to prepare a special feast in honor of your return." Laird Sinclair turned and continued down the hall.

"I canna believe he willna listen to me. What am I tae do?" Edina pressed her hand to her temple. "I canna marry Duncan. I would sooner die."

"Och, m'lady, you dinna mean that. You never know, it might not be as bad as you think. I am told Duncan Sutherland is quite handsome and charming. You may be surprised," Helen said, then touched Edina's arm. "Hopefully William will bring the Mackenzie lass back and you willna have tae marry him after all. You must have faith in the Almighty and in my William."

Helen's cheerful, optimistic attitude did nothing to change Edina's state of mind. She was convinced she would never be happy with Duncan and would not give up hope until the dire end.

The ladies followed Laird Sinclair into the great hall and Edina took her place at her father's left side. Helen sat at a trestle table with her mother and father. The drone of voices filled the hall, the primary topic of conversation Callum and the events leading up to his death.

"Good morning, sister. How do you fare this fine day?" Jayden bowed and took Edina's hand in preparation to kiss the back of it, but she tugged it away.

"Dinna fine day me, Jayden Sinclair. Why did you leave Alasdair alone with a jug of whisky? The man was well in his cups when I saw him last and lacking any manners whatsoever because of it," Edina snapped.

"I dinna tell him tae stay up all night drinking. He is my friend, not my charge. I offered him a drink and how much he chose tae down is his affair. He is a warrior and accustomed tae battle, drink, and women. Mayhap not the kind of man a soon-tae-be married woman should be associating with." Jayden's reply was brusque and to the point.

Edina's mouth gaped open. "I thought he was your friend."

"Aye, but you are my sister and I want what's best for you."

"Your brother is right. You should be thinking about your betrothed and how to please him, not a drunken warrior. I expect Duncan will arrive late this afternoon or on the morrow at the latest. Once you are wed, he will be your main focus of attention, along with providing him an heir," her father cut in.

Edina shook her head. There was no point in trying to talk to her father or her brother. Neither was prepared to listen. Thankfully she had taken matters into her own hands and sent for Duncan's former lover.

"I heard about Callum." Edina decided it best to change the subject for the time being. "Is it true he fell tae his death?"

Her father lowered his head and gave it a slow nod. "Aye. The fool attacked the guard, nearly killed the bugger, then made a run for it. He should have known better than tae try. I sent out a party of men at dawn tae search for his remains. However, I dinna think they will find him. The current is strong and the tide has gone out, likely taking his body with it."

Edina placed her hand on her father's forearm. "I am sorry he let you down, Da. I know you put your faith in him."

"He and I have been friends since we were lads. The fact that he would betray me came as quite a shock, but I was bent on seeing him punished. I suppose his death has saved me the task of deciding his fate."

"The blackguard got what he deserved. Had I gotten my hands on him, I'd have lopped off his ballocks and fed tae the dogs," Jayden interjected. "Even that would have been too good for the bastard."

"His fate was not yours tae decide, son. But we dinna have tae worry about that now." Sinclair pointed to the platters of meat, cheese, fruit, and fresh bannock that were placed on the table before them. "Cook has gone to a lot of trouble tae prepare your favorite foods. Eat, Edina."

"I'm not hungry," Edina replied softly. "If you dinna mind, I am still verra tired and wish tae return to my chamber." She stood to leave, bowed to her father, and was about to exit the room when a messenger entered.

"I bring word from Duncan Sutherland," the man announced.

Laird Sinclair ushered him in with a sweep of his arm. "Tell us and make haste."

The messenger bowed, then plucked a piece of vellum from his sporran, and handed it to her father. Edina waited with baited breath while he read the note.

A broad smile crossed her father's face as he read the missive. "Duncan has been delayed, but will be here first thing in the morning. It appears you have another day tae prepare for your husband-tae-be's arrival."

Chapter 17

Edina now understood the angst and desperation a condemned man must feel as he awaits execution. Duncan's delay gave her a brief reprieve, but an extra day didn't change the fact that she would be forced to marry upon his arrival. Unless her plan to reunite him with his true love succeeded, she'd have no options but to follow through with her father's arrangement.

An attempt to busy herself with needlework failed, as did walking about the parapets and castle grounds until she was exhausted. She hid out in her chamber for hours, brooding about her fate, wishing she could find the answer to her dilemma. She refused to join the clan for the evening meal, opting to eat in her chamber, then retired early. But she was unable to sleep.

Despite being angry with Alasdair for the way he'd abandoned her and showed no concern for her plight, she could not get him off her mind. An unsavory mix of antagonism and desire churned in her belly. The voice in her head told her that she should curse the ground he walked upon, and be thankful he would soon be out of her life forever, but her heart told her otherwise.

He'd managed to keep his distance. Since their confrontation prior to the morning meal, she'd not seen a sign of Alasdair. Mayhap he'd spent the entire day sleeping off the effects of too much whisky? Nay, her gut told her the man was deliberately avoiding her.

The possibility that he may have left to rejoin the Bruce without saying goodbye crossed her mind, causing her heart to plummet. But surely Jayden would have told her if he'd departed.

Fretting over things she could not change was a fruitless task, so she closed her eyes and prayed for sleep.

Morning came far too quickly. Edina arose before the sun, still toying with the idea of running away before Duncan arrived. But her sense of duty and honor would not allow her to humiliate her father in that way. At least by facing the situation head on, she'd have a chance to reason with Duncan.

A commotion in the bailey prompted Edina to move to the window. She threw open the shutters and peered into the inner courtyard. Her stomach clenched and her breath caught as she beheld the elaborate entourage proceeding through the iron gates.

Bright colored flags flapped in the breeze. A tall, handsome man on a white destrier led the group of warriors. He sat proud in the saddle, his back straight, and his head held high. He wore a saffron tunic that stretched across a broad muscular chest and a sash of Sutherland plaid. His shoulder length, blond hair hung loose and was tousled by a gust of wind. Helen was correct. Duncan was a striking man and an impressive sight.

But it mattered not. Edina did not wish to marry this man and hoped he would feel the same way once she'd had a chance to speak with him in private.

As she drew in her head, the patter of feet approaching from behind caused her to spin around.

"I hope I dinna startle you, m'lady. Since you were looking out the window, I guess you're already aware of your betrothed's grand entrance. Your da sent me tae help you get ready tae meet the young laird and bid you join them in the great hall as soon as possible."

"Aye. I saw him enter the bailey." Edina moved toward the bed and sat.

"From what I've observed, he is a braw warrior. You are verra lucky tae have such a dashing man ask for your hand," Helen said cheerfully. She selected two gowns from the shelf and held them up for Edina's perusal. "Do you fancy the blue or the green? Both would look lovely."

"I have no desire tae impress the man. There is a grey, wool servant's frock hanging on a hook in the kitchen, mayhap that would be my best choice," Edina replied.

"Och, you dinna mean tae wear that old rag." Helen chose the green gown, then returned the blue one to the shelf. "I think this will complement your bonny eyes and beautiful flaxen locks." She placed the garment on the bed beside Edina, before retrieving a pair of matching slippers.

"I canna believe your lighthearted attitude. I thought you were my friend." Edina rose, threw her hands in the air, and began to pace. "You know I am opposed tae this union."

"Aye, I am your friend. But until William returns with the Mackenzie lass or you come up with another plan tae get your father tae reconsider this arrangement, best you approach the arrival of Laird Sutherland with an open mind. Defying your da and insulting your betrothed will only make a bad situation worse."

Edina offered a hesitant nod. "You are verra wise, Helen, for a lass so young. If I anger my father, he will be even more intent on seeing me wed as soon as possible. I must stall until William returns." She reached for the hem of her nightrail and tugged it over her head. "I will meet with Duncan as Da commands and be as cordial as possible. Hopefully he is a reasonable man and will listen tae what I have tae say."

Edina donned the gown and allowed Helen to assist her with her hair, but as she readied herself to meet the man she was to marry, she was revisited by thoughts of Alasdair. Despite his strong aversion to marriage, she held out a glimmer of hope he might have a change of heart.

"Have you seen Lord Fraser this morn?" Edina had to know if he was still at the castle.

"Nay. I havena seen him since yesterday when you spoke with him in the hallway." The young maid's face flushed red. "That is a conversation I willna forget."

"Do you know if he is still in the keep?"

"I heard rumors that he spent the entire day in his chamber, drinking." Helen shook her head and clucked her tongue. "Cook told me that when the maid went tae change his bed clothes, she dinna return for some time. When she did, her hair was a mess, her cheeks flushed, and her gown rumpled. She refused tae say what, if anything, happened. But then again, the knave is only living up tae his reputation."

"What do you mean by that?" A mix of anger and jealousy tormented Edina's stomach. How could he humiliate her so and take a maid into his bed when he knew how she felt about him? Mayhap Jayden was right about Alasdair's morals or lack there of.

"My brother was with him at Methven and Loudon Hill. While Darius says Lord Alasdair is a brave, fierce warrior, he also told me the man likes his whisky, carouses with tavern wenches, is crude, and certainly not known for his manners. I am surprised you found him tolerable."

"I heard similar things about Alasdair, but once you get tae know him, and if given a chance, he can be quite charming." Again she found herself defending his character and actions.

"Do you plan tae stay holed up in here for another full day?" Jayden asked as he stomped across the room and threw open the shutters. "High time you got up."

"What does a man have tae do around here tae get some sleep? First there was a ruckus in the bailey and now you barge in." He threw his arm over his eyes, shielding them from the unwelcome sunlight. "Leave me be," Alasdair growled."

"I've left you be too long by the sorry look of you. Not tae mention the chamber smells like some sort of animal lives in here," Jayden commented, then whacked the bottom of Alasdair's foot with flat of his hand. "You need tae get up and take a bath."

Alasdair glared at his friend. "I dinna need you tae tell me what tae do."

"Obviously someone has tae point you in the right direction, afore you drink yourself tae death." He picked up an empty jug from the floor and then another. "I see you managed tae find Da's supply of whisky. No wonder you dinna come out of your cave."

Alasdair grunted, then rolled over, turning his back to Jayden. Despite what people thought, he did not usually drink to excess unless he had a very good reason. "I said leave me alone."

"Nay. I insist you get out of bed and wash up. Now." He yanked the pelt from the bed, leaving Alasdair naked and shivering. "Da will be expecting you tae join him in the great hall tae break your fast and tae greet Duncan Sutherland."

A rock-sized knot formed in Alasdair's stomach at the sound of the man's name. So Edina's betrothed had arrived. "That would explain the noise in the bailey. The bride's future husband has finally come tae claim his prize. I am sure your sister will be pleased." He was unable to curtail the cynicism in his voice.

"I canna speak for Edina. She may not agree with Da's decision, but I know she willna do anything tae embarrass him. I suggest you honor him in the same manner . . . with your presence."

Jayden retrieved a large bowl from the shelf, then filled

it with water. "I would suggest you wash and mayhap shave afore you come down. You look like a bear and smell like one as well." He threw back his head and laughed.

"As far as hosts go, you are sorely lacking." Alasdair groaned when he sat up, quickly dropping his throbbing head into his hands. He spied the jug on the table beside the bed and reached for it. Just as Jayden snatched it away, marched over the window, and dumped the remaining content.

"No more whisky. Get up and ready for the day," Jayden snapped. "And for God sake, put on some clothes." He tossed the pelt over Alasdair's lap.

Alasdair licked his parched lips and coughed to clear his throat. "Then we are in agreement. The time has come for me tae leave. I will clean up, pay my respects tae your da, and be on my way. Robert will be engaging the MacDougalls soon, so I shall be returning tae camp and will prepare for battle."

"There is no need for you tae go. We have had verra little opportunity tae catch up on old times. Besides, my father has invited the chiefs of several prominent Highland clans tae the wedding and is expecting you tae represent Clan Fraser."

"I am not the Laird of my clan, Connor is," Alasdair snapped. "I need to rejoin the Bruce."

"That may be, but you are still the eldest son of my father's dear friend. If you depart after the wedding, I will join you in the fight against the MacDougall's. The time has come I had my chance at the buggers."

The more Alasdair thought about Edina's upcoming nuptials, the more eager he was to depart. He could not offer her a future, but he sure as hell did not have to stick around and torture himself. Seeing her wed to Duncan Sutherland, knowing she'd warm his bed, and grow round with his bairns, was more than he could handle. While Laird Sinclair might find his abrupt departure offensive, it was a risk he was willing to take.

"I canna make any promises. My brothers were expecting me tae visit afore the confrontation. I have not seen them in over a year and dinna want tae disappoint them."

"Are Connor and Bryce not joining Robert in the fight? You mentioned they were." Jayden cocked his head to the side and waited for an answer.

"Aye, but I'd hoped to see my nephew and Bryce's daughter as well. Andrew was a babe, only a fortnight old, when last I saw him and he has now seen two summers. I have yet tae see Bryce and Fallon's wee lassie and according to his last missive, Connor and Cailin were expecting another tae be born any day." Alasdair was making excuses, looking for reasons to justify his hasty departure. Anything but the truth.

After rising to a wobbly stance, he trudged across the chamber to the washbasin. "Once I've cleaned up, I'll meet you in the great hall." He dipped both hands into the bowl, then splashed water on his face.

"I'll hold you tae your word. Dinna take too long," Jayden replied, then left the chamber.

Alasdair washed his face several times before picking up the pitcher and pouring the remaining liquid over his head. Rivulets of cold water running down his back made him shiver, but it felt refreshing. After rinsing his teeth and scraping two days worth of stubble from his chin, he was ready to don his clothes and face Edina and her father for the last time.

Chapter 18

Edina ran her sweaty palms down the front of her gown. Her heart raced and she found it hard to breathe. Preparing to meet Duncan for the first time proved to be more difficult than she'd ever imagined. "You can do this. You have no choice," she muttered to herself.

After taking a minute to steady her nerves, she reached for the latch then shoved the door to the great hall open. The din of conversation ceased when she stepped into the room, and as she proceeded to the laird's dais all eyes were upon her.

What are they staring at? Have they never seen a lamb led to slaughter afore? That is exactly how she felt at the moment.

Her father, deep in discussion with his guests, stopped mid-sentence and rose to his feet. "Duncan. May I present my daughter, Edina, your betrothed?"

His statement caused her chest to tighten and she found it hard to breathe. She wanted to turn tail and run while she still had the chance, but managed to stifle the urge.

"It is a pleasure tae finally meet you, m'lady." Duncan stood, then bowed.

"And you, m'lord." She had to force the words. Edina responded to his gesture with a curtsy, but could not bring herself to look him in the eye.

"Your da has told me so much about you and I feel as though we are already acquainted. However, I must say his description dinna do you justice. You are far lovelier than I anticipated." Duncan stepped around the end of the dais and took Edina's hand.

Her stomach knotted and her breath caught when he brought her palm to his lips. How dare he be so bold? But then again, she would soon be his wife and he'd be at liberty to do with her as he pleased.

"I look forward tae getting tae know you a lot better, Edina. Your father said he plans to see us wed in the next few days. I hope it will be sooner."

Edina withdrew her hand and tucked it in her skirts. While she had to admit Duncan Sutherland was charismatic and dashing—mayhap the handsomest man she'd ever laid eyes upon—his touch did not ignite the same unbridled passion as Alasdair's. Despite his good looks and charm, she still had no desire to marry this man.

"If my da told you all about me, I am surprised you still wish tae go through with the nuptials," she said for lack of a better reply.

"On the contrary, my dear, I am quite taken by your beauty and intrigued by your father's tales. This should prove to be an interesting union."

"We can talk about that later. First we must break our fast," Laird Sinclair announced. "Be seated next tae Duncan, Edina, I am sure he would share his trencher with you."

"Aye." Duncan held out her chair and waited for her to sit.

"Och, I'm glad you decided to join us, lad. Come in," her father called out across the room and waved.

Edina's heart leapt when she saw Alasdair standing in the doorway with freshly washed hair, clean shaven, and looking every bit the gentleman. If not for the scowl on his face, she'd almost think he was pleased to join them.

Alasdair strode across the room with purpose, stopping a few feet from the dais. "I've come tae thank you for your hospitality, Laird Sinclair, and tae bid you farewell."

Edina almost choked on the piece of oatcake she had just popped into her mouth. Was he really leaving? Alasdair spoke directly to her father and never once looked in her direction.

"You canna leave." Jayden sprang to his feet. "I thought we agreed you would remain at the castle until after the wedding."

"You agreed, my friend. I told you Robert is expecting me to join him in battle, and I want tae stop by Fraser Castle on the way."

"And I said I'd be happy tae accompany you and join in the fight if you could wait a few days," Jayden replied sharply.

"You've obviously made up your mind. Can you not at least stay long enough tae break your fast?" Laird Sinclair pointed to an empty chair between Edina and her brother. "Have a seat beside Jayden, lad. Cook has prepared a feast."

A tidal wave of emotions hit Edina. She didn't want Alasdair to leave, but she was also angry he was not prepared to fight for her hand. She was falling in love with him, of that she was certain, but reality hit when she looked at the man sitting beside her. Duncan was her betrothed, not Alasdair, and she'd soon be married to man she neither knew or loved.

"Again, I thank you for your kindness, but I'm not hungry. I have a three-day ride ahead of me and need tae be on my way. I hope tae cover many miles afore making camp for the night," Alasdair replied.

Not hungry? Edina fought to keep her mouth from dropping open. If she knew anything about Alasdair Fraser, it was that he had a healthy appetite. She stood. "Father is right. You canna leave before you've had something tae eat."

Laird Sinclair continued to speak as if he'd not heard what either Edina or Alasdair had said. "Forgive me for being remiss. This is Duncan Sutherland, the man Edina is tae marry. And this is Alasdair Fraser, the man who saved my daughter's life, and is responsible for her safe return."

Duncan rose and offered his hand. "I owe you a debt of gratitude, Fraser." He slid his arm around Edina's waist and drew her to his side. "I'd been told Edina had died at sea and was pleased to hear the rumor wasna true. I would be honored if you could attend our wedding."

Alasdair bowed, but kept his hands at his sides. "Laird Sinclair has chosen well. I hope you and Edina will be verra happy together, but I must depart."

"Well, if you insist on leaving, may the Almighty guide your way and watch your back," Laird Sinclair said and raised his tankard.

Speechless, Edina moved from Duncan's side and returned to her chair. She could not believe Alasdair was leaving. By the time she found her tongue, he'd already departed.

Edina nibbled on her lower lip and shifted in her seat, tempted to race after him, to beg him to stay. But by doing so, she would embarrass her father and insult Duncan before her entire clan. Despite what was in her heart, she did not act on her impulse.

"He seems like a nice fellow. I've heard tales of his valor in the battles with the English." Duncan sat, picked up his tankard of ale, and took a sip. "Have you known him long?"

"Aye. Since we were bairns. His da was one of my father's dearest friends." She answered Duncan's questions, but her eyes remained on the door. Dare she hope Alasdair would have a change of heart and return for her? But as the minutes passed, she resolved herself to the fact she'd likely seen the last of him.

The thunder of his pounding heart resonated in Alasdair's ears. Anger threatened to consume him as he stomped toward the stable with his fists balled. Had he not contained himself and acted on instinct, he'd have taken Duncan by the throat and pummeled him for being so forward with Edina.

It was plain the man had no sense of decency or respect for the lass. The suggestive way Duncan spoke to her and kissed her hand in front of her kin and the entire clan infuriated him. The familiarity with which he put his arm around Edina, acting as if he already owned her, caused Alasdair's blood boil.

Alasdair refused to stand idly by and watch Duncan take inappropriate liberties, but it was not his place to intervene. The sooner he left, the better, lest he end up in a brawl and wound up in the pit again.

"Will you slow down?" Jayden shouted as he raced up from behind, almost running into Alasdair when he came to an abrupt halt and turned to face him.

"I have nothing tae say and must be on my way. There is no reason to tarry here any longer and there are things I must do afore I rejoin the Bruce. Naught you say will change my mind," Alasdair growled. Why his friend could not accept his decision was a puzzle.

"You could stay and fight for her. Is that not reason enough tae remain?" Jayden blurted out. "Nay-say it if you want, but any fool could see you care for my sister a great deal and my guess is she feels the same. If not for you, she'd have died on the beach. She owes you her life and I know she would like you tae stay."

"You're daft. She is merely grateful. Women are nothing but trouble and I have no desire tae take a wife. Even if I was interested, which I am not, she is promised tae Sutherland, a man who has far more tae offer her and your clan. The battle with the MacDougalls and MacCanns will soon take place and I must get back. Robert needs every man he can round up."

"If you werena so thrawn and in such a rush tae leave, I'd join you."

"Then come with me. But make haste. I have delayed long enough," Alasdair replied.

"You know I canna leave afore the wedding. If you are too bull-headed tae speak up for her, I willna insult Duncan by my absence. One day, I will be laird of Clan Sinclair and I refuse tae do anything to disgrace my father or my kin."

"You've made your choice. I respect your right tae choose loyalty tae family over friendship, just as I wish you would respect my decision to go. I may not have a future with your sister, but I'll not stand by and see Edina wed tae another man." Alasdair turned to leave, but Jayden placed his hand on his shoulder, halting his retreat.

"I wish we'd had more time to catch up. Once Edina is married, I will join you. Together we will face the MacDougalls." Jayden held out his hand, but when Alasdair grasped his wrist, he yanked his friend into a tight embrace. "Take care, Alasdair. If you stop tae see your brothers afore you join the Bruce give them my regards."

"I will if I can ever be on my way." Alasdair laughed and backed out of Jayden's embrace.

Jayden nodded. "Godspeed. I will see you in a sennight."

Alasdair heaved a sigh of relief when Jayden trotted back toward the castle. Had he kept up his relentless badgering much longer, he might have succeeded in convincing him to stay, and to fight for Edina's hand. A battle he had no hope of winning and no intention of waging. Sutherland had so much to offer, and he had naught but himself. A poor comparison by any man's standards.

Despite the inevitable, Jayden was right in his assumption. Alasdair's chest felt like it was being crushed by bands of iron. Edina had managed to worm her way into the carefully guarded heart. He'd miss her sweet smile and the soft lilt of her voice, along with her strong will and dogged determination. Her offer to run away with him had been tempting, but they were not destined to be together.

He cursed. He wanted no woman in his life, but Edina had him questioning his chosen path. She was better off without him and the sooner he left Sinclair Castle the sooner he could forget about the little minx.

Determined to purge her from his mind once and for all, he gritted his teeth and resumed his trek toward the stable. He'd saddle Odin and be on his way. If he rode hard all day, he'd be able to put a good deal of distance between them.

"Lad, fetch my horse," Alasdair said to a young stable hand.

"Are you leaving, m'lord, or just going out for a ride?" the lad asked.

"What difference does it make? I need my mount either way. If you must know, I willna be returning." Alasdair softened his tone. It was not the lad's fault he was in such a foul mood.

"Then I'll put some oats in a sack for you tae take along." The lad limped over to a large barrel in the corner, picked up a canvas bag, filled it with grain, and handed it to Alasdair. "I'll go fetch your horse."

"Never mind." Alasdair brought his fingers to his lips and whistled.

Odin trotted into the stable and stood a few feet away from his master. "Good lad. You've never let me down." Alasdair stroked the animal's mane before addressing the lad again. "What ails you? I saw you in the bailey yesterday. The other bairns were playing, but you stood off to the side watching." He noticed on closer scrutiny that the lad's left leg was not nearly as well muscled as the right.

The lad lowered his eyes and kicked at a stone with his good leg. "I'm not like the others."

Alasdair cocked his head to the side and studied the lad's downtrodden expression. "I dinna understand. You appeared tae be the same age as the other bairns, mayhap even a tad older."

"Aye, I have seen twelve summers, but they dinna wish tae play with me." He balled his fist and pounded it against his left thigh. "I'm small for my age and my leg gives me trouble. I canna keep up. They taunt me because I'm different and call me names. My da told me I had better learn tae accept it. He said I was cursed with poor health and a game leg when I was born and would never be like the other bairns, or grow tae be a strong warrior. Sometimes, I think he is ashamed tae call me his son." He dropped his chin and stared at the ground.

Alasdair swallowed hard as memories of his youth, his own afflictions, and the frustration he'd felt when he was not much older than this lad came crashing back. "Your da is wrong," Alasdair blurted out, allowing the depth of his emotions to color his words. "You can be or do anything if you want it badly enough. I was a sickly bairn and there was a time when people said the same things about me. My two younger brothers fought my battles for me because I couldna do it myself."

"You, m'lord?" The boy's mouth gaped open. "You are a brawny warrior, mayhap one of the largest, strongest men I have ever seen. I've heard tales of your ferocity in battle, that men fear you."

"I was born with a weak constitution and spent most of my younger days in a sickbed. Many believed I wouldna live tae see manhood. Tall, but spindly for my age, with my ungodly hair, the bairns teased me as they do you, about my size, appearance, and limitations. But I proved them all wrong and so can you." He placed his hand on the boy's shoulder. "If you work at it, you can become stronger than, and as fierce as any warrior in King Robert's army." I would stake my life on it."

The boy's eyes widened. "Do you really think so?"

"I would stake my life on it. Dinna listen to what others say. Follow what is in here." Alasdair thumped his chest.

"And here," he concluded and tapped his brow.

The lad nodded. "I will do my best, m'lord." A broad smile crossed his lips.

"I can offer you one more bit of advice, and it pays tae mind. You canna go wrong with a horse for a companion. But stay as far away from woman as you can."

"I'll keep it in mind, m'lord," the lad replied. "Will you be needing me for anything else?"

"Nay, you can run along. I am sure you must have plenty of work tae keep you busy."

The boy bowed and turned to leave when Alasdair called him back. "You've taken excellent care of Odin. Accept this with my thanks." He tossed the lad a piece of silver.

"Och, thank you, m'lord." Beaming, the lad clutched the coin in a tight fist.

"You're welcome. Now be off with you." Alasdair tousled the lad's hair, then patted him on the backside.

"What do you say, Odin? Shall we be off as well?" After tightening the cinches, Alasdair threw his leg over the animal's back, and pulled himself into the saddle. With a sharp kick to the flanks, his mount bolted forward. He dipped his head as they passed under the doorframe of the stable and did not look back as they sped across the bailey and through the iron gates of the castle.

Chapter 19

Edina pretended to listen as Duncan told her about himself and his plans for their future. She nodded politely, but her thoughts kept wandering back to Alasdair. Was he really gone?

"Good riddance," she muttered under her breath. If he was too blind to see they were meant to be together, he deserved to be alone.

"Did you say something?" Duncan asked.

"Nay. Please tell me more about your clan." Edina forced a smile and gently touched his forearm, but she averted her eyes, afraid he would know she was lying.

"I am sure you will like living at Sutherland Castle. My da has not been well and I'd like tae return as soon as possible. If you are agreeable, I will speak tae your father and see if we can be wed on the morrow."

"I'm sorry tae hear your father hasna been well. Is that why Laird Sutherland dinna accompany you?" She was determined to keep the discussion away from the topic of their upcoming marriage. Albeit unsuccessful.

"Aye, he has been ailing for a while and plans tae step down as laird once I am married. He will be anxious for me tae produce an heir, so I want tae try for a babe right away."

Edina swallowed hard, a lump forming in her throat the size of a boulder. She nibbled on her bottom lip, not sure how to broach the subject foremost on her mind. "Can I ask you something?"

"Certainly. What is it you want tae know," Duncan replied.

"Is this agreement between our fathers, the wedding I mean, what you truly want?" she blurted out.

"Why would you ask?" Duncan's brow furrowed.

She shifted her weight from one foot to the other and stared at the floor, searching for the right words. The last thing she wanted to do was offend him. And she certainly did not want to make him angry. But the need to know gave her the courage to press on.

"I've heard rumors about a lass from the Mackenzie Clan. I was told the two of you have been in love since you were bairns, and would understand if you wished tae marry her in my stead."

There, she'd said her piece. Edina peered up at Duncan, waiting for his response.

Duncan coughed to clear his throat. "The past means naught. We canna always follow our hearts, Edina. Especially if we are destined tae lead a clan and must abide by tradition."

"That isna what I asked you." Edina wrung her hands and shuffled her feet. "Do you still love her?"

"Whether I love Oceana or not doesna matter. Our fathers entered into a pact and it is our duty tae honor their wishes. The King has also sanctioned this union in hopes of uniting the clans and we are bound tae abide by his decree. Are you not pleased with your father's choice?"

"You are a dashing warrior, Duncan. Any woman would be proud tae call you husband. But I dinna wish tae marry a man who is in love with another."

"I can promise I will be a good husband, Edina. I'm sure in time we will grow tae care for each other," Duncan replied.

Care for each other? That is not what she'd hoped for in a marriage. Unlike her parents, she wanted to wed a man she loved, someone who felt the same way about her. "I have known since I was a wee bairn that a mate would be chosen for me, I just hoped that we would love each other."

Duncan did not answer. Instead, he changed the subject. "After the fine meal your cook has provided, I would like to go for a walk. Will you accompany me, mayhap give me a tour of the castle grounds?"

Edina covered her mouth to stifle a yawn. "As you know, I am still recovering from my tumble intae the water and near death. I find myself verra tired. If you dinna mind, I would like tae go tae my solar and rest awhile."

Duncan took her hand and kissed the back of it. "I understand. If you'll permit me, I will escort you tae your chamber."

She placed her free hand on his chest. "Thank you, but it willna be necessary. I am sure my father and brother have many things tae discuss with you. I have lived in this castle since I was a babe and can find my way." She slid her hand out of Duncan's grasp, curtsied, turned on her heel, and scurried out of the great hall.

When she arrived at her chamber, Edina entered and quickly closed the door. She rested her back against the wooden slab, her heart racing. What was she going to do? William had not returned with the Mackenzie lass, and even if he did, she was no longer certain her plan would work. Duncan seemed bent on honoring the pact between their fathers and wanted the wedding to take place as soon as possible. If only Alasdair had been willing to fight for her.

She ran a shaky hand down her gown as she crossed the room, a sense of dread suddenly washing over her.

Something was amiss.

A strong arm snaked around her waist and hauled her against a solid wall of muscle. A dirty hand covered her mouth.

"I'll bet you thought you'd seen the last of me. Thanked the Almighty when you assumed he'd seen tae my demise," the man hissed in her ear. "Did you think you'd get off that easily? You got away once, but it willna happen again."

Her chest constricted. She recognized the gravelly cadence of Callum's voice. When her struggle to break free failed, she bit down on his hand, tasting blood.

"Satan's bitch," he yelped, then released her, bringing his injured hand to his lips.

Edina backed away and rubbed her eyes in disbelief, but when her vision cleared, he was still standing before her. "How can this be? You're dead."

"Am I?" he growled, then tossed back his head and laughed. "Then I suppose you are about to be bedded, then flayed by a spirit."

"This canna be! My father's men saw you fall to your death from the cliffs." Edina gasped for air as she continued to back away, but her eyes remained focused on Callum. He was blocking the doorway, her only means of escape, so she frantically searched for a weapon, something she could use to defend herself.

"That little slip played nicely into my plans. The fools never found my body, did they? Suffice tae say, they were mistaken when they presumed I was dead." He pulled a dirk from his boot and took a menacing step forward.

"You are a wanted man. Why would you return to the castle and risk capture?" Edina asked on a strangled breath. Her heart hammered against her ribs and fear squeezed, but she refused to show any weakness. A blackguard like Callum would use that to his advantage and she had no intention of giving up without a fight.

He lurched forward with his hand outstretched, but she managed to sidestep his grasp. "You were meant to be mine and I am here to collect my prize."

"Damn you, Callum." The curse left her lips before she could stop it, the words feeding his anger. "You willna get away with this. If they dinna catch you in the act, my father will hunt you down and see you punished."

"I am already damned. Your father has seen tae that. You may not be a virgin anymore, but I can still sate my needs afore I slit your throat. No one betrays me and gets away with it. You should have heeded my warning when we were on the ship." He inched closer.

"You dinna have tae do this, Callum. If you leave now, you can escape afore anyone knows you were here. I always thought of you like an uncle, and my father trusted you, treated you like a brother." While she was certain trying to reason with the man would do no good, she had to try.

"Your father is a fool. Were it not for my guidance, he would never have been a great leader. I run this clan, not him, and have for many years," Callum boasted. "But you had to ruin everything."

"I did naught. It was you who tried tae accost me against my will, betrayed my father's faith in you. But despite your treacherous acts, I am sure my father would have shown you mercy, that he had no intention of seeing you hang."

Callum spat on the floor. "I dinna want his kind of mercy. If he banished me, I'd have nothing tae live for. I would rather he'd run me through. But your da willna get the chance tae humiliate me before the clan. Once I finish with you, I will help myself tae some coin from the village coffers, then be off afore anyone knows I have been here." An evil smirk crossed his lips. "By the time they find your body, I will be long gone. Since everyone believes I am dead, they will have no idea who committed the deed and I will be free to start my life anew."

When Callum tried to grab for Edina's arm, she picked up a tankard from the table and tossed it, striking him on the side of his head. He cursed and lunged at her again, catching the sleeve of her gown as she tried to scoot around the bed, but she managed to twist free.

"It will do you no good tae fight me, lass. You'll only prolong what is destined tae happen." He groaned when he struck his toe on the leg of the bed. His face flushed red with anger and a string of ribald curses spewed from his mouth.

"Come any closer and I'll scream for help." Her heart raced as he slinked forward. She stepped backward until she could go no farther, her spine pressed against the wall beside the hearth.

"Go ahead and shout for all it is worth. The walls are thick and the door a heavy plank of oak. Your father and brother are in the great hall trying tae impress your pompous husband-tae-be and the servants are busy tending to their duties in another part of the castle at this time of day."

"Someone will hear me and when they do, you'll wish you had died when you fell from the cliff."

"Mayhap you are right." Callum ran his finger along the blade of his dirk. "Helen might hear your cry for help. Should she dare tae interfere, after I am finished with you, I will take great pleasure in bedding her as well, then take pleasure in killing her slowly. Whether I sate my needs with one or two women it matters not."

"Bastard!" Edina balled her fists at her sides. She was not going to give in without a fight. But she could not risk putting Helen in danger. She shuffled to the side, her hand brushing cold metal. Her fingers furled around the shaft of an iron poker.

He paused a few feet from where she stood and tilted his head to the side. His eyes roamed her body from top to bottom, as if she were a prize steer up for auction. "I had forgotten just how lovely you are. You look so much like your mother. We were lovers. Did you know that?" His devilish grin broadened. "She never loved your da and warmed my bed more than once. I wonder if you will taste as sweet or sheath me as tightly as she did."

Edina fought to keep the bile rising in her throat. She could not believe her mother had given herself to Callum. "Liar!" she shouted and raised the poker in the air. "My mother may not have loved my father, but she would never dishonor him by lying with the likes of you, and neither will I."

"Still the feisty wench. Your mother said the same thing until she sampled my wares, then she couldna get enough." He cupped his groin and thrust his hips forward. "Put down the poker or I will have to teach you a lesson in manners. One that is long overdue."

"What would a swine like you know about manners?" Edina swung the poker as if wielding a sword.

"Foolish bairn. You canna possibly think tae best me with that." He dropped the dirk on the bed, slid a sword from the scabbard at his side, then brought the hilt to his nose in challenge. "I will give you one more chance tae put it down, lass, afore I flay you."

"You can try," she replied boldly, her chin held high. "You know my father saw tae it that I learned tae handle a sword and a bow. I can hold my own in a fight with any man. Mayhap you will be the one flayed."

"Bold and haughty as ever and like your mam, soon tae be my whore," Callum taunted. "It would be a shame to kill you afore I have the chance tae bed you, but if you insist on a challenge, so be it." He raised his sword. "Tell me, Edina. How would you like tae die? Fast or slow? I can lop off your head or gut you like a fish and watch you squirm in agony. The choice is yours."

"You willna have the chance to do either." Edina brought the poker down in a sweeping motion, connecting with Callum's blade.

"Well done, but you willna best me." He widened his stance and swung his blade, the strike countered by Edina this time.

They exchanged blows, Edina more determined than ever to beat Callum and kill the bugger. "Do you take pride in fighting a woman?" she asked as she swung the poker toward him, time after time.

"What you wield matters not. You dinna have a prayer of winning." Callum quickly met each blow with his sword, finally disarming Edina with the final swoop of his blade.

Panic squeezed her chest and her breath caught. Callum was about to make good on his threat. But she'd not stand there and let him kill her. She ducked when he swung his sword, coming very close to her neck, and stumbled toward the bed.

He grabbed her hair and yanked her head back, pressing the cold steel against her throat. "Beg me for mercy and I may let you live long enough tae enjoy what I am about tae do." He lifted her skirt and forced her facedown onto the bed.

Using his body weight, he pressed her into the mattress, his hand sliding between her thighs and fondling her most intimate place. Tears welled in her eyes, but she refused to cry. "I curse you, Callum, and willna give in to you, while a breath remains. I demand you release me at once." She tried to call out for help, but her plea was muffled when he buried her face in the pelts until she was sure she'd smother.

"You are wasting your breath and energy. No one is going to help you and remember my promise. If Helen should come to your aid, she will be next in line," he snapped.

When he eased up on his hold, Edina rolled her head to the side and gasped for a much-needed breath.

"My brother and father willna give up until they've hunted you down and seen you executed. Let me go now and there's a chance you'll survive."

"You are not in any position tae barter or tae tell me what tae do." Callum rolled her to her back. "I want you tae see what is coming, tae watch your face as I drive intae you." He clutched her wrists with one hand, and tugged at the waist of his trews with the other, quickly exposing his burgeoning shaft. "Hold still and you may just enjoy your last minutes on earth."

"Nay!" She twisted to free herself, but he outweighed her. She kicked with all her might, but Callum only laughed. "Suit yourself. Either way this is going tae happen." He flipped her onto her stomach, pressing his knee to her back in order to hold her in place.

Cold hands encircled her bottom and her effort to squeeze her knees together was fruitless. He was too strong and easily pried her legs apart. She choked back a sob. He would not make her cry. What was she going to do?

"There's nothing you can do tae stop him," a tiny voice at the back of her brain insisted.

Nay. She would not give in. Struggling in earnest, her hand brushed against something metal buried amidst the bed covering.

"Coward! At least have the nerve tae face me," she said, her voice never wavering, despite the overwhelming terror she felt. "You have won. I want tae look intae your eyes when you kill me."

"Happy tae oblige, m'lady." Callum lifted his knee and rolled her to her back again. "Now be a good lassie, spread your legs, and let me—" His eyes widened and his mouth dropped open as Edina plunged the dirk into his chest and twisted.

Callum gasped and clutched the dagger protruding from his body, blood oozing between his fingers. He tried to stand and retrieve his sword, but fell to the floor before he could reach it. "Damnation, bitch," he groaned as he slumped forward and his eyes closed.

"May you rot in hell." Edina scrambled to her feet. There was no time to dally or to let her pulse and breath return to normal. She had to get out of there. Now.

In her haste to step around his crumpled body, she caught her foot on his arm and tumbled to the floor, striking her forehead on the stone. A sharp pain lanced through her skull, and for a moment, the room began to spin, then everything faded to darkness.

Calling on every ounce of courage and strength, she fought to remain conscious. But when she finally opened her eyes, the blackguard was standing over her, blood dripping from his wound.

"I will take you tae Hell with me. You will be my bride in death if not life," Callum hissed.

Edina kicked out with her free leg, connecting with Callum's shin, throwing him off balance, and sending him crashing to his knees. She tried to stand, but a bloody hand wrapped around her ankle, thwarting her escape. Why wouldn't he die?

This time when she kicked, she connected with his jaw. When the first blow proved unsuccessful, she repeated the action with as much force as she could muster.

Finally, his fingers unfurled and she was able to crawl a few feet away, and out of his reach. She scooped up the sword and was about to end his life when the door opened behind her.

"Saint's teeth, Edina, what goes on in here?"

From a distance, Edina heard Jayden's voice, then her eyesight started to dim. She felt someone take the sword from her hand just as she collapsed.

Chapter 20

The sound of familiar voices echoed in Edina's ears. Her head throbbed, her stomach churned, and the struggle to open her eyes failed. Someone was carrying her. Was it Callum? Fear seized her heart.

Nay. Callum was gravely injured and in no condition to carry himself. She could see the blackguard standing before her, the wild look in his eyes, his dirk protruding from his chest, and blood oozing between his fingers as he clutched the wound. A string of curses that no maiden should hear spewed from his mouth. But as the horrible memory dissipated her brother's face came into view. She remembered he was leaning over her, tapping her cheek, and calling her name.

"Jayden—" she mumbled.

"Aye, Edina. Dinna fash, you're safe."

Relief washed over her at his words of comfort, and she relaxed in his arms. "W-where are you taking me?"

"Callum attacked you and judging by the bump and cut on your brow, you must have hit your head during the struggle. The wound is in need of tending so I am taking you tae my chamber, then I will fetch the healer."

"What of Callum?" she managed to ask. Another attempt to open her eyes proved fruitless. Something warm and sticky trickled down her cheek, but she could not muster the strength to wipe it away. She ground her teeth against the pain in her skull, and she could feel herself drifting in and out of consciousness. But she had to stay awake, had to know what happened to her assailant.

"He is dead and a good thing, too. Had I gotten my hands on the bugger, he'd have suffered far worse than he did at your hand." Jayden growled, then he softened his tone. "Try not tae talk, Edina. You need tae save your strength." Wasting no time, he continued his trek down the hall.

"Och! What ails my lady?" Helen asked and touched Edina's arm.

"H-Helen?" Edina mumbled. While hazy memories of her encounter with Callum faded in and out, she vividly recalled his threat to kill her, then attack her maid. Thank the Lord she was unharmed.

"Callum tried tae kill her."

"Och, I should have done something tae help," Helen sobbed.

"Nay. I'm glad you had the good sense tae summon me when you heard the commotion, or he might have succeeded."

"Callum? How could that be? After his escape from the pit, my brother and the others who gave chase saw the devil fall from atop the cliff and ontae the rocks below."

"He obviously survived the tumble, but there is no question that the blackguard is dead now," Jayden replied.

"May the Lord be praised. But my lady is injured and in need of a healer. She should be abed." Concern resonated in Helen's voice.

Edina wanted to console her friend, to let her know she would be fine, and had done the right thing in fetching Jayden, but she could not manage the simple task.

"I'm taking Edina tae my chamber. Will you fetch the physician, then summon my father and Duncan?"

"Right away, m'lord."

Helen's footfall faded and Edina once again relaxed in her brother's protective embrace. She moaned and Jayden shifted her in his arms.

"Hold on Edina, we are almost there," he reassured her.

She heard the soft thud and felt a slight jar as he pushed open a door with his elbow. He carried her a short distance before placing her on a soft mattress, and covering her with a pelt.

"There you go, try tae rest. I've sent for a healer," Jayden whispered in her ear as he stroked her cheek.

Edina groaned when Jayden wiped her brow with a damp cloth and rolled her head to the side. She brought her hand up to brush his away, but he caught her wrist.

"Easy, lass. I only mean tae clean the blood from your forehead."

"How in damnation did that traitorous bastard get intae the castle unnoticed, let alone intae my daughter's chamber?" her father bellowed. "I should have had him beheaded when first I found out about his treachery, showed him no mercy." He lifted her hand and patted the back of it. "Thank the Lord you came along when you did, son. Is she badly injured?"

"She took a nasty blow tae the head, but other than that, appears tae be unharmed. We will know more when the healer arrives and has had a chance tae examine her."

"Is it true she killed the bugger?" her father asked.

"Aye. Teaching Edina tae defend herself with a sword and dagger proved useful," Jayden answered, and Edina could hear the satisfaction and pride in his voice.

"I came as soon as Helen told me what happened," Duncan said as he entered the chamber. "How does Edina fare?"

"She'll be shaken I'm sure, but right now I am having difficulty waking her," Jayden said as he touched her cheek.

"My head hurts." Edina opened her eyes, but closed them again when her vision blurred and the room began to spin.

"Shhhh. Rest, daughter. You've come from hardy stock and willna let a wee knock on the head keep you down for long," her father said. "What is delaying my physician?"

"He is on his way, m'lord," Helen replied as she entered the chamber. "Is there anything I can do tae help, Lord Jayden?"

"Aye. Fetch me a bowl of clean water and see what is keeping the healer."

Edina raised heavy lids, glanced up at her brother and father, waiting for them to come into focus. "There is no need for all the palver. Da is right, I'll be fine."

"Let me be the judge of that," a man said as he crossed the room.

Edina narrowed her eyes in an attempt to see his face. As he neared the bed, she recognized the clan's physician.

"Please step outside while I examine the lass," the physician said. "Unless you wish tae be present, Laird Sinclair. Would you like me tae check if she has been violated?"

"There is no need." Her voice trembled as she spoke. "Callum threatened tae ravage me afore he killed me, but he dinna have the chance tae complete the deed. He tried, but I fought him off and stabbed him with his dirk. I thought he was dead, but tripped when I tried tae escape, fell, and struck my head."

"When I entered her chamber, Edina was standing over Callum's motionless body with his blade in her hand. I approached and she collapsed. It was at that time I noticed the cut on her brow," Jayden informed the physician.

"Saints be praised he dinna take her innocence. She remains a virgin and a suitable bride." Her father patted Duncan on the back.

Edina could not believe her ears. Was her suitability for marriage her father's only concern? Her heart sank. He was never going to relent in his quest to see her wed.

"Talk of our nuptials can wait," Duncan interjected. "Let the physician tend tae the lass's needs." He brought Edina's palm to his lips. "I'm glad you were not injured more seriously. After a few days of rest, I am confident you will be up and about, as bright as a silver coin."

The physician coughed to clear his throat. "I'd like tae examine her now. If you gentlemen would wait in the great hall, I will summon you once I have completed my assessment."

Laird Sinclair nodded, turned on his heel, and left the chamber. Duncan and Jayden followed.

Edina nibbled on her lower lip as her father's physician tended to her cut, then checked her for other injuries. Her head continued to pound and nausea twisted her belly. After emptying the content of her stomach twice, in a bucket provided by the healer, she groaned, then lay back on the pallet.

"You were verra fortunate. Callum could have killed you," the physician said as he tucked a pelt beneath her chin. "Any deeper and the wound on your brow would require stitching. But your brother managed tae staunch the bleeding and the cut should heal nicely on its own. However, you did take a hard knock on the head and will continue tae feel poorly for a while. If you remain in bed for the next day or so, your stomach will settle and vision will clear."

She needed more time than that to convince Duncan this marriage was a mistake. But right now, she'd take any reprieve she could get.

He mixed some herbs into a tankard and handed it to Edina. "Drink this elixir and try to get some sleep. I will go and speak tae your father."

Edina downed the bitter content of the cup. A few days abed would buy her some time. If only she could delay the wedding longer. Mayhap if she appealed to Duncan's sense of decency and compassion, he would agree to a postponement while she recovered from her ordeal. By then, William would be back, hopefully with the Mackenzie lass in tow.

Edina balled her fists and slammed them down on the pallet, wishing she had handled matters with Alasdair in a much different way. Why didn't she act on her impulse and go to his chamber when she had the chance? She should have pleaded with him to take her along, and if necessary, offered him her innocence in hope that he would have a change of heart. Desperation can make people do things they normally would never consider. But better judgment had prevailed and she'd not grovel before any man.

The fact that Alasdair was honorable and would not betray her father's or Jayden's trust was an obstacle she could not hurdle. He'd also made it clear he would not take a maiden to his bed unless he could offer marriage, and that was never going to happen. Feeling defeated, she closed her eyes and tried to sleep. Mayhap her plan to reunite Duncan and his love would do the trick.

Edina picked up her needlework, but it was no use. She could not get Alasdair or her upcoming wedding off her mind. She placed the craft on the table, then stood and stretched before wandering over to the window. Three days had passed since the attack and there was still no sign of William. Despite the fact she was feeling much better, she'd remained in bed the entire time as instructed by the physician and other than a brief visit from Jayden on the day she was injured, Helen had been her only companion.

The door opened, causing Edina to spin around. There was no time to climb back into bed so she prayed it would be her maid and not her father or Duncan. The longer they believed her too weak to marry the better.

"Guid morning, m'lady. You are looking chipper today. Are you ready tae break your fast?" Helen entered the chamber carrying a tray of food.

"I'm not hungry." Edina crossed the room and sat in a large overstuffed chair by the hearth.

"Och, m'lady, you must try some of this porridge and fresh bannock. You havena eaten enough to keep a bird alive these last few days."

"Then I shall be too weak tae stand afore the priest and marry Duncan," Edina answered on a shuddering breath.

"Mayhap the tidings I have tae share will brighten your day and your mood," Helen said as she placed the tray on the table beside Edina.

"What news do you bring?" Edina's eyes widened and she anxiously bit her lip in anticipation. Could this be what she'd been waiting for?

"William has returned from his quest, and he has the Mackenzie lass with him. He took her tae his croft and awaits your instructions," Helen said with a broad smile. "I knew he wouldna let me down."

Edina leapt from the chair and threw her arms around Helen, pulling her into a tight hug. "Oh, Helen, I can think of no better tidings. Have William bring her tae my chamber at once. But dinna let anyone else know she is here. I want tae surprise Duncan and need tae speak with the lass alone afore I do."

Helen bobbed a curtsy. "Aye, I will fetch her right away." She brought her finger to her lips. "Dinna fash, I willna breathe a word of it tae anyone, m'lady. You can count on me."

"I know I can, Helen. Please hurry. I wish to speak with the lass as soon as possible."

As Helen reached for the door latch, Edina called her back. "Wait. Have you seen her?"

"Aye, for a few minutes afore I came to tell you they'd returned. Why do you ask?"

"Is she a comely lass?" Edina had to know if seeing her again would be enough to turn Duncan's head and prompt him to follow his heart.

"Oh, aye, she is lovely. A fine lady with raven locks, large blue eyes, and porcelain skin. I can see why Lord Sutherland would be taken by her."

"Guid." Edina rubbed her hands together and smiled. "That will make my task easier." She dismissed Helen with a wave her hand. "Please bring her to me at once."

Edina watched as the maid left the room, then threw her hands in the air and spun around in a circle, excitement and renewed hope burgeoning in her chest. If her scheme worked, her betrothed would be so thrilled tae see his lost love, he'd opt to marry her instead.

But Edina's euphoria dissipated as quickly as it came. The first part of her plan had come to pass. Now, she had to complete the second half. Given his strong sense of duty, convincing Duncan to break the pact and marry his love could prove to be difficult. Of that she was certain.

But it was her only hope, and she had to try.

Chapter 21

"We are almost home," Alasdair announced to Odin as he leaned over the horse's sweat-soaked neck and dug his heels into the animal's flanks. He'd ridden hard for three days, again pushing his mount to unreasonable limits. But the sooner he arrived at Fraser Castle and was reunited with his brothers, the sooner he could resume doing what he was born to do. Being a warrior was in his blood, it was his destiny. Any foolish notion he might have briefly entertained about a wife and family needed to be struck from his mind. He'd rejoin the cause, defending his king and country with his last breath if necessary. In time, he'd forget about Edina, or so he tried to convince himself.

Wind whipped though his unbound hair and he caught the smell of the village fires. As he raced to the top of the moor, the impressive home of his clan came into sight. A swift kick had Odin galloping towards the heavily manned curtain wall, alerting several guards who took their positions upon the stone barricade with their weapons drawn.

He raised one fist in the air and shouted the Fraser war cry. "A Mhor-fhaiche! Tell my brothers I have returned."

"All my hope in God," the men on the wall responded in unison as they hoisted their swords before raising the iron gates.

Alasdair rode into the bailey at full speed, then pulled back on the reins, causing Odin to halt abruptly and to rear on his hind legs.

The door to the castle opened and two men stepped out onto the stone steps.

"Will you look who has decided tae pay us a visit," Alasdair's youngest brother, Bryce, proclaimed as he trotted down the stairs. Connor followed.

Alasdair threw his leg over Odin's neck and slid from the saddle in one swift move. Once his feet were firmly planted on the ground, he ran his hand over his beard-stubbled chin, then twisted and stretched, working out the kinks in his back and legs. Three days in the saddle, stopping only long enough to eat, rest the horse, and to sleep for a few hours each day had taken its toll.

"Welcome home, Alasdair. I'm glad tae see you," Connor said as he approached with his hand outstretched.

"It feels great tae be on home soil," Alasdair replied as he clutched Connor's wrist, drew him into a quick embrace, then took a step back. "You look hail and hardy. Married life obviously suits you." He laughed and patted his brother on the stomach. "You've put on a stone or two. Cailin must be feeding you well."

"She doesna let me miss any meals," Connor replied with a chuckle.

"I'm surprised he's gained weight given how busy he is beneath the sheets. Cailin just gave birth a short time ago and she's breeding again," Bryce said as he joined his two older brothers.

"You should talk. Fallon is with child again too, and the healer thinks it might be twins." Connor thumped Bryce on the back.

"Well I canna have it said my brother is a better lover and sire." Bryce stood toe-to-toe with Connor and poked him in the chest with his finger. "But then again, everyone knows you're the leader and I'm the lover."

"That is a matter of opinion. Yours," Connor countered, then stepped forward and crossed his arms over his chest.

"While you argue over which one is a more virile stud, I'm heading intae the castle tae find some food and a tankard of ale. My throat is as dry as dirt and I'm starving. I could eat an entire wild boar by myself. After that, I plan tae sleep for an entire day, mayhap for a sennight."

"Things never change. I canna remember a time when you werena hungry or ready for a nap." Bryce threw back his head and laughed, then yanked Alasdair into a hug. "Welcome home, brother."

Connor summoned a squire to take Alasdair's mount. "You should have sent word you were coming home, brother. I'd have had Cook prepare a feast and asked the maid tae put fresh rushes on the floor in your chamber."

"We dinna expect tae see you until the battle against the MacDougall's was set tae take place," Bryce said as the three men walked toward the castle. "Fallon told me something was amiss and you were coming home early. She saw it in a dream. But as you know, I dinna set much store in dà shealladh."

"Best you not let her hear you say that about her gift of second sight. Unless you wish tae be sleeping in the stable tonight," Connor warned.

Edina's face flashed before Alasdair's eyes, as did the image of Duncan with his arm wrapped possessively around her waist. His gut twisted and he gave his head a shake. "Plans have a way of changing," he replied curtly, then picked up the pace, leaving his brothers in his wake.

Alasdair stomped into the great hall. "Cook!" he shouted. "Bring me something tae eat and a tankard of ale. Better make it two, I'm parched," he said to a portly man who entered the hall, wiping his hands on an apron.

"The evening meal will be ready soon, m'lord. I was not aware of your return. Could you wait a wee bit longer?" Cook asked with a frown.

"I dinna mean to cause you any trouble, but anything will do tae tide me over. I've ridden with very few provisions for three days and am famished." Alasdair sat on a chair by the dais and leaned back so it balanced on two legs. He was glad to be home. That was until he saw his brothers enter the great hall and he could tell by Bryce's determined expression he was not about to give up his inquisition.

"Are you going tae tell us what happened when you were at Sinclair Castle or do we need tae drag it out of you?" Bryce asked as he strode toward the dais.

"There is naught to tell," Alasdair snapped. "Let it be, Bryce."

Bryce shook his head, pulled out a chair, and took a seat beside his brother. "You sent a missive, informing us of your intent tae delay your trip home, said you'd meet us afore the battle. Then you show up ahead of time, looking like the devil was on your tail, and expect us to just act like everything is fine. Something happened."

"Enough, Bryce, give him a chance to breathe," Connor said as he joined them. "It dinna matter why Alasdair came home early. I'm glad he did." He slapped his older brother on the back and sat beside him. "We've missed you."

Cook entered the hall carrying a tray of roast meat, cheese, and bread. A maid followed with three tankards and a pitcher of ale. The repast was placed on the table, then the two servants left the room as quickly as they entered.

Alasdair reached for a chunk of bread, but Bryce caught his wrist. "Not so fast. It has been well over a summer since I've seen you, brother and longer for Connor. You promised tae return after the battle at Loudon Hill. But instead, you continued tae fight. When the campaign in the north of Scotland ended, you said you'd return. Why did you choose tae visit Jayden Sinclair instead of coming home?"

Alasdair twisted free of his brother's grasp, tore off a chunk of bread, and popped it into his mouth. "I've been at war for over two summers and was in need of a wee bit of time tae relax. I was in the north of Scotland, only a stone's throw from Sinclair Castle and havena seen Jayden since I was a lad. I decided tae pay him a visit. Not that it should be any of your concern what I do or why."

"Was it Jayden you stopped tae see or his sister?" Bryce raised a brow. "Is she still as unappealing as stray dog? If memory serves me, she was quite a homely bairn and you called her a pest." Bryce closed his eyes and shuddered. "I only met her once, when she was 5 or 6 summers old, but if she looks anything like she did then, I canna say, I would be knocking on her door any time soon. At least not in the daylight."

Anger churned in Alasdair's gut. He wanted to grab his youngest brother by the throat and squeeze until he begged for mercy. Instead, he did his best to ignore the comment and downed a tankard of ale.

"I'd mind my tongue if you value your life, brother. You know naught of what you speak and I am not in a mood tae listen to you," Alasdair said through clenched teeth, before taking another drink of ale, then dragging his hand across his mouth and belching. Bryce was goading him, exactly as he'd done since they were bairns. It was always in jest, but this time Alasdair would not let his brother get to him.

But Bryce refused to let up. "I can tell at a glance that something has caused a change in you. True, you tote several days worth of grime and stubble, but you've been shaving and cut your hair. This is the first time since we were lads that I've seen you without full beard, unkempt locks well beyond your shoulders and dinna come home smelling like a dung heap. If I dinna know you better, I would say you have been smitten." He turned to face Connor. "Can it be our older brother has fallen under the spell of a lass, or mayhap, he is running from one?" Bryce chuckled and downed the content of his tankard.

"You know better than tae even suggest it. Settling down with a wife might be fine for you and Connor, but you know I have no desire to complicate my life with a woman."

"You protest too much, brother. Who said anything about marriage? You're a Fraser, and I think you spent the last fortnight beneath the sheets. Mayhap—" Bryce began, but spun around when he heard a woman's voice.

"Is this any way to welcome home your brother? Leave the poor man be, Bryce. I canna understand why you must torment him so?" A raven-haired beauty with eyes the color of sapphires entered the great hall and moved toward the dais. "It is wonderful to see you, Alasdair. Please dinna pay my husband any mind."

"He has no use for women, yet he lets one fight his battles for him," Bryce remarked smugly.

Alasdair ground his teeth and cursed beneath his breath, but he refused to let his brother get a rise out of him.

"If you must know, I found a lass on the beach when heading tae Sinclair Castle. I thought her dead, but on closer examination, realized she was still breathing, so I took her to the hunt croft of Jayden's da. I remember going there when I was a lad and it wasna far."

"Why didn't you go and fetch Jayden. Better yet, take her to Sinclair Castle?" Bryce badgered.

"It was too far and in her weak condition, I dinna think she would survive the trip. When she woke up, she had no idea who she was or how she came tae be on the beach. She also injured her ankle and couldna walk or sit a horse."

"So how long did you and this mystery woman stay at the croft?" Bryce wiggled his brows and grinned.

"A sennight, mayhap a wee bit longer. When she was well enough tae ride, I took her home," Alasdair snapped.

"You spend more than a sennight alone in a croft with a woman and naught happened between you? I find that hard tae believe," Bryce said, his grin broadening.

"What would you have me do, take her by force when she was ill? Unlike some, I dinna bed a maiden unless I have asked her consent and am in a position tae marry her. Since I dinna plan tae do either, naught happened between us."

"Say what you will, but I dinna believe a word of it." Bryce crossed his arms over his chest and stared at Alasdair. "Unless of course she was so ugly you couldna stand the sight of her. Did you ever find out her name?"

Alasdair downed his drink, then glanced up at Bryce. "It turned out tae be Edina, Jayden's sister."

"Och, well that explains why you dinna bed her." Bryce inclined his head and laughed.

"How can you just sit there and let this nonsense go on, Connor? You are not only their brother, but laird of the clan." Fallon planted her hands on her hips and glared at her brother-by-marriage.

"I learned a long time ago that it was useless tae try and intervene between them. You know verra well that Bryce is like a deerhound with a bone. Once he bites into it, the only way to get him tae stop is tae throw a bucket of water on him." Connor grinned. "Unless there are blades drawn and blood about tae be shed, I have found it best tae let them have at it. This banter has gone on since we were wee bairns. I dinna think it is about tae cease any time soon."

Alasdair finished his ale, rose, then rounded the table. "Dinna fash. I pay Bryce no mind when he spouts off at the mouth. Which is most of the time." He lifted Fallon's hand and kissed it. "You are as comely as ever. It is good tae be home."

Fallon's face paled when he touched her and she swayed on her feet as if ready to faint.

"Is everything all right, lass? Alasdair clasped her elbow to steady her.

"Aye," she muttered on a strangled breath.

Bryce leapt to his feet, bolted to Fallon's side, and shoved Alasdair out of the way. He wrapped his arm around her waist. "What happened? Are you ill? Is it the babe?"

When she didn't reply and swayed again, he lifted her, then carried her to a chair. "Cook, bring me some water, right away," he shouted.

Cook responded immediately, and Bryce held the cup to Fallon's lips. "Drink."

"What's wrong?" Alasdair demanded, concern making his voice harsh.

"I dinna know. Stand back and give her some room," Bryce ordered and waved his brother off.

"I'm fine, Bryce." Fallon glanced up at Alasdair. "I had another vision is all. I saw a stunning lass with flaxen locks and lovely hazel eyes. Was she well when you left Sinclair Castle?"

"I knew it." Bryce approached Connor and thumped him on the back . "He's been holding out on us."

"Why do you ask? Has something happened tae her?" Alasdair's heart clenched and he fisted his hands at his sides as concern for Edina's safety engulfed him. Like Bryce, he'd never set much store in the gift of second sight, premonitions, or superstition. But in the past, Fallon's visions had proved to be correct on more than one occasion.

"This isna the first time I've had this vision. The first time was a few nights ago. I saw a man hiding in her chamber, with the intent tae do her harm. He was wielding a dirk and threatening tae kill her if she dinna comply with his demands. I heard her calling out your name."

"I mean no disrespect, Fallon, but you must be mistaken. True, Edina was attacked in her chamber, but it was well over a fortnight ago, while she was on ship, returning to her kin. The man responsible for the attack is dead."

"Are you certain?" Fallon scratched her head. "I suppose it could have been the attack aboard ship I envisioned. I have had dreams involving past events afore, but they are usually not this vivid."

"When I left, she was safe and well. Besides, she lives in a well fortified castle and has her brother and betrothed tae take care of her." Alasdair ran a shaky hand through his hair. "She isna my responsibility or my concern," he lied. It took every ounce of self-control to keep from jumping on Odin and racing back to Sinclair Castle.

"Mayhap you are right about the attack, Alasdair, but I fear the lass is verra unhappy and about tae make a grave mistake. That is unless you do something tae stop her."

Chapter 22

As Edina anxiously awaited Helen's return, she paced her chamber, a myriad of questions flooding her mind. Did the Mackenzie lass come willingly, or did William have to use some form of deception in order to get her to accompany him? Did he use force or does she love Duncan enough that she would do anything to win him back? She prayed for the latter.

A rap on the door disturbed her musing. "Aye, who is it?" She swallowed against the lump in her throat. If it were her father or Duncan, how would she explain when Helen returned with the lass, or that she had not been truthful about her quick recovery from the attack.

"Helen. May we enter?" she asked, her voice barely above a whisper.

Edina hurried across her chamber, threw open the door, and peered down the hall. "Aye, come in." She motioned with a sweep of her arm, then stepped aside so the two ladies could enter. "Did anyone see you, Helen?" she asked as she closed the door.

"Nay. We stayed in the shadows and were as quiet as two wee mice."

"I dinna understand the need for secrecy," the Mackenzie lass said as she glanced around the room. "Where is Duncan?"

"Forgive the confusion. I will do my best tae explain." Edina escorted the lass to a chair. "Please have a seat. I must also apologize for my bad manners. I am Edina Sinclair. Welcome to our home."

"I am Oceana Mackenzie," the lass said then glanced around the room. "Where is Duncan? I thought he'd be here."

"Your name is beautiful, as are you." Edina shifted her weight from one foot to the other and twisted her hands in her skirt. Now that the lass had arrived, she had no idea where to begin. "Duncan isna here at the moment, but I am sure when he returns, he will be pleased tae see you."

"I dinna understand. I have made a long journey and would verra much like tae know what this is all about. The man who came for me said that Duncan needed me and bid me tae come. He said it was urgent. Is he well? I have been worried he might have fallen ill or is injured. When can I see him?"

Edina glanced at Helen. "What did William tell her?"

Helen shrugged. "I dinna know, but if you would grant me leave, I will find out."

With a curt nod, Edina dismissed her maid, and waited for her to leave the room before addressing Oceana. "I can assure you Duncan is well. Can I get you something? Mayhap you would like some mead." She quickly changed the subject and moved to a table by the window. "You must be thirsty after your trip." She picked up a clay jug, filled two pewter goblets, then handed one to Oceana.

Oceana took a sip then placed the cup on the table. "I appreciate your kindness, and this is verra good, but I am not used tae drinking spirits."

"If you dinna mind me asking, how auld are you?" While Edina found Oceana to be every bit as beautiful as described, the lass didn't appear much older than a bairn, mayhap fifteen or sixteen summers at best. It was commonplace for a man to wed a much younger bride, but Duncan did not strike her as the kind of man to consort with a young woman of such a tender age. True, she was old enough to breed, but could not possibly be aware of the ways between a man and a woman. "You are so young. How long were you and Duncan courting?"

"People often think I am younger than I am. I've seen nearly eighteen summers and Duncan has seen twenty and seven. I know there is a gap in our ages, but I have what the clan seer calls an auld soul and am wiser than my years. Duncan and I first realized there was an attraction between us when I was not quite fourteen. He came tae visit with his father, Mam's distant cousin. The draw between us got stronger each time we were together, and afore long, we couldna deny it." She stopped speaking and lowered her gaze. "But our union isna tae be."

Edina's heart twisted in her chest. Oceana obviously cared a great deal for Duncan and would make him a good wife. Now, if she could convince him to free her from their betrothal, they could be wed. "You are aware that Duncan and I are betrothed?"

Oceana nodded. "Aye. I was told his father and yours entered into an agreement as a means tae unite the clans."

"Do you still love him?" Edina asked.

"It doesna matter. Duncan is a man of honor and will do as his da asks. You're a verra comely woman, Edina. I am sure he wasna disappointed with his father's choice."

"It matters a great deal how you feel about each other. Our fathers entered into a pact, but Duncan and I had no say. Had they not made a deal, do you think the two of you would have married?"

"Aye. But you and Duncan are tae be united, and there is naught that can be done tae change that." Tears ran down Oceana's cheeks as she spoke.

Edina squatted beside the chair and took Oceana's hands. "What if there was something we could do?"

Oceana sniffled and shook her head. "There is no hope for Duncan and me." She tugged her hands from Edina's grasp and stood. "Your fathers have an agreement and the king sanctioned the union. The marriage will take place regardless of how Duncan and I feel about each other, or. . ." Her voice trailed off and she slid her hand over her belly. Her face blanched and she began to sway.

"Are you unwell?" Edina grasped her arm and ushered her back to her seat.

"I just need a minute to catch my breath. I guess I am wearier than I thought." Oceana closed her eyes and inhaled slowly.

Edina studied her guest and waited for the color to return to her cheeks. She hadn't noticed when Oceana first arrived, but judging by her profile, the willowy lass had a slightly swollen abdomen. "It might be bold of me tae ask, but are you breeding?"

Oceana buried her face in her hands and sobbed. "Och, I dinna think it showed. I should never have come, but couldna resist the chance tae see Duncan one more time." She wiped her eyes with the sleeve of her gown and peered up at Edina. "Please dinna tell him I am here or about the babe. I will leave at first light."

"He doesna know about the babe?" Edina found it hard to hide the shock in her voice.

"Nay, and you must promise not tae tell him. I dinna wish to complicate his life or tae put him in a position where he feels he must break his word. I also havena told my parents and dinna want them tae find out. My father would demand Duncan's head on a pike for violating me."

Edina started to pace. "What are you going tae do? It willna be long afore you can no longer hide the fact you are with child. Duncan has a right tae know he is going to be a father." This information could be used to break the marriage contract, but Edina felt pity for Oceana's plight. "How will you conceal a babe?"

"I told my father I wished tae take the vows and will go tae the priory when I leave here. He thinks that is where I am now. Once the babe is born, he, or she, will be given tae strangers and raised as their own. They will never know who sired the child or who gave birth. The sisters and priests will keep my secret."

"How sad. I canna believe Duncan would take your maidenhead and not consider the consequences. Especially when he knew he wasna free tae marry you." Edina clucked her tongue and slid her hand over Oceana's shoulder, hoping to offer a modicum of comfort.

"When Duncan found out about your arranged marriage, he came tae tell me we could never see each other again, but I fear we got caught up in the moment. Afore we knew it, we had consummated our love and it was too late tae go back."

Oceana paused to draw in a slow shaky breath before she continued. "Neither of us thought a babe would come from just one joining. A bastard that will be taken from my arms at birth, a son or daughter Duncan will never know." Oceana lifted her chin and gazed into Edina's eyes. "Please dinna hate him. He and you had not yet met and it willna happen again. Losing the man I love and my babe is my punishment."

"You will lose your babe, only if we allow that tae happen." Edina paused, softly nibbling her bottom lip. "If Duncan knew about the babe, he might be willing tae stand up tae his father and demand he be allowed tae marry the mother of his heir. I am sure an alliance between the Mackenzie and Sutherland clans would be equally suitable tae the king."

"Nay! He must never know. I love him too much tae ask him tae shirk his duty tae his clan or tae go against King Robert's decree."

Edina saw the desperation on Oceana's face and could hear the angst in her plea.

"Are you not happy about the marriage, Edina? I can assure you that Duncan is a gentle and caring man. You are verra lucky he was chosen for you. Please dinna hold this one mistake against him." Oceana twisted her hands in her lap.

"Duncan is a guid man and I have no doubt he would make a wonderful husband—for the right woman," Edina added. "While it is tradition for the daughter of a laird tae marry her father's selection, I dinna want my husband chosen for me. I wish tae marry a man I love, one who shares my feelings. Tae be honest, I sent for you, not Duncan. I hoped that when you saw each other, he would decide tae marry you in my stead."

"Is there a man you do wish tae marry?" Oceana asked.

Alasdair's face flashed before Edina's mind's eye and her chest tightened. "There was a man I thought loved me, or could in time, but it was not tae be. He is a warrior and has no plans tae take a wife. However, it doesna mean you and Duncan should be kept apart."

"I know Duncan verra well and regardless of what he wants, he willna go against his father's wishes. He is tae be the next laird of Clan Sutherland and must command and earn the respect of his kin."

"Dinna fash, we'll think of a way for the two of you tae be taegether. But you are correct. From what I have seen, Duncan is duty bound and we must wait for the right time tae let him know you are here. For now, I will ask Helen tae take you somewhere safe. I will send for you once I figure out a plan."

Edina summoned Helen. "Please take Oceana tae the chamber at the top of the north tower. But I dinna want anyone tae know she is here."

"Not even Lord Duncan?" Helen asked.

"Especially, Duncan. No one is tae know," Edina answered, a little more abruptly than she intended. "See that she has everything she might need and ask William to bring wood for the hearth. He must also promise to remain silent about Oceana's presence."

Helen bobbed a curtsy. "As you wish, m'lady. And you needna worry about William. I will see that he holds his tongue."

Edina took Oceana's hand and patted it. "Go with Helen. You can trust her, and for now, I promise tae keep you secret. I must think on what you've told me and will come tae see you this evening."

"I want you tae give me a horse ride!" Andrew shouted as he climbed onto Alasdair's back, squeezed his chubby legs against his uncle's sides, and dug in his heels. "Da gives me rides all the time, but you are a much bigger mount. I look like a warrior."

"That you do, laddie." Alasdair obliged his nephew by crawling around the chamber on all fours and snorting like a warhorse.

"Andrew Fraser, leave your uncle be. I am sure he has better things tae do than appeasing your whims." A red-haired beauty entered the chamber. She pressed her hand to the small of her back and released a soft sigh. "I have my hands full with two bairns, but fear I will be run ragged with three."

"You look as lovely as ever, Cailin." Alasdair placed Andrew on the ground, then stood. He tousled the wee one's hair and patted his behind. "Go and play with your cousin, Elise. I will give you another ride later." He pointed to Bryce and Fallon's daughter. The curly-haired tot was sitting in the corner, chewing on a rag doll.

"Nay. Elise is a babe and I am a warrior like my da," Andrew protested and stomped his tiny feet. "I am almost auld enough to train in the lists."

Alasdair fought hard to stifle a laugh. "That may be, but you have not yet seen three summers and I think your mam would like you tae wait until you are wee bit aulder. Now, be a guid laddie and play with your cousin." He covered his mouth, snickering as Andrew trudged across the room grumbling.

"He's a brooder like his da and too proud tae give in like his uncle Bryce," Alasdair remarked.

"You are very much at home with the bairns, Alasdair. Mayhap you will soon have some of your own. You'd be a wonderful father."

"Bah." Alasdair gave his head a shake and held both hands in front of him, in hope of staying any further comment about bairns. "I will leave breeding tae my brothers. You look weary, lass, mayhap you should sit for a while." He took Cailin's arm and ushered her to a chair by the hearth. "Would you like a pelt or tae put your feet up?"

Cailin smiled and touched his cheek. "You've changed, Alasdair."

Alasdair coughed to clear his throat and backed away. "Why does everyone keep saying that? I am still the same man I always was."

"I dinna mean tae offend you. On the contrary, it is a compliment. You seem much more at peace than I've ever seen you, and there is something else, but canna put my finger on it exactly." Cailin sat in the chair and peered up at her brother-by-marriage.

"Naught has changed about me. I am still as ill-mannered, hot tempered, and as slovenly as ever. I remain a clumsy brute who eats too much, drinks tae excess, and has no use for women," he grumbled.

"I dinna believe that for one minute and never thought of you as any of those things. Even though you've tried verra hard tae make people believe it," Cailin countered. "True, you were quick tae anger and put on a gruff front, but I saw beyond that not long after we met. Inside, you are a compassionate, caring man, and you deserve tae find happiness."

Alasdair threw his hands in the air. "You're mistaken. What I described is exactly who I am and always will be. You are not about tae change me. Not you or . . . anyone else." He caught himself before he revealed too much.

"Connor told me you met someone you care about. There is no shame in admitting it. I believe there is a mate for everyone. It is our destiny tae find that person. The difficult part is recognizing when tae accept what fate offers."

"Connor needs tae mind his tongue and you sound like Fallon with her prophecies. I set no store in fate or superstition. I make my own luck." He picked up his sword and fastened the scabbard around his waist. "There is no woman in my life and never will be. I have no need of one."

Despite his efforts, Cailin gave him a knowing glance and her brow knit together. "If you dinna wish tae confide in me or your brothers, I understand. Connor and Bryce can be difficult tae deal with, and you are a verra private man. Just know that I am here tae listen if you ever do wish tae talk."

"That willna be necessary. I am a warrior and my destiny is tae fight for my king and country," Alasdair replied curtly.

"Say what you will, but I think you'd make a fine husband and father. Any woman would be proud to be your bride." Cailin slowly stood and ran her hand over her swollen belly. "As you are aware, Connor never planned tae marry and neither did Bryce. But I honestly believe they are both happy. You are entitled tae the same. If you have met a lass who touches your heart, tell her. Dinna wait too long because you never know what life has in store."

Alasdair bit back a curse. Was he that poor at hiding his emotions? Did everyone know that Edina had breached the protective wall around his heart? "We canna always have what we desire." The words escaped before he could stop them. He lowered his gaze and turned away.

Cailin caressed his forearm. "Anything is possible if you truly want it. Look at Connor and me. I was tae marry a man I detested and my father wouldna listen to reason. Then, I was falsely accused of murdering the English soldier, taken prisoner by Borden, and slated for execution. Yet, we ended up together and I love Connor with all my heart."

"Some men are luckier than others," Alasdair muttered as he recalled the difficulties and danger Cailin and Connor faced on their way to happiness.

"Alasdair, there you are," Bryce called out as he entered the chamber. "I have been looking everywhere for you. Jayden Sinclair is here and asked tae see you right away."

Alasdair's stomach clenched and his pulse began to pound. "I did not expect him for several days. Something must be amiss. Where is he?" He didn't bother to hide the anxiety in his voice.

"In the great hall. He said—" Bryce began but never had a chance to finish. Alasdair pushed past him and ran down the hall.

Chapter 23

With his heart pounding like it was trying to escape his chest, Alasdair raced into the great hall, and stopped short when he saw his friend standing by the dais talking to Connor. "Jayden!" He stomped over to where they stood and grabbed him by the arms.

"What are you doing here? I dinna expect you for several days, if at all. Has something happened tae Edina? Tell me." Fallon's prophetic word echoed in his head, and the twisting of his gut told him she was right. She'd said Edina was in danger. Mayhap she was injured, or worse, dead. Why else would her brother be here ahead of time?

I should have listened to Fallon, should have return to Sinclair Castle as soon as I heard her prophecy.

His mind reeled. But then again, what could he have done when she was a three day ride away?

"Damnation, Jayden, Tell me why you are here. If something has happened to Edina, I'll never forgive myself for leaving her alone." Alasdair tightened his grip. "Speak up, man!"

"Calm yourself, Alasdair. Edina is well, or she will be after a wee bit of rest. Now, let me go afore you break my arms," Jayden replied.

"For a man who claims he isna in love, Alasdair is verra concerned about Jayden's sister." Bryce chuckled.

"Hold your tongue, brother," Connor snapped.

Alasdair ignored Bryce's comments. His only concern was for Edina. He released his grip on Jayden and took a step back. "What do you mean she will be fine? Tell me."

"Edina was attacked in her chamber not long after you left the castle. She—"

"Who?" Alasdair cut in before Jayden could finish.

"Callum. He was bent on revenge and determined tae kill her for giving him away. If you ask me, he waited until you were gone afore making his move," Jayden concluded.

"Callum? I thought the bastard was dead," Alasdair snapped.

"So did we. My father's men swore he fell tae his death, but they were sorely mistaken."

"Saint's teeth, how did he get intae Edina's chamber unnoticed? Where were the guards? Where was Duncan?" Anger knotted Alasdair's belly. He cursed. He should never have left until he saw Callum's body for himself, until he knew for certain Edina was safe. But then again, she was to marry Sutherland and her welfare wasn't really any of his affairs.

"Duncan had seen her tae her chamber after the morning meal, but there was no reason tae suspect what happened after he left her tae rest," Jayden replied. "Callum was waiting for her tae return. When she entered the room, he attacked her. He told her he planned tae bed her, then kill her."

"How did she manage tae get away?" Connor asked.

"She fought him off the best she could, but a slender lass like Edina dinna have the strength tae wrestle a man of Callum's size and weight." Jayden shook his head. "He got the better of her and threw her on the pallet, prepared tae take her innocence."

"Yet she somehow survived his assault," Bryce cut in.

"My sister is as gifted with a sword, bow, and dirk as any warrior. My father insisted upon it. When he tried tae take intimate liberties, she killed the bugger with his own dagger."

"Did he succeed in violating her? Was she injured in the scuffle?" Alasdair's heart rate kicked up another notch as he waited for answers.

"Nay, she plunged the blade intae his chest afore he had a chance tae bed her. Thank the Almighty." Jayden paused and crossed himself. "After she stabbed him, she tried to escape, but she tripped and fell, striking her head on the floor. She received a nasty bump, but the feisty lass stood and grabbed his sword, prepared tae finish him off when he made another attempt tae kill her. But the Lord saw tae that for her. Or mayhap I should say the devil, as I am sure he went straight tae hell," he concluded and spat on the floor. "May he rot there for all eternity."

Alasdair blew out the breath he'd been holding and his shoulders slumped as relief washed over him. "Aye, may he rot in Hell."

"She is married then?" Bryce asked.

"Nay. My father and Duncan agreed tae postpone the nuptials until Edina got over her latest ordeal. After falling from the ship, nearly drowning, and now this, both agreed to give her a bit of time to recover. I left as soon as I knew she was well and the marriage was not about to happen." Jayden raised a brow. "There is still time for you tae go back and ask for her hand."

Connor approached his older brother and cupped his shoulder. "What do you plan tae do, Alasdair? Will you go tae her?"

"Nay," Alasdair replied adamantly. "She is going to be fine and Sutherland will take care of her. I have no intention of returning tae Sinclair Castle and dinna want to discuss this any further. We have a battle tae plan. Does anyone know where I can find Robert?" He quickly changed the topic of conversation.

"The last I saw him, he was in the lists, watching the men train," Bryce answered. "We were heading there when Jayden arrived."

Alasdair nodded. "Then let us not keep Robert waiting. We have the English on the run and I am sure he is anxious to keep the momentum moving."

"From what I've heard, he has made great headway, taking possession of most of northern Scotland in a relatively short time. I wish I could have been there," Connor added.

"Aye. After his return tae the mainland and the victory at Loudon Hill, he began the trek north tae settle the Highlands. We sailed up Loch Linnhe with a fleet of galleys, prepared tae confront those who supported Balliol and kin tae Red Comyn. We captured the lands held by allies of the English. That included the lands held by John Comyn, the 3rd Earl of Buchan. Red Comyn's cousin. The campaign lasted through the winter, the final battle in May at Inveurie. He is now prepared tae continue with unfinished business, drive the English out of Scotland, then take the Scottish throne where he belongs," Alasdair said and slammed his balled fist against his open palm.

"Are you sure his only purpose is tae rid Scotland of the English, or could he be trying tae settle an auld score?" Jayden asked. "Edward II is not nearly as concerned with keeping his army in Scotland as his father was. Once Longshanks died, his son turned his attentions internally and spends his time concentrating on English affairs. In time he will forget all about his da's obsession with ruling Scotland, and Robert will take the throne unchallenged."

Bryce lunged forward, anger flashing in his eyes. "Are you saying we should forget about all that has happened, years of tyranny, hardship, cruelty, and murder? Edward's attentions might be diverted for a time, but the English will return. They always do. Robert means tae leave a strong message so that doesna happen."

"Many still think the Bruce's motives are not as pure and selfless as he leads us tae believe. Especially those who supported Red Comyn's bid for the crown and believe he was murdered by the Bruce. The unrest between the clans started long before the war with English. I am not sure that is about tae change. A country divided by political differences is tough tae govern and an easy target for those who wish tae take over," Jayden said.

"If you dinna believe in the cause, in Robert's right tae the crown, why are you here?" Alasdair clenched his fists and straightened his spine. "The MacDougalls swear fealty tae the English crown and still control most of Argyll. Robert intends tae see that all of Scotland belongs tae those are who not under Saxon influence." He spat on the ground and stepped forward.

"Calm yourself. I am only making an observation." Jayden held his hands out to the sides, palms facing skyward.

"You werena with us at Methven and Dalry, Jayden. You dinna witness the carnage when the English bastards attacked before dawn and killed men as they slept. Thousands perished and the MacDougalls lay in wait, ready tae attack the survivors as we retreated to the mountains tae regroup. You dinna live for almost a year as a fugitive, dwelling in caves like animals on the Aisle of Arran," Alasdair replied.

"I am not questioning Robert's right tae seek revenge for the years of injustice and despair brought upon us by Longshanks. True, I was not there, but I lost many kin tae the war, including my brothers. I am fully aware of the need tae rid Scottish soil of the English or wouldna be here offering my support. I just want tae be sure I fight for the right reasons." Jayden stood toe-to-toe with Alasdair and looked him in the eye.

Connor stepped between the two men and placed is hand on Alasdair's chest. "You and Jayden have been friends since you were lads. You need tae respect each other's opinions and work together on this. Jayden has his points and so do you, Alasdair. What's important is that he supports our bid against the MacDougalls and is prepared tae fight. If the clans dinna unite, this civil unrest will never be over."

Alasdair raked his fingers through his hair and bobbed his head. "My brother is wiser than his years." He held his arm out to Jayden, who accepted the gesture by clasping his wrist.

"I wouldna be here if I dinna wish tae fight for the cause," Jayden said as he hauled Alasdair into an embrace. "You are like my brother and always have been. I will stand by you in battle, or anywhere else you choose tae go."

Alasdair coughed to clear his throat and broke free of Jayden's hug. "I am ready to fight the MacDougalls. Who's with me?" He turned and stormed out of the hall. Jayden, Connor, and Bryce followed.

Aug 1308, near Loch Awe in Argyll.

"Will we be confronting Alexander MacDougall, head of the MacDougalls of Lorne, by laying siege tae Dunstaffnage Castle?" Bryce asked.

"Nay. Although that is what they'll be expecting us tae do. Rumor has it their leader, Laird MacDougall, is too ill tae fight, but has sent John Bacach in his stead. My informants tell me his men have taken a position in the Pass of Brander, at a place where the River Awe slices past the southern slope of Ben Cruachan. There they lay in wait, planning tae ambush us from behind if we attack the MacDougall stronghold. Another informant told me that Bacach is observing from a galley on Loch Awe."

"So they intend tae attack from the rear, trapping us between the castle and Bacach, similar tae the way they did at Dalry?" Alasdair stroked his chin and smiled. "But we are wise tae their trickery and willna be easy prey this time."

"If they expect a repeat of Dalry they are in for a grand surprise." Robert grinned. "We have learned much since that fateful day and are about tae turn the tables. They may have fooled us once, but never again. I have already sent John Douglas and his Highlanders tae a spot on the slope, behind the MacDougalls. We will confront them from below, but as they retaliate, Black Douglas will catch them from behind. Once we have destroyed their army, we will go forth tae Dunstaffnage."

"If anyone can offer support it is John Douglas. He proved a valuable ally at Loudon Hill and after," Alasdair added.

"Rally the men and I will brief them on our plan. The hour of battle is at hand. I can taste the victory." Robert raised his sword in the air. "May the Almighty bless us and guide our weapons."

Alasdair nodded, then trotted off to gather the men.

After a brief benediction, Robert divided his army into several groups. "Alasdair, you will lead the men on heavy horse. Connor, take charge of the spearmen, and Bryce, the archers. I will lead the men fighting with sword and targe on foot."

Alasdair mounted Odin and swung his sword above his head. "Aye, Bruce!" he shouted, and when the roar of his men died down, he turned to his brother and Jayden. "Watch your backs, lads, and keep your head on a swivel. I'll see you when we converge on the castle. "All my trust in God." He called out the Fraser war cry, then pressed his heels to the horse's flanks.

Being careful to remain out of sight, Alasdair and his men watched with anticipation as a selected group of fully armed Scottish soldiers marched into the valley, in order to draw the attention of their enemy. As Robert predicted the MacDougalls fell for the trap, attacking from behind. But this time the Scots were ready for them.

While the men on foot confronted the MacDougall army, Douglas attacked from the rear, trapping the enemy in the middle. Connor led his band of spearman into the fray as Bryce's archers released a volley of arrows. Robert's scheme worked exactly as planned.

Obviously confused by the turn of events, the MacDougalls broke ranks after a brief offensive, and retreated across the river, heading for the castle with Robert's army on their tail.

With his adrenalin pumping and the smell of victory at hand, Alasdair rallied the horsemen, dug his heels into Odin's flanks, and gave chase. But by the time they caught up with their fleeing quarry, the battle was all but over.

Bodies of their fallen enemy lay strewn across the moor. As they approached the unmanned curtain wall, Alasdair brought his mount to a halt and summoned two of him men. "Brian, I want you and Keith to remain behind. Care for any of our lads you find wounded and bring them tae the castle."

"What about the dead and the MacDougalls' wounded?" Brian asked.

"We have our own tae worry about. They can see tae theirs and we will bury our dead once we have secured the castle." Accompanied by the remainder of his men, Alasdair fisted the reins and urged his horse forward, racing to the keep with a vengeance.

Entering the bailey with little resistance, Alasdair dismounted and began searching for his brothers. While his horsemen suffered very few casualties, he was not certain how those on foot fared. Relief washed over him when he saw Bryce and Connor walking toward him.

Connor raised his sword in the air and waved. "Guid tae see you, brother," he called out.

Alasdair narrowed his eyes and frowned when he noticed a blossoming blood stain on the sleeve of Bryce's tunic. His youngest brother was on his feet, but was also cradling his right arm, an arrow protruding from his shoulder. He raced to his side. "The bastards got you?"

"Aye, but I'll be as good as new once someone gets this damned shaft out of my arm," Bryce grumbled and ground his teeth.

"You were supposed tae duck," Alasdair said and scooped his brother into his arms when he wavered on his feet. He carried Bryce across the courtyard to a stone bench and set him down. "Rest here and I will fetch a healer."

Bryce grabbed his brother's wrists, preventing his departure. "Nay. It is a flesh wound. There are men worse off than me. Just snap the damned thing in half and push it on through."

Alasdair nodded, broke off the feathered end of the arrow, then turned to Connor and Jayden. "Hold him down while I do this. He has no idea how much it will hurt."

"I'm not a bairn and I know exactly what it feels like. This isna the first time I have been wounded and won't likely be the last. Just do it, Alasdair, and stop wasting time. A man could bleed tae death while waiting for you tae help," Bryce groaned.

Despite Bryce's protest, Connor and Jayden took their positions, one on either side, and grabbed Bryce's arms, holding him steady. "Ready when you are," Connor said and closed his eyes.

Alasdair grabbed the arrow by the shaft. Ignoring his brother's bucking, cursing, and shouts of pain, he shoved the shaft through in one swift move. "The tip missed the bone by the look of things, but the wound will need tae be cleaned and dressed."

"Seal it and make haste," Bryce growled. I dinna want it tae fester."

"Are you certain?" Jayden asked and swallowed hard.

"Aye, it is the best way tae tend tae a wound like this. I would do it myself, but that might prove difficult," Bryce replied.

Alasdair recalled the day Bryce arrived at the Bruce's camp, following the ambush on Loch Ryan, like it was yesterday. When, in fact, over a year had passed. His youngest brother had been injured in a scuffle with the MacDougalls and left for dead. Had Fallon's uncle not found him, he would not have survived. He remembered the black, puckered wound on Bryce's chest. "He is right. To seal a wound with a hot blade is the best way."

"I'll do it," Connor said as he slid a dirk from his boot and stuck it into the flames of a nearby cook fire. "You and Jayden will have tae hold him steady."

Once Bryce's injury had been tended, Alasdair released his brother and stood. "If you dinna need me, Connor, I must find Robert. He went in search of the MacDougall. My guess is he plans tae give him the chance tae surrender and swear his fealty. Will you stay with Bryce?"

"I've had enough torture for one day," Bryce said through clenched teeth. "I wish tae rest a wee bit and if my brother would be kind enough tae locate some whisky, I would be eternally grateful." He peered up at Connor and forced a smile.

"You see tae Robert, Alasdair, and I will ferret out the spirits. Jayden, will you stay with Bryce?" Connor rose, then brushed the dirt and leaves from his trews.

"I dinna need a nursemaid," Bryce grumbled.

"You will do as you're told. Fallon wouldna forgive me or Connor if we dinna take care of you. Now, be a good laddie and rest." Alasdair laughed, ruffled his youngest brother's hair like he would a bairn, then trotted off.

Chapter 24

"Can we talk to you?" Connor asked as he, Jayden, and Bryce approached.

"Aye, Connor, what is on your mind?" Alasdair replied, but instead of looking at his brothers, he continued to wipe the blood from his sword. "You should be resting, Bryce."

"I'm fine. I've been injured far worse in the past," Bryce replied curtly.

"The battle is over and the MacDougall's are finished. We have the English on the run so it willna be long afore Scotland has seen the last of them. The warriors who so valiantly defend her soil will soon be able tae go home tae their families.

"Aye." Alasdair glanced up at his brother. "And your point is?"

"I wondered what your plans are. Will you be returning with us tae Fraser Castle? And if so, are you home tae stay?" Connor shifted his weight from one foot to the other as he awaited his brother's response.

"Saint's teeth, Connor, just ask the man and be done with it," Bryce blurted out. "Are you still pining over Jayden's sister and do you plan to marry her? You must be anxious tae get her between the sheets."

Alasdair's blood began to simmer, but he did his best to remain calm. After the rigors of battle, men were often excitable for hours, some still looking for a fight. However, Bryce was walking a fine line and his patience grew thin.

"How many times must I have tae tell you there is naught between us and never will be? Edina is tae be married, and I havena decided where I will go from here," Alasdair replied through clenched teeth.

"I still dinna believe you could spend more than a sennight together at her father's hunt camp and remain celibate." Bryce wiggled his brows in a suggestive manner. "No true-blooded Fraser man could be alone with a woman for that long and not act on the opportunity many times over. Unless he is a eunuch that is."

Alasdair jumped to his feet, grabbed Bryce by the throat, and lifted him off the ground. "Hold your wheest! Not every man has rutting on his mind, all the time. Edina is by far the most respectable woman I have ever met. She is not only beautiful, but she is brave and smart." He continued to squeeze his youngest brother's neck until he was gasping for air and clawing at his hand.

Connor clutched Alasdair's wrist. "He's injured and a fool. Let him go afore you make Fallon a widow."

Alasdair grunted and released his grip. "He's lucky I dinna cut out his tongue."

Bryce rolled on the ground and sucked in several short, sharp breaths. He managed to rise to his knees, but shoved Jayden hand away when he tried to help him up. "Leave me." He stood, using a nearby tree stump for leverage, then staggered forward, clutching his wounded shoulder. But rather than apologize or retaliate against his older brother, he began to chuckle. "I told you I could get the big ox tae open up. Why he must act like such a stubborn arse is beyond me. It is clear you're yearning for Edina, so why not marry her and have at it?" he goaded then gave Alasdair a shove.

In spite of his brother's injury, Alasdair lunged forward, but Connor blocked the way and held him at bay. "You know better than tae pay Bryce any mind when he is prodding you. We gave him some whisky to dull the pain and mayhap we gave him too much." He glared at Bryce. "Our younger brother may not have a tactful way of making a point, but he is right. If you are in love with the lass, you should fight for her."

"I'm not in love with anyone," Alasdair snapped. He turned his back to his brothers, least he give away his true feelings. He ached for Edina with every fiber of his being. Constant thoughts of her were about to drive him mad with longing.

"Jayden said she loves you and not Sutherland. Why not go back and claim her afore it is too late? Speak tae her da and ask for her hand," Connor continued.

"It is not that simple. I am not worthy of Edina and I've done and said many things she may never be able tae forgive. Besides, you're forgetting, she is the daughter of one of the most powerful lairds in northern Scotland. For that reason, she must marry well and in accordance with her father's wishes."

"We're forgetting naught." Bryce threw his good arm up in the air. "You're a Fraser and that should be enough for any lass or her da. A finer husband she willna find. No better clan with which tae form a bond."

"I'm na a wealthy man. I hold no title or land and have naught tae offer but myself." He lowered his head and blew out a heavy sigh. "Nay, I willna make her choose between me and duty tae her clan."

Connor slid his hand over Alasdair's shoulder and squeezed. "Do you love her?"

"It matters not. She is promised tae a powerful man and the king has sanctioned the marriage in order tae unite the clans. There is naught I can do to stop it."

"You're wrong, brother. Speak to Robert and tell him you wish tae ask for Edina's hand. You've served him well and I have no doubt he will consider your request," Connor said.

"And if that doesna work, I say you steal her away and marry her anyway," Bryce added.

"Aye and end up losing his head because of his impulsive actions," Connor interjected. "He must first speak with Robert and then with Laird Sinclair."

He had no doubt his brothers meant well, but Alasdair wished they would leave him to make his own decisions. "I told you afore, I've naught to offer that can rival the alliance or wealth that will come from her joining with Sutherland. Is there naught the two of you could be doing aside from pestering me?"

"An alliance with the Clan Sutherland would prove beneficial, but so would a stronger bond with Clan Fraser." Connor pointed out. "Laird Sinclair was one of our father's closest friends and allies. I'd wager he would be pleased tae have you as a son-by-marriage."

"I'm willing tae speak tae my father on your behalf. I dinna wish tae see my sister marry Sutherland any more than you do. An arranged union might be customary and suitable for most women, but not a free spirit like Edina. She willna be happy living with a man she doesna love," Jayden said.

"Is no one listening tae me? Sutherland will soon be a laird, I am naught, and I have naught." Alasdair held out empty hands, then balled them into fists. "Edina is better off with Duncan."

"If the lack of a title and land is all that stops you from fighting for the lass, I will stand down as laird. I am certain the clan elders would not hesitate tae appoint you in my place. As the oldest living son, it is your birthright after all," Connor announced.

"I'll not hear of it. You are a fine chief, Connor." While the gesture touched his heart and might be a solution to his problem, Alasdair would not allow his brother to make the sacrifice on his behalf. "The clan thrives under your leadership and you have proven yourself a great leader many times over. I willna see that change tae suit my own selfish needs. It was my choice to relinquish the title of laird when asked, but you dinna hesitate tae accept the responsibility."

"The situation was different then," Connor argued. "You dinna feel you possessed the qualities necessary tae lead the clan at the time, had no plans or the desire tae settle down in one spot. Marriage and heirs were the last things on your mind. You were driven by anger and the need for revenge. You acted first and asked questions later."

"What makes you think I am a different man now?"

"Whether you are ready tae admit it or not, you've changed in many ways, Alasdair. You have always been a brave warrior. No one would dare challenge that point. I've stood beside you in battle more times than I care tae count. The men look up tae you and will follow you without question," Connor began.

"There is far more tae being a chief than brawn on the battlefield," Alasdair countered.

"True, but in addition tae those attributes and the alteration in your overall appearance, I've seen you with my bairns, have noticed the glimmer in your eyes and the longing on your face when ever Edina's name is mentioned. And if that were not enough, your patience with Bryce's constant banter had been that of a saint . . . for the most part anyway." Connor laughed.

"It does take more than brawn tae lead a clan. It requires, dedication, quick wits, temperance, and a cool head in the face of adversity. You possess all of those qualities and would make a fine laird. What you dinna know, you will learn. I will be proud tae serve under you, as will my sons." Connor bowed before his brother.

"Think about it, man. This would solve a lot of your problems, and I am confident my sister will forgive you for being a buffoon . . . in time." Jayden thumped Alasdair on the back. "Best you decide quickly. The hour grows late, and it will be a long hard ride if we wish tae make it back tae Sinclair Castle in time tae prevent the wedding."

"I'm not going anywhere," Alasdair replied harshly.

"Are you planning another trip?" Robert the Bruce joined them. "Or am I interrupting a private conversation."

"You are interrupting naught," Alasdair answered.

"The big ox is in love with Jayden's sister. He wishes tae ask for her hand, but is too thrawn tae do so," Bryce blurted out.

Alasdair retaliated with a sharp jab of his elbow into Bryce's ribs. "Mind your tongue and your own affairs."

"If what Bryce says is true, why did you not ask for the lassie's hand when you were at Sinclair Castle?" Robert asked. "Tae be honest, I never thought you would marry, but if the woman is agreeable, it would be a fine match."

"You have already sanctioned her marriage to Duncan Sutherland," Connor said as he slid his hand over Alasdair's shoulder. "Alasdair did not tell the lass about his feelings because he dinna think himself worthy and had naught to offer her. I have since told him I will step down as laird and allow him to take over, but he refused to give it any thought."

"This does pose a problem." Robert rubbed his bearded chin and hesitated for a minute before he continued. "What of the lass? Does she share your feelings?"

"I'm certain she does," Jayden interjected. "She just might not know it yet."

"You canna speak on Edina's behalf. Besides, Duncan arrived at your clan's castle with the intention of honoring the pact made by his father on his behalf. Arranged marriages have been our way for centuries and I have no right tae interfere," Alasdair snapped.

"My sister loves you, Alasdair. But, like you, she is just too thrawn to declare it. Edina has never been one to grovel or admit weakness. Growing up with four boisterous brothers, she dinna have much choice. If forced tae marry against her will, I pity the poor sot."

"She sounds hard-headed like someone else we know," Bryce commented snidely and glared at Alasdair. "If you decide tae marry the lass, it will prove an interesting match tae be sure."

"I may not have a right tae reveal what is in my sister's heart, but I know beyond a shadow of a doubt, Edina doesna wish tae marry Duncan. When last we spoke, she still held out hope he would change his mind. If I know my sister, she will remain optimistic until the bitter end."

"And you think Duncan is too blind tae see she isna pleased about the union?" Connor asked.

"Edina will do her duty regardless of how she feels. Duncan is a man of honor and dedicated to his clan. He will do what ever it takes to fulfill his obligations. He willna disgrace his father, or defy the king's decree." Jayden lowered his eyes and shook his head. "Unless someone steps up and convinces him otherwise, I believe he will go through with the marriage."

"Then there is no need tae continue this conversation." Alasdair turned to leave, but his youngest brother grabbed his arm.

"If Robert were to withdraw his consent and sanctioned the union between you and Edina, would you then declare your intent?" Bryce asked.

"I would still have naught tae offer her, so there is no point tae this discussion. Now, if you value your good arm, let go of me." Alasdair glared at his brother.

Bryce released Alasdair's arm, then approached the Scottish King. "My brother has been steadfast in his support of the cause. Could you not see fit tae give him land and a title so he can ask for the lass's hand?"

Jayden stepped forward. "That willna be necessary. Nor will Connor need tae give up his position as chief. I will someday be laird of Clan Sinclair. Our holdings are vast and growing all the time. For one man tae oversee it all is a difficult task, and I am not too proud tae admit I could use some help. Were Edina and Alasdair tae marry, I could have a castle built on the western border of Sinclair land and supply an army large enough tae defend the territory around it."

"That might be a viable option had you asked tae have one of your brothers assist you, but Alasdair is no relation," Robert replied. "However, if your da would agree tae the change of husbands, and Duncan was prepared tae step aside, I would consent to the union between Alasdair and Edina."

"My brothers perished in battle, but if Alasdair married my sister, he would then be my brother-by-marriage. Besides, there are rumors Duncan is still in love with a lass from the Mackenzie clan. Apparently, they had plans tae marry until his father decided otherwise. An alliance between the Mackenzie and Sinclair clans would also prove beneficial to the cause. I am certain if you were tae order it, my father would be agreeable."

"Why would Edina's father permit a change of suitors when Sutherland has so much more tae offer? I dinna believe Laird Sinclair will change his mind or break the pact made with Duncan's da," Alasdair replied.

"You willna know unless you try, brother. If you truly love Edina, then fight for her hand," Connor said. "It is time you found happiness. I've already told you that I will turn the leadership of the clan over tae you, Jayden has made you a generous offer, and if Robert agrees to sanction your union, the final decision will be yours tae make."

"You appear tae have my life all figured out, but have omitted one verra important thing," Alasdair replied.

"What might that be?" Connor frowned.

"Edina. She will be the one tae have the final say who she marries, not me."

"You see. He already knows what it will be like tae have a wife. As long as they believe you care about what they think, you will live in bliss." Bryce threw back his head and roared with laughter.

"If Fallon hears you talking like that, you will wish you'd held your tongue." Connor laughed.

"I willna allow you tae relinquish your seat as clan leader, Connor, no matter what the cost," Alasdair said adamantly, then raked his fingers through his hair. Mayhap his brothers were right. He did love Edina and he had always felt at home on the northern shore of Scotland. The thought of never seeing her again caused his heart to ache. Jayden's suggestion was looking better and better.

"What say you?" Jayden badgered. "If you wish tae stop the wedding, I'd suggest we leave right away. I received a missive from home prior tae the battle. A priest has been summoned and the nuptials between Duncan and Edina are set tae take place three days hence."

"I will go with you, but I willna take Connor's place as laird." Alasdair faced Jayden. "If you are serious about needing my help, I can think of nowhere else I would rather live."

"About time you did the wise thing." Jayden slapped Alasdair on the back and grasped his forearm, giving it a hardy shake. "But if you dinna make haste this will all be for naught and my sister will be a married woman."

Connor reached for his brother's forearm. "We will miss you, Alasdair, but you canna deny what is in your heart. Godspeed and good luck."

After exchanging embraces with both his brothers, Alasdair turned to face Robert. "You will sanction the union?"

Robert nodded, picked up a piece of vellum, and penned a note. "Give this tae Laird Sutherland. But if he doesna choose tae honor it, you must abide by his wishes, and allow the wedding tae take place as planned."

Alasdair took the document and bowed. "Hopefully that willna be necessary." After tucking the missive into his sporran, he turned on his heel, and jogged toward his horse. "If you are coming Jayden, make haste."

Jayden trotted to his mount and climbed into the saddle. "I will see him married and would be honored if you and your wives could pay us a visit in the near future."

"Try and stop them," Bryce chuckled. "Once Cailin and Fallon learn of Alasdair's marriage, there will be no appeasing them until they have seen it for themselves, and have offered their best wishes."

"Safe journey, brother and we will see you soon," Connor added.

"Enough chatter, we must be off." Alasdair dug his heels into Odin's sides and the horse lunged forward.

"We've made guid time, much better than I had expected." Alasdair reined in Odin and brought him to a walk. "We should be at Sinclair Castle well afore the noon meal and in time tae stop the wedding."

"Aye, but we've ridden nonstop for two days and three nights. I'm exhausted, covered in dirt, and we have nearly run our horses intae the ground. My arse is numb and I have no feeling in my legs, not tae mention we havena eaten since yesterday. But I guess for a man with an important mission time is of the essence and the necessities of life, like food and sleep are not an option." Jayden dismounted by a stream.

"You complain worse than Bryce." Alasdair jumped from the saddle and strode toward the water. "We dinna have the luxury of time. Mayhap Edina is already wed." Alasdair shuddered at the thought and balled his fists at his side. "I hope we are not too late."

"You really do love her." Jayden patted Alasdair on the back.

Alasdair grunted and squatted by the brook. He dipped his hand in water and scooped out enough water to quench his thirst, then began to fill his wineskin. He was not accustomed to talking about his feelings and when it came to Edina, he had no idea what to say or think. He'd never been truly in love before.

"I am positive my sister will be elated tae see you. I'm not sure my da will be as pleased. He can be a verra thrawn man. But once I tell him you are willing tae stay and help me to oversee Sinclair land, I am sure he will be agreeable."

"I pray you are right, my friend. The more I think about Edina being married tae Duncan, the less I like the idea." Alasdair took another drink, then capped his wineskin, and hung it at his side. "Is it much farther?"

Jayden threw his leg over his horse's back and hauled himself into the saddle. "While we are on the Sinclair land, we still have a wee way tae go. Best we be off."

Alasdair didn't need any prompting. He could not wait to see Edina and hoped Jayden was correct in his assessment. The thought that she might say no troubled him, but his worst fear was that she might already be wed. He dug in his heels and Odin lunged forward.

They covered the next few miles at breakneck speed, both of their mounts frothing from the mouth and nose as they entered the bailey. Alasdair barely allowed the destrier to come to a stop when he flung himself from the saddle. "See that someone tends tae Odin," he shouted over his shoulder as he raced toward the castle.

"Walk the horses for a bit tae cool them down, then see them well fed and watered," Jayden instructed a lad who approached. He handed over the reins, then hurried after Alasdair. "Haud on, man, you canna rush in like the castle is afire. That is no way tae make an impression on my father."

Jayden paused, doubled over at the waist and sucked in a deep breath. "You are going tae be the death of me."

"I canna help it if you have the stamina and strength of an auld woman," Alasdair said as he stopped to open the castle door. "There is no time tae dally."

"I'd not be so quick to pass judgment or to rile me, Alasdair. You need an ally when speaking tae my da, not an enemy." Jayden climbed the castle steps and joined his friend. "It might be wise tae clean up afore we talk to him."

"There isna time for such things. I must see your father afore the wedding." Alasdair yanked open the door.

"Look at yourself, man. You're covered in dirt. Anyone would think you've been dragged by your horse, not riding him. It is still early. I dinna expect the ceremony tae start until just afore noon. That is when the messenger told me it was tae take place."

Alasdair dragged his hand across his beard-stubbled chin, then glanced down at his dust-covered trews, muddy boots and sweat-soiled tunic. "Mayhap you're right. Clean and shaven I could stand a better chance with both Edina and your da. But we must hurry."

Chapter 25

Edina fussed with the bodice of her gown. "This was worn by my mother on her wedding day. My father asked me tae wear it. But I have lost weight and it is too large."

"Och, you look lovely. A comelier bride I havena seen," Helen said as she tied a sash of Sinclair plaid around Edina's waist to improve the fit, then placed a ring of heather atop her mistress's head.

"I dinna know why my father decided tae start the wedding earlier than planned. He said noon and if true tae his word, I'd still have a couple of hours of freedom left."

"I am told the priest must leave early. He has a funeral tae reside over in the next glen and must leave afore noon. If the wedding happens an hour or two early, it canna make that much difference," Helen replied.

Edina sighed as she sat on the end of her pallet. "I dinna wish tae marry Duncan at all, but unless I betray Oceana's confidence and tell him about the babe, I fear there is no choice. I will find myself wed tae a man I dinna love and the poor lass will end up at a priory. She will lose her babe and Duncan will never know he has an heir."

"Aye, her quandary is verra sad indeed. Mayhap you should tell your betrothed about the babe and let fate decide the outcome. Tae begin a marriage with such secrets isna prudent."

"I hear what you're saying, Helen, and agree, but I gave my word tae Oceana. She was so distraught when she found out I wanted tae tell Duncan she was here and made me swear I wouldna betray her."

A loud rap at the door caused Edina's heart to jump. "Aye, who is it?"

"Your father. Duncan is in the great hall with the priest and they are awaiting your arrival. Dinna tarry lass, your husband-tae-be grows impatient. This is no way tae start a marriage."

"I come anon," Edina replied. She turned to Helen and grasped the lass by the hand. "Fetch Oceana and bring her tae the great hall. Please hurry."

"Are you planning tae tell Lord Sutherland about the babe, m'lady?"

"I dinna have a choice. You're right. If Duncan and I are destined tae be married, I canna conceal something that could ruin any chance of our happiness. He has a right tae know he has sired a bairn. Once he learns the truth, I pray he will wish tae marry the lass and be a father tae his babe."

Helen touched Edina's arm and smiled. "I pray that happens for everyone's sake as well, m'lady. Try tae stall the priest as long as you can. I will go and get Lady Oceana right away." She turned and scurried out the door and down the hall.

Edina sucked in a deep breath for courage and followed in Helen's wake. She hoped Oceana would forgive her and that Duncan would do the right thing by her.

"Here is my lovely daughter now," Laird Sinclair announced as Edina entered the hall to the cheers of those in attendance. "This is indeed a fine day for both our clans. I only wish your da could be here to witness your joining."

"As do I. We will drink tae his health during the feast." Duncan approached Edina and took her hand. "You look lovely, my dear."

Edina bobbed a curtsy. "Thank you, m'lord. If it would be possible, could I speak with you in private afore the wedding takes place?"

Duncan's brow furrowed. "Of course." He took her hand and escorted her toward the corner of the room.

"What is the meaning of this delay?" her father asked.

Edina turned to face her father. "Da, please. There is something I need tae discuss with Duncan. We will be but a moment."

"I'll not hear of it. There will be plenty of time tae talk once you've exchanged your vows," her father argued.

Duncan stepped forward. "We have waited this long tae marry, a few more minutes willna matter. Obviously, Edina feels this is important and I wish to hear what she has tae say." He bowed. "We will return promptly. I promise." He slid his hand from Edina's hand to her elbow. "Come, m'lady. Let us speak in private."

Edina twisted her hands in her skirt, worried she was making a mistake by telling Duncan the truth, but she honestly believed it was the right thing to do.

"What is it you wish tae say? The priest is waiting and best we not anger your father any more than we already have," Duncan warned. He took a step in her direction and once again clasped her hand. "Tell me what troubles you."

Edina straightened her posture and swallowed hard against the lump building in her throat. "What are your thoughts on a married couple having secrets from each other?" she asked.

"That would depend on what it is, Edina, why do you ask?"

"If I had a secret and failed tae tell you about afore we were wed, one which might affect your decision tae take me as your bride, would you want tae know?" Her heart raced like a runaway horse and she found it hard to look him in the eye, but she had to make him understand.

"Is there something you've done, something I should know afore we marry?" Duncan released her hand. He crossed his arms over his chest and tapped his foot, waiting for her to respond.

"It is not what I have done, m'lord, rather what you have done . . . you and someone else." Edina nipped at her bottom lip.

His frown deepened. "I dinna understand. Explain yourself, m'lady."

"I know about you and Oceana, that you were verra much in love, and if not for the agreement between our fathers, you would have likely chosen tae marry her and not me," Edina began, but Duncan cut her off.

"We have already talked about my involvement with Oceana at great length. That is in the past and we have our future ahead of us. Just as we discussed that people in our positions, the sons and daughters of powerful lairds, often must sacrifice our happiness for the good of our clans. We dinna always have a say in who we marry. This tradition of having our mate selected and my relationship with Oceana prior to our betrothal are not secrets or anything new," Duncan said.

The fact that Duncan implied he did not want this marriage, but felt he had no options was evident in his choice of words. "Aye, we have discussed this afore, but there are things you arena aware of. T-things about Oceana you have a right tae know," Edina stammered. Her nerves were getting the better of her, but she had started to tell Duncan the truth and could not turn back now.

"There is naught about Oceana that I dinna know," Duncan replied. "Even if there was, this isna the time tae be bringing it up. We are about tae be wed."

"Did you or did you not consummate your love for each other?" Edina blurted out.

"What are you asking?" Duncan turned around and began to pace.

"Is everything all right?" Laird Sinclair called out. "We are waiting to complete the ceremony. Can this not wait until later?"

"Nay, it canna wait." She raised her hand to stay her father's advance, then touched Duncan's arm. "Did you take Oceana tae your bed?" she asked softly.

"It is not uncommon for men tae have bedded women afore they are wed and some still do it after. What difference does it make? I never claimed to be celibate afore we met," Duncan snapped, then turned his back to her and started to walk away. "Your father is right. This can wait until later."

"Please answer my question, Duncan. Did you bed Oceana?" she asked again.

He stopped and spun around. "Aye, but I am here tae marry you. Now, if you are satisfied, I'd suggest we get on with the nuptials."

"Would you be in such a rush if I told you Oceana is with child? That she will birth your babe in a priory afore the snow flies, then hand the bairn over tae a family she doesna know?" Edina could not stop the words that needed to be said. "Forgive me, Oceana," she muttered under her breath.

Duncan grabbed her by the arms and glared down at her. "You lie. Oceana isna having my babe. We were only together once. This is but a ruse tae get out of marrying me. Well it willna work. I dinna want this union any more than you do, but it has been arranged by our sires and we will go through with it."

Gasps of shock and the din of voices rumbled through the great hall. It was obvious everyone had heard Duncan's comment, since he did not bother to lower his voice.

Heat rose in her cheeks. "It only requires one joining, and I wouldna lie about something so important," Edina replied with her chin held high.

"You dinna know Oceana. How could you be privy tae

such personal information? It is a trick I say and in verra poor taste. This is not the way I pictured our marriage beginning, Edina." Duncan grabbed her wrist and tugged her toward the priest. "Father Cullen, we are ready to complete the union."

Edina dug in her heels, refusing to take another step. "I know Oceana better than you think. She is here Duncan and she is verra much in the family way. What you chose tae do about that is up tae you. But I willna be dragged tae the altar and marry a man who thinks me a liar."

Duncan's face blanched. "How long has she been here? Why was I not informed?"

"Because I asked Edina not tae tell you about my presence or the babe." Oceana entered the great hall and approached Duncan and Edina.

"What is the meaning of this intrusion and who is this lass? Duncan, you had better have a guid explanation," Laird Sinclair shouted.

Duncan glared at Edina. "How did she come tae be here?"

"I invited her. I thought mayhap if you had the chance tae see each other one more time, you would realize how much you care for her, and break our betrothal." Edina spoke softly and lowered her eyes in shame. "I had no idea she was expecting a babe until she arrived. Once she was here, Oceana told me she was on her way to a priory, and planned tae give up the babe, I dinna know what tae do."

Duncan faced Oceana. "Why? I had a right tae know you bore my babe." He slid two fingers beneath her chin and lifted until their eyes met. "Talk tae me, lass."

"Because I love you and wouldna ask you tae choose between me and your duty tae the clan. I know how much your honor means tae you." Tears streamed down Oceana's cheeks. She wiped them away with one hand and slid the other over her belly.

"This marriage is sanctioned by the king of Scotland and

was arranged in accordance with Highland tradition. You have brought shame upon yourself and your family name, lass, but your dalliance, and the spawn thereof has no bearing on the marriage between Duncan and Edina." Laird Sinclair shook his fist at Duncan. "You will marry my daughter or suffer the consequences."

Edina grasped her Laird Sinclair's forearm. "Father, please give us time tae sort this out. How can you expect me tae marry Duncan after learning this news? He loves Oceana—"

"Fail tae honor the pact, Duncan, and I will have your head, after I've severed all ties with your clan." Laird Sinclair threatened. "As for the lass, I will have one of my guards escort her tae the priory where she can give birth tae your bastard, and we willna speak of the bairn again."

"Father, you are being cruel and unreasonable. At least let Duncan and Oceana have a few minutes tae talk afore you force them tae make such a difficult and unfair decision," Edina pleaded.

"He should have thought about that afore he bedded the chit. He has only himself tae blame," Sinclair replied harshly.

Duncan glanced between the two ladies. "I wish you had told me about the babe sooner, Oceana. I might have been able tae get my father tae speak with Laird Sinclair and make alternate arrangements. But he is right, I must honor the pact for the sake of the clan."

Oceana lowered her eyes and sniffled. "I understand, Duncan, and wish you both much happiness."

"Now we have that settled, let us get these nuptials done and over with, afore we have any more interruptions," Laird Sinclair growled as he clasped Duncan and Edina's wrists and hauled them toward the priest.

"Do something, Duncan. You love Oceana and she loves you. This isna right and the Almighty willna bless a marriage based on lies," Edina pleaded.

"Hush, daughter. We willna speak of this unfortunate incident again." Laird Sinclair called to the priest, "They are ready. Make haste."

The priest nodded, then wrapped a length of Sinclair plaid around the couple's wrists and repeated the act with a length of Sutherland colors. But as he began to read from the bible, reciting prayers in Latin, the door to the great hall opened.

"Wait!" someone shouted. "I must speak tae you Laird Sinclair."

Edina's heart leapt when she recognized the deep rumble and familiar cadence of Alasdair's voice. Had he returned for her? She wanted to tear the bonds of marriage from around her wrist, run to him, throw herself into his arms, and kiss him. Instead, she glanced over her shoulder and stood her ground. If he had returned with the intent of asking for her hand, she wouldna give in so easily.

"Jayden, what is the meaning of this?" Laird Sinclair asked. "Can you not see we are in the middle of a wedding?"

"It is mid-morning, Da, and we have ridden hard in order tae arrive afore noon, the time I was told the ceremony would take place. There is something urgent we must discuss," Jayden replied. "Let me talk with my father afore you speak your mind," he said to Alasdair.

"Plans change. If you will give us a moment, Father Cullen will hear their vows. We can talk when the union is completed." Laird Sinclair turned tae the priest. "Forgive yet another interruption. Continue, Father."

"Nay. This canna be postponed until after the wedding," Alasdair blurted out.

Laird Sinclair threw his hands in the air. "I canna believe this is happening. What is so blasted important that it canna wait a few minutes? I canna understand why everyone suddenly has something urgent tae discuss."

"If these proceedings continue, it will be too late. I wish tae make a bid for Edina's hand," Alasdair blurted out.

Edina had waited and prayed to hear those words from Alasdair. Once uttered, she could no longer fight the urge to go to him. She damned the idea of being coy and prideful and turned to Duncan. "You are a fine man, but I am in love with Alasdair and this would solve all our problems. You will then be free tae marry Oceana."

"I willna allow it and my daughter willna accept. Damn it, man, are you daft? You have known about this arrangement for over sennight. How can you burst in now and make an announcement such as this?"

"Alasdair saved Edina's life. The least you can do is hear him out, Father. Once he has said his piece, you may have a change of heart," Jayden said.

"What he has tae say will make no difference. Robert the Bruce has sanctioned this union, and while he may be the son of my dearest friend, and there was a time when he would have been considered a suitable husband, he isna now." He faced Alasdair. "You have naught tae offer my daughter, no land or title. She must enter intae a marriage that will benefit the clan. Uniting the Sinclair and Sutherland clans will also make a stronger Scotland."

"He could have taken over as laird of Clan Fraser had he chosen tae do so. It is his birthright and Connor offered tae step down. But Alasdair refused tae accept—" Jayden began, but was cut off.

"That is exactly why his isna the man tae marry your sister," Laird Sinclair snapped.

"Alasdair is a guid man and a brave warrior. He could see the Fraser clan was thriving under Connor's leadership and wouldna put his own desires ahead of the clan's best interests. That in itself is a testament to the kind of man he is," Jayden continued. "He has also accepted my request tae oversee the western portion of Sinclair land once he and

Edina were wed. Provided you give your consent, Da."

"Why would he do that?" Laird Sinclair inquired.

"I need a strong leader to protect the outer reaches of our holdings and canna think of a finer man tae do it. He may not be wealthy, but has earned a goodly sum of coin as reward for his service for the King and country. He also has Robert's blessing and sanction if you and Duncan are in agreement."

Alasdair moved forward, handed Laird Sinclair the missive from the Bruce, then stepped back."

After reading the note, Laird Sinclair scrubbed his hand over his chin. "And you are willing to remain in the north of Scotland and help Jayden?" he asked.

"Aye. I have always been drawn tae this part of the country. I feel verra much at home here and would like to remain," Alasdair replied.

Laird Sinclair turned to Edina and Duncan. "This does put a new light on things. If you are willing tae release Edina from the betrothal and Edina is prepared tae—"

"Oh, aye, I will marry him, Father." She raced to Alasdair's side. "I prayed you would come back for me."

Alasdair hauled her against his chest, dropped his head, and pressed his lips to hers. "I've been a fool, can you ever forgive me?" he asked when he finally broke the kiss.

"Aye, you have been a fool, but we have a lifetime for you tae make it up tae me." She smiled and nipped at his lower lip. "I love you, Alasdair."

Strong arms engulfed her. "And I love you, Edina. I have since the day I first laid eyes upon you. I would be verra happy if you would consent tae be my wife." He didn't wait for an answer. Instead, he captured her mouth with a kiss that curled her toes and made her swoon. An act of boldness that could very well cost him his head.

Laird Sinclair coughed to clear his throat. "This is verra touching, but there is still the matter of her betrothal tae Duncan."

"He has a point." Alasdair raised his head. "What say you, Duncan?"

Duncan didn't answer. He stood in the corner talking to Oceana cradling her in his arms.

"I think that answers your question." Jayden slapped Alasdair on the back. "Welcome tae Clan Sinclair, brother."

Chapter 26

"When do you plan tae marry my daughter?" Laird Sinclair asked.

Alasdair smiled and tugged Edina to his side. He had never thought about marriage in the past, but now that he had made up his mind to take Edina as his bride, he did not want to wait. "Father Cullen is here now, and you have already planned a feast and ceildh. If your daughter is agreeable, I say we do it right away. Mayhap Duncan and Oceana can exchange their vows as well. What say you, Edina?"

Edina glanced up at him, her eyes filled with passion. "I think it a fine idea. That is, if Duncan has a mind tae marry Oceana without her father's consent."

"Do you think your da would approve?" Duncan asked.

"My father will be verra pleased. I'm certain of it," Oceana replied. "He dinna want me tae enter the priory and he has always liked you, Duncan. He, too, thought we would marry someday and was disappointed when he learned about the arrangement made between you and Edina."

"What about the babe?" Duncan slid his hand over her belly and smiled. "Were your mam and da verra upset when they learned you carried my bairn? I am surprised your father doesna want tae see me drawn and quartered."

"He might if he knew. But my parents dinna know I am with child." Oceana lowered her chin and stared at the ground. "I was ashamed tae tell them I had surrendered my innocence out of wedlock."

"Then we must rectify that right away." Duncan cupped her chin and raised it until their eyes met. "This is my babe,

Oceana, and I mean to do right by you and the bairn. We will work things out. Together." He leaned in and brushed her lips with a kiss. "Will have me as your husband?"

"Aye, Duncan. I would be proud tae be your wife." Oceana threw her arms around Duncan's neck and kissed his cheek.

"It is settled. Alasdair and Edina will be wed and so will Duncan and Oceana," Laird Sinclair announced, then turned to Father Cullen. "Will you perform the services?"

"I am anxious to become your wife, but what about your brothers, Alasdair? Do you not wish them tae be present?" Edina whispered.

Alasdair brushed her cheek with his fingertips, then kissed the tip of her nose. "My brothers will be verra happy about our union and they promised tae visit us, along with their wives and children afore the snow flies. We can plan a feast when they come, but I dinna want to wait." He looked to Father Cullen. "I'm told you have a funeral to preside over in the next glen, best you start."

Father Cullen nodded and took his place atop the dais. He motioned with a wave of his hand. "Would the couples please stand afore me and pledge their intent?"

"Aye." Alasdair ushered Edina to a spot before the priest and Duncan did the same with Oceana.

"Now if there are no more objections, changes, or interruptions, I will begin," Father Cullen said as he glanced around the great hall. When no one spoke up, he began to read a scripture from his bible on the sanctity of marriage.

Alasdair listened intently as the priest prattled on in a mix of Latin and Gaelic, outlined the responsibilities of marriage, and listed the duties of a husband.

"Do you, Alasdair Fraser, of the Clan Fraser, agree tae take Edina as your wife?" the priest asked.

"Aye," Alasdair responded, but his eyes were fixed on Edina's beautiful face.

"Will you protect her and provide for her, will you honor and . . .?"

As Father Cullen continued, Alasdair looked down at their hands, bound together with strips of plaid representing both their clans and smiled.

As he recited his vows, Alasdair could not believe his good fortune, or how close he'd come to losing the only woman he had ever truly loved. Now that he was here, he couldn't imagine his life without her by his side and he offered a silent prayer of gratitude to the Almighty for blessing him with Edina. He'd never planned to marry, but he could not think of a more perfect bride.

Father Cullen turned the page and began to read aloud the duties of a wife. "Do you, Edina Sinclair, of the Clan Sinclair promise tae honor you husband as I have just described?"

"Aye, I do," she answered promptly.

Alasdair found himself lost in her beautiful hazel eyes. He'd never noticed the flecks of green and gold until now, making them look even more magical. When Edina smiled up at him, his heart missed a beat. If she had this kind of power over him while they were standing before a crowd of people, he could not begin to imagine the heat and passion their joining would create. The very thought made him dizzy with desire.

"You may kiss your bride," Father Cullen announced and tapped Alasdair on the shoulder, causing him to jump. "Kiss your bride, lad," he repeated and untied the plaids joining their wrists.

As Alasdair lowered his head and pressed his lips to Edina's, the room erupted in cheers. "Aye, Sinclair!" those in attendance shouted.

"Congratulations, brother." Jayden linked arms with Alasdair, then thumped him on the back. "Take guid care of my sister or you will answer tae me." He turned and hugged Edina. "I am verra happy for you."

Laird Sinclair joined them. "Welcome tae Clan Sinclair, Alasdair. I know you will do your da proud." He turned and raised his sword. "All present are invited tae join us for a feast and the grandest ceildh this clan has ever seen."

After hearing Duncan and Oceana's vows, the priest turned to Laird Sinclair. "If you have no more need of my services, I will take my leave."

"Will you not stay long enough tae toast the bride and groom?" Laird Sinclair asked. "Cook has prepared a feast and there will be music and dancing after the meal."

"I thank you for the invitation, but I must be off. I will be back this way in a fortnight on my way tae Inverness. I would welcome a hot meal and soft bed at that time if you are so inclined to offer," Father Cullen said.

"You are always welcomed, Father." Edina took his hand. "Thank you for a lovely ceremony."

"You are most welcome, my dear." The priest patted her hand in return. "I must say it got a wee bit confusing for a while, but the outcome was worth it. God bless you both and may you have many bairns."

"The feast grows cold and the musicians anxious. Let's not keep either waiting any longer." Laird Sinclair placed one hand on Alasdair's shoulder and the other on the small of Edina's back, urging them forward.

As they approached the dais, Oceana and Duncan crossed the room and joined them.

"Thank you for everything, Laird Sinclair. Oceana and I will now take our leave." Duncan bowed and took Edina's hand and kissed the back of it. "I owe you so much, I dinna know where to begin."

"As do I," Oceana added and hugged Edina. "If not for you, Duncan and I would never be together. Thank you."

"I am just glad things worked out the way they did." Edina snuggled against Alasdair's side. "Must you leave so soon?"

"Aye. We have a long journey ahead of us and I dinna want to rush. Oceana needs tae go easy in her delicate condition." Duncan slid his hand over his wife's swollen belly. "I dinna want to put off facing Oceana's parents any longer than necessary."

"Godspeed and safe journey." Alasdair held out his hand and Duncan grasped his wrist. "I wish the two of you much happiness."

"I have tae admit that I dinna like you verra much when we first met, Fraser. But I can now see why Edina loves you so. You are a guid man and I know you will make her happy." Duncan turned to Oceana. "Best we be on our way, wife. Enjoy the ceildh," he concluded and ushered his bride out of the room.

Alasdair hugged Edina and kissed her brow. "If you dinna mind, I would like tae make our attendance at the festivities brief as well. I dinna want tae offend your da, but I want tae be alone with you. I canna wait tae—"

Edina pressed two fingers to his lips, then replaced them with a quick kiss. "I am anxious tae be alone with you as well," she whispered in his ear then pulled the lobe between her teeth.

He was shocked at her boldness, but it caused his blood to heat. He snaked his arms around her waist and kissed her soundly. His groin stirred as their bodies molded together like they were made for each other.

Laird Sinclair coughed to clear his throat. "There will be plenty of time for that after the feast." He slapped Alasdair on the back. "Come, lad, it is time tae eat. You need to keep up your strength for the night ahead."

"I'm not hungry. At least not for food," he murmured in Edina's ear, his words causing her to blush.

She poked him in the side and giggled. "My father is right. There will be plenty of time for that later."

They joined Jayden at the dais, and watched as platter after platter of roast meat, fruit, cheese, breads and vegetables were placed on the table before them.

Jayden tore off a leg of lamb and began to chew on it, juices running down his chin. "Cook has outdone himself. Dig in." He picked up a tankard of ale and downed the contents.

Edina nibbled on a bit of fruit and cheese, while Alasdair absently chased some turnip and venison around his trencher with a knife.

"What is wrong with you, brother? You usually have a hardy appetite," Jayden asked as he pushed a tray of meat in Alasdair's direction, then helped himself to some bread and honey.

"I have other things on my mind," Alasdair replied hoarsely when Edina's thigh brushed against his. "In fact, if you would excuse us, Edina and I would like tae take our leave." He stood and held out his hand in her direction. "Will you join me, wife?"

"Aye, husband," Edina replied and rose to her feet.

"Where are you going?" her father asked. "It is still early and the festivities have yet tae start."

Edina faced father. "Everything is lovely, Da, but Alasdair and I would like tae—"

Laird Sinclair lifted his hand and grinned. "Say no more. I was once young and with any luck, you will make me a grandfather afore spring. If you can manage tae produce a lad that would make me verra happy."

Alasdair took Edina's hand and kissed her palm. "Are you ready tae retire?"

"Aye." She nodded and her cheeks flushed red when Alasdair scooped her up in his arms and carried her across the great hall.

She buried her face in his tunic when the guests began to chant and make bawdy comments. "You can put me down," she said as they exited the room.

"I dinna wish to set your feet on the floor until we reach our chamber," he replied on a ragged sigh and kissed her neck.

He took the stairs leading to the above floor two at a time, then marched with purpose down the hall, pausing only long enough to open the door to her solar.

Once inside, he set her down beside the hearth, then took her in his arms. "You are so beautiful, Edina. I wish tae truly make you my wife."

He'd waited so long to lay with her flesh-to-flesh, to taste her fragrant skin, to feel the rub of her silken thighs, and to hear her sharp intake of breath as he entered her for the first time. Then, he planned to revile in her whimpers of pleasure as he buried himself to the hilt in her hot, moist sheath, bringing her to the height of ecstasy until neither could take any more. Only then would he be truly satisfied.

Chapter 27

Caught in the heat of passion, they stood by the hearth entwined in each other's arms, hearts pounding in unison, and their lips locked together. Bombarded by an array of emotions she'd never before experienced, Edina didn't want the moment to end.

"I canna believe you came back for me, and that we are married." She fisted her hands in his tunic, afraid if she let go, Alasdair would disappear, or that she might be dreaming. If the latter was true, she didn't ever want to wake up.

"Believe, mo gaol." Alasdair kissed her lips, her cheeks, and the tip of her nose as his large hands roamed her body, taking in every dip and curve. "I was a fool for ever leaving you."

Alasdair nibbled on her earlobe, sending a shiver of excitement down her spine. Her legs grew weak and she clung to his arms when he trailed his lips along her jaw, down her neck, and came to rest in the hollow at the base of her throat. While she tried to stifle a moan, it escaped as she closed her eyes and dropped her head back. Surely anything that made her feel this amazing must be sinful, but she could not seem to get enough.

Edina trembled when his fingers fumbled with the laces of her gown. "Are you afraid?" he asked on a ragged breath, his hot, moist lips still pressed against her tingling flesh.

She raised her heavy eyelids and smiled. "I fear naught. Have I done something tae displease you?"

"You could never displease me, Edina." He brushed her mouth with a brief, but passionate, kiss, and then swept a lock of hair from her forehead. "I thought you might be uncertain about our first joining."

For a warrior of his size, Alasdair was surprisingly tender. Her heart soared at the thought of spending the rest of her life with a man she truly loved.

"We can go slowly and take as long as you like, Edina. There is no need tae do anything but hold each other until you are ready for more."

"Nay. For a husband and wife tae become one in their marriage bed is what the Lord intended. I can only imagine how wonderful it will be," she replied on a breathy sigh.

Alasdair held her at arm's length and their eyes met. "I have bedded women in the past and have made no secret of that fact. However, you will be my first maiden. I am told there is a moment of discomfort for the lass, but it will pass quickly, replaced by pleasure the likes of which you have never known. I am larger than most men, but give you my word, I will be gentle."

Edina found his concern and consideration touching. "I trust you, Alasdair, and believe you will do everything in your power to make our first time, every time, experiences we will never forget." She pressed her palm to his chest and glanced at the floor. "But while I may be a woman grown, with a woman's heart, and needs, I have no experience in such things. I hope I dinna disappoint you. Will you teach me how tae please you?"

Alasdair nuzzled his nose against the curve of her neck. "We will learn together, mo gaol," he whispered in her ear. "But we are both wearing far too many clothes," he said as he unlaced her gown, then lay it open, exposing the swell of her breasts.

He'd called her his love. Words Edina had longed to hear. She was truly blessed and at this moment, the happiest woman in the world, of that she was certain.

"You are exquisite, mo gaol, he said as he slid her gown over her shoulders and let it drop to the floor in a pool of fabric at her feet.

Her kirtle followed next and she stood in the glow of the firelight naked before her husband. She'd never considered her slight body and lack of womanly curves, full bosoms, and a plump round bottom to be one a man would desire. Yet, Alasdair gazed at her with such appreciation, as if he could devour her. He made her feel beautiful and desirable.

Dark eyes filled with passion moved over her body from top to bottom, causing her skin to tingle, her breasts to grow heavy, and her nipples to stand erect. Suddenly feeling ill at ease, Edina tried covering herself with her arms, but Alasdair insisted she drop them to her sides.

"Why do you hide yourself from me, Edina?"

"I fear I am not as shapely as the tavern wenches you are accustomed to bedding," she said and lowered her eyes.

"Nonsense. You are by far the most beautiful, alluring woman I have ever seen." He cupped her chin and raised it. "I've thought so since the day I found you on the beach and couldna purge your image from my mind. Do you have any idea how difficult it was to stay my lust and desire to bed you?"

She could never forget their time in the hunting croft, or that he'd seen her naked on more than one occasion while tending to her injuries.

"I think I do know how you felt. I wanted you, too, Alasdair, but dinna think you found me appealing. I also couldna offer myself tae you, tae anyone, when I dinna know who I was or where I belonged. When I remembered my name, you were so angry. I—"

He silenced her with a kiss. "I was a fool and should have asked for your hand the day we returned to Sinclair Castle. I will never tire of looking at you, or touching you." Alasdair tightened his embrace. "Nor will I tire of the way you smell, like a field of heather after a spring rain, or the way you taste." He swept her hair aside and nipped at her shoulder.

Edina's head began to swim, her pulse raced, and her uncertainty faded. He caressed her breasts and teased the sensitive tips with his fingers, rolled them and squeezed, the sinful mix of pain and pleasure causing her to grind her hips against his. He groaned aloud and she felt the proof of his arousal pressing against her belly.

"Keep doing that and I willna be able tae resist the need tae make you mine." He lifted her, carried her to the pallet, and laid her onto the overstuffed mattress.

"I thought you said we were wearing too many clothes." She smiled and reached for the ties of his trews. "I no longer have on a stitch. Mayhap you would care tae join me?"

Alasdair yanked the tunic over his head and tossed it into the corner. His boots and trews followed. He stood beside the bed, his finely honed, muscular body like that of a Norse god.

"Oh my." She gasped when she beheld his manhood for the first time, marveling not only at the size, but at the combination of rigidity and smoothness." How she would accommodate his length and girth was suddenly a concern. "Does it hurt?"

He nodded, took her hand, and laid it on his shaft, encouraging her to wrap her fingers around it. "It aches for you, m'lady."

"Then join with me and make me your wife." She reclined on the pallet, a combination of excitement and anticipation laced with fear washing over her.

He lay beside her. "There are many ways a man can pleasure a woman. Would you like me tae show you?"

"Aye." She wrapped her arms around his neck and drew him toward her. "Show me. I want tae learn."

When he positioned her on her back, then knelt between her knees, Edina was uncertain what to expect. He nudged her thighs apart, her stomach flipped and her heart began to race.

"Dinna fash. I willna do anything you dinna want, Edina."

Without saying another word, Alasdair slid his fingertips along her inner thigh, his thumb brushing her most intimate place.

Edina gasped and tried to sit up. "What are you doing?" she asked, unable to hide the apprehension in her voice. She was prepared to join with her husband in the traditional way, but this was something she had never considered.

"Relax, and enjoy, mo gaol." He placed his hands on her shoulders and eased her back against the mattress. "I thought you trusted me."

"Aye. I do trust you, husband," Edina replied, even though she had no idea what he had planned.

He cupped her heel, lifted her leg, then proceeded to feather kisses along her calf. She trembled when he licked the back of her knee, surprised by a rush of hot moist heat released between her thighs.

As his sensual journey continued, she rolled her head from side-to-side. "Please . . . Alasdair," Edina moaned.

"Please, what?" He raised his head and wiggled his brows. "Tell me what you like."

She moaned again. "I dinna know. I have never done this afore."

"That makes it all the sweeter, mo gaol. Do you not like what I am doing now?" He lowered his head and nibbled on the flesh where her leg and torso joined.

"Nay . . . I mean, Aye. It feels wonderful, but it must be sinful," she moaned.

"For a husband and wife tae share intimate pleasures

is not a sin, Edina. If you allow yourself to accept what is happening, I can take you places, you never knew existed."

"You are the devil tae be sure, Alasdair Fraser."

"Aye. And that makes you the devil's woman." He laughed and placed her heel on his shoulder, giving him better access and exposing her for his perusal. "Lovely." A wolfish grin tugged at his lips as he dipped his head, then snaked his tongue around her bud of arousal. He fed hungrily, slow at first, then picked up the tempo.

Edina whimpered and squirmed, but couldn't bring herself to ask him to stop. He lapped at her sensitive feminine folds, licking from front to back and then in reverse, igniting a wild fire of passion, the pressure building until she didn't think she could take any more.

"Enough," she pleaded on a strangled breath, but he paid her no mind. Instead, he brought her to the precipice of release, time and time again.

Her breathing came in short sharp pants, her heart pounded, and every part of her body was alive with sensations she could never have imagined. Her legs began to quiver and her core clenched as a dizzying, bone-melting euphoria engulfed her. She thought she might perish from pure ecstasy.

He continued to suckle until the last waves of her release subsided, and she lay motionless on the mattress, gasping for air. Only then did he release her from the intimate torture.

She struggled to open her eyes and smiled. "That was like nothing I could have anticipated. I dinna know it could be like that."

"This is only the beginning. We have an entire night of discovery ahead of us." He stroked his engorged manhood. "I ache for you, Edina. Are you willing tae join with me?"

Alasdair positioned himself above Edina and nudged her legs apart with his knee. "Will you have me, wife."

Edina nodded. "Aye, husband."

His heart thundered in his chest, his blood heated, and he found it difficult to control his unbridled passion. But instead of taking her, he paused, hypnotized by her beauty. The sight of her lying before him stole his breath away. Edina had the face of an angel and a body that drove him mad with desire. Perfectly sculpted, creamy white breasts, tipped with delicate pink buds, rose and fell with each shallow breath. Her long shapely limbs were topped with a soft nest of curls, the color of summer wheat and the perfect match to her waist-length hair strewn across the mattress.

"Make love tae me, Alasdair," Edina muttered softly.

He entered her slowly, giving her time to adjust to the stretch and fullness of their joining. He slid in a little, pulled out, then eased in further with each thrust. He wanted her to feel every inch of his arousal, he wanted to bury himself to the hilt, to pound into her with wild abandon, but he stopped when he reached the barrier of her innocence.

Her eyes opened wide. "Is something amiss?"

"Nay. But it can take time for your body to adjust to the union and I dinna want tae hurt you, lass. I want—"

He didn't have a chance to finish. Edina thrust her hips forward until they connected with his, foiling his plan to take things slowly.

Her nails dug into his shoulders and he felt hot tears on his neck when he broke through her maidenhead, but she didn't utter a sound.

"Are you all right?" he murmured softly against her ear.

She nodded and began to move her hips in a slow, rhythmic motion. His body responded and he followed her lead, his bold, brave lass, his woman, his wife.

Alasdair had bedded his share of women in the past, but this was the first time he'd ever made love. He could not believe the exhilaration, possessiveness, and pride he felt when he began to rock into her hard and fast.

He covered her mouth with his own, swallowing her whimpers of pleasure. When her feminine muscles clenched around his engorged shaft and she called out his name, his groin tightened. He increased the speed, coming close to release, then rolled to his back taking her with him.

Speechless, Edina straddled his hips, staring down at him, a shocked expression on her face. But when he began to move beneath her, she smiled and matched him stroke for stroke.

She arched and curled her spine, rose and lowered herself, riding him like a warhorse. A feral growl rose from deep within his chest.

Alasdair never dreamed Edina, his virgin bride, would teach him things about making love he didn't already know. The room began to spin, the pressure building from deep within his core, until he could take no more. With one final thrust, he shouted out a war cry, and released his seed.

She joined him in his release, then collapsed, her head resting on his breast, her hair covering his chest.

Alasdair woke several hours later and glanced down at Edina, sleeping peacefully in his arms. He closed his eyes and inhaled deeply, the scent of their lovemaking still lingering on the air. While he never thought he was destined to marry, he could not remember ever being so happy, or feeling so much at peace. He leaned over and pressed a kiss to her brow.

Edina stirred, opened her eyes, then brought her hand up to stifle a yawn. "Is it morning?"

"Aye, dawn has come, but it is still verra early. Go back tae sleep if you like. Last night was our wedding night and no one expects us tae rise afore noon," Alasdair said, then brushed a strand of hair from her cheek and tucked it behind her ear.

"I hope you werena disappointed," Edina said then lay her head on his chest.

"Last night was amazing. You are a very quick study." Alasdair stroked his hand down her back.

"I had a verra good teacher." Edina pressed her lips to his chest, then placed her hand over his heart, and sighed. "Are you happy, Alasdair?"

"Aye. Why do you ask?"

"I fear you may grow restless and someday regret your decision tae marry," she replied softly.

Alasdair wrapped his arm around her shoulders and pulled her close. "I love you, Edina. More than I ever dreamed was possible. I willna regret my decision. On the contrary, I will give daily thanks tae the Almighty for bringing us together."

"Will you not miss your brothers and your home? Jayden told me Connor offered to step down as laird of Clan Fraser so you could take your rightful place."

"This is my place, Edina, and my home. With you is where I belong. Connor is a fine laird and I have no desire tae replace him. My brothers and their wives know they are welcome tae visit us any time they wish. Once our castle is built, we will have plenty of space. However, given the way my brothers breed, we are going tae need many chambers tae house all their bairns," he tossed back his head and laughed.

"What about you, Alasdair? Will we need many chambers for our babes?" she asked, then lowered her gaze and began to nibble on her bottom lip.

Alasdair lifted her chin and kissed her. "I am the eldest brother. You dinna think I will let Connor and Bryce outshine me beneath the sheets, do you?" He slid his hand over her belly and smiled. "After last night, your father may get his wish and he will have a grandbabe in the spring." He rolled Edina beneath him and smiled. "But tae be safe, I think we should try again."

Also by bestselling author B.J. Scott
HIGHLAND LEGACY

Faced with an abhorrent betrothal, Cailin Macmillan flees her father's castle and quickly learns that a woman traveling alone in Medieval Scotland is an easy target for ruthless English soldiers. When Highland patriot Connor Fraser comes to her aid, his steadfast dedication to king and country is challenged by his overwhelming desire to protect Cailin—even if he must marry her to do so. Accused of murdering one of her attackers and determined to rely on her own resourcefulness, Cailin dresses as a lad, intent on seeking refuge at the camp of Robert the Bruce. Can she elude an enemy from her past-a vindictive English lord bent on her utter demise-or will she fall prey to his carnal intent and be executed for a crime she did not commit?

Available now on Amazon.com
http://www.amazon.com/Highland-Legacy-B-J-Scott/dp/1619351013/ref

HIGHLAND QUEST

No longer content in the shadows of his older brothers, and on a quest to find his destiny, Bryce Fraser's chosen path is fraught with danger, passion, and decisions. Can his unspoken love for spirited, beguiling Fallon be triumphant in a time of war and uncertainty, or will they both fall prey to the devious plans of a traitorous laird from a rival clan?

Available now on Amazon.com
http://www.amazon.com/Highland-Quest-ebook/dp/B00AQKYPU0/ref